A SLIP ON GOLDEN STAIRS

A Slip on Golden Stairs

WANTED: DEAD OR ALIVE

Joanne Sundell

FIVE STAR

A part of Gale, a Cengage Company

GALE
A Cengage Company

Farmington Hills, Mich • San Francisco • New York • Waterville, Maine
Meriden, Conn • Mason, Ohio • Chicago

LIBRARY OF CONGRESS CATALOGING-IN-PUBLICATION DATA

Names: Sundell, Joanne, author.
Title: A slip on golden stairs / Joanne Sundell.
Description: First edition. | Farmington Hills, Mich. : Five Star, a part of Gale, Cengage Learning, [2019] | Series: Wanted: dead or alive | Identifiers: LCCN 2018059026 (print) | ISBN 9781432855055 (hardcover)
Subjects: GSAFD: Ghost stories. | Love stories. | Christian fiction.
Classification: LCC PS3619.U557 S58 2019 (print) | DDC 813/.6—dc23
LC record available at https://lccn.loc.gov/2018059026

First Edition. First Printing: August 2019
Find us on Facebook—https://www.facebook.com/FiveStarCengage
Visit our website—http://www.gale.cengage.com/fivestar/
Contact Five Star Publishing at FiveStar@cengage.com

Printed in Mexico
1 2 3 4 5 6 7 23 22 21 20 19

To all the ghosts and ghost towns of the Old West,
a treasure trove of inspiration

ACKNOWLEDGMENTS

History of the Old West is the star here, whether found in libraries, on the internet, on a bookshelf at home, at a writing conference, in shared conversation, in movies watched on the big screen or on television. The rich heritage that is the West is a part of American culture and accessible by car, train, or plane if one isn't fortunate enough to live in frontier territory already.

Outside "all of the above," I found three books particularly helpful in writing *A Slip on Golden Stairs: Skid Road: An Informal Portrait of Seattle* by Murray Morgan; *Gold Rush Women* by Claire Rudolf Murphy and Jane G. Haigh; and *Colorado Ghost Tours: Haunted History and Encounters with the Afterlife* by Ann Westerberg.

The rest, as they say, is history.

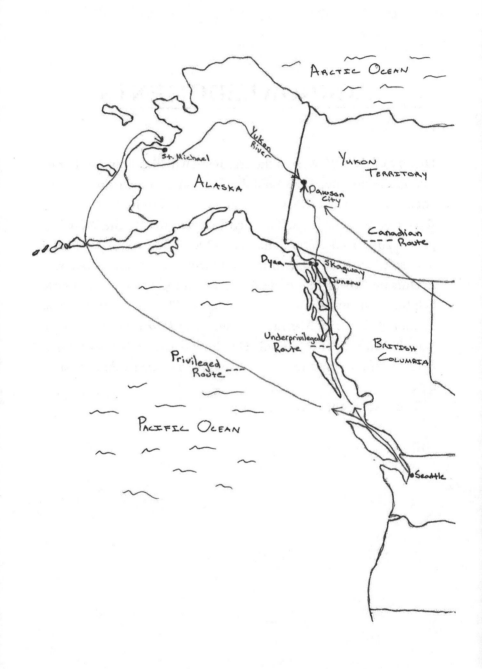

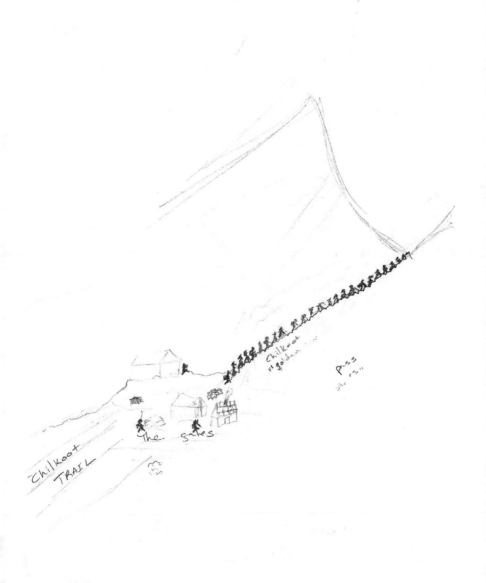

Pass
Steps

Chilkoot
"golden"

The   gates

Chilkoot
TRAIL

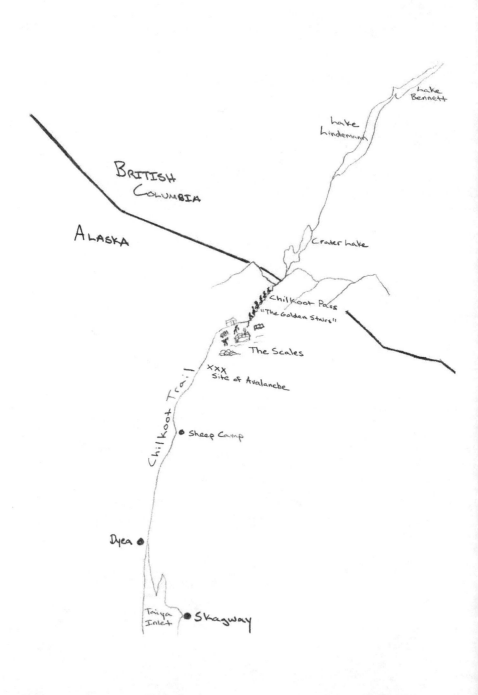

PREFACE

This frontier ghost story is a romantic slip in gold-rush time, inspired by an actual EVP recording made in the Slide Cemetery, Dyea, Alaska, in which a haunting male voice can be heard calling, "Abigail . . . Abigail." Historic Dyea is a true ghost town. There are portals to all ghost towns. They rarely open but when they do, you'd best slip through. A different choice would be foolhardy.

Unsigned Letter

April, 1898

Chilkoot Pass, Alaska

I'm setting this down so there will be a record of me climbing the Golden Stairs. Everybody's life counts for something and I was here. The Alaska wild doesn't much care.

Today will be a bad day. I feel it in my bones, settled in deep along with the cold. I should sleep. It's snowing again. The winds quit their howling. I'm unnerved by the silence. Like when you die. But I'm not dead. Just beat up by this trail. I'm sick with the ague. So are most others but they only talk of gold. Few say hello. Few are kind. The glimmer from my lantern burns low.

I broke from the party I arrived with from Seattle, they being a band of actresses headed for the next boomtown. I traveled with them to Skagway, then set out for Dyea. I am not an entertainer. I have another purpose.

I did what I needed to earn my way up the Chilkoot. I'm heartsick over helping tend pack animals for sale to stampeders. The rumors drifting down from White Pass are true. I've seen as much firsthand. Greedy men can inflict pain and suffering easy as spitting out a tobacco chew. What's happening is unforgivable. Gold fever is a poor excuse.

Today is Palm Sunday. You wouldn't know it from any talk up and down the Chilkoot. Stampeders only worship at the feet of the Golden Stairs. I get the queerest shivers sometimes. I could swear I *hear my name called out but when I turn to see who's there, no one ever is. It's a man's voice I hear. I don't know any man who'd be calling out to me. I am no beauty. I must be making this up in my head. Loneliness can do that. I've only my lantern light for companion. When it dies, I'll be alone on this cold mountain.*

CHAPTER ONE

April, 2017
The Dyea Tidal Flats, Alaska

Fifteen-hundred ice steps up the Golden Stairs. Fifteen-hundred women determined to climb them, Abby mused, and she imagined herself one of those determined women. The Klondike Gold Rush loomed large up the trail ahead, the notorious Chilkoot. Abby shut her eyes to better see the iconic photograph taken by Eric Hegg, of stampeders climbing those same ice steps in single file to reach the summit and the gold fields beyond. That black line in history—the rush of 100,000 stampeders pressed into the snowy scape—pulled at her whenever she pictured the scene. Gold-rush history always sparked her fanciful side, which she denied she had.

Today had been a long day and a good one. Palm Sunday in fact. It was getting late, and Abby wanted more time in Dyea, a true ghost town abandoned and forested over except for the false front of an old real estate office and a few rows of splintered pilings where a wharf once stretched to the waters beyond. What made the ghost town real to Abby were the three cemeteries here; real in the sense people had lived and died in this one-time frontier boomtown. She heaved a mournful sigh. No more lingering in cemeteries. She should start back. The trek to Skagway would take some time.

"Abigail . . . Abigail . . ."

Abby froze. A male voice had whispered her name, she was sure. Or maybe the wind had suddenly picked up? A quick look around showed no one there. She hugged her arms, shaken by the strange rasps. Her tour group left long ago. She had a purpose in staying behind at the Slide Cemetery, but not this. Her mind must be playing tricks and her imagination getting the better of her. Not like her. She shrugged off the bothersome shivers and straightened. *No man would be calling out to me. I am no beauty.*

"Abigail . . . Abigail . . ."

Abby broke into a run and never looked back. Cold and alone, she prayed no one chased her.

Every day since Abby ran out of the Slide Cemetery in Dyea had been a bad day. Her bones ached with this overhang of . . . what? She couldn't identify the bothersome feeling, and she couldn't get rid of it no matter how hard she tried. Too young for hot flashes and too old for childhood complaints, she kept her head buried in her college texts and her body on the move. If she wasn't out hiking in the Colorado foothills, she'd jog along the trails weaving in and around the School of Mines. The strange aching didn't disappear, but at least she could put her thoughts to study and wear herself out. Exhaustion helped her sleep. She didn't want to dream, just sleep. Since the Slide Cemetery, she feared her dreams.

Not one for fanciful daydreaming or nighttime romantic yearnings, Abby had come to hate the young man's face she kept trying to conjure in her dreams. She wasn't stupid. She knew she tried to conjure the face of the one who had called out, *"Abigail . . . Abigail."* It had been weeks since Abby had returned to Golden, Colorado, and the last month of her freshman year at the School of Mines. She'd set aside the exact amount of money needed to spend spring break backpacking in

16

Klondike gold-rush country, and had to put her focus on her finals, only that. She was determined to be a mining engineer. She'd come too far to let some bothersome, random phantom stand in the way of her ambitions.

The grandfather clock in the living room of the Lace House struck midnight. Abby hated that it was late and hated that she might struggle in her dreams to make out the stranger's face all over again. Lucky to have part-time work and housing at the popular Golden bed and breakfast, Abby rolled to her side and pulled the chain to shut off the Tiffany-style bedside lamp. Her wrought-iron single creaked a bit during the maneuver. She settled deep under the patchwork quilt and heaved a discontented sigh.

Moonlight poured into her little room, giving life to her surroundings and the room's Victorian décor. The pedestal sink beamed in shadow. The oval mirror above the sink did not. No moonlight shone from it. The wall sconce nearby did. Just as well, Abby thought. Mirrors never reflect anything worth seeing. The old-fashioned glass sconce brought Abby back on track. Her room was cozy. One didn't have to try hard to imagine them in the West as it was over a hundred years ago. That's one of the reasons she loved this historic hostel and often wished she'd been born to the pioneer west. Actually she had been. A perplexing thought to be sure.

Abby rolled onto her stomach and beat at her pillow a few times before laying her cheek against the soft muslin. Rows of mountain wildflowers drifted in view from the wallpaper before her. She could almost smell their sweet fragrance. *Wallflowers*, she thought, and could have kicked herself for doing it. She'd never cared about this kind of thing before—before the Slide Cemetery. She'd never cared about how she looked and, in fact, didn't much like mirrors. At that, Abby hopped out of bed and pulled down the tasseled shade. Nuisance moonlight! Flopping in bed on her back, she stared at the dark ceiling. Better. Shrouded in darkness, maybe she could get some peaceful sleep. Spring finals started tomorrow.

Her freshman year at Mines had gone well so far. The last thing she wanted was to screw up and not become a sophomore. She'd made it to this school by some miracle and wanted to stay and earn her engineering degree. Abby rolled onto her stomach again, relieved to see nothing but darkness; no wildflowers, no wallflowers. This time when she laid her cheek against her pillow, she mentally outlined her physics notes and the mathematics needed in support.

Classical mechanics related to electricity and magnetism, while quantum mechanics spoke to statistics, she mused, already a bit off-subject. The interrelationship between theory and observation made for a fascinating overlay of ideas and facts. Abby never tired of pondering the probable and the improbable, or separating empirical from actual. She loved the science and mathematics of any and everything involved with mining, especially gold mining. She loved that the School of Mines sat right in the heart of mining country, and only eighteen miles from Denver. No better place to be. On that pleasant thought, she drifted off to sleep.

Jolted awake, Abby shook all over. Steel cold penetrated to the bone. Her lungs felt imploded. Gasping for air, she forced herself to grab her cell phone off the nightstand. *Cough. Cough.* The phone read *4:00.* Her head pounded. She didn't move beyond that since she still had the shakes. At least she could get a breath now. She blinked hard. It was too dark for her to see much of anything in her room that might give her a clue about what was going on.

Was it the flu? She'd had a flu shot. The school had made her. No, shouldn't be the flu. Fear tried to set in with the cold, but she refused to let it. *I have exams in four hours.* That thought panicked her more than this bizarre awakening. Failure wasn't an option she could afford.

Only then did Abby realize her t-shirt and pajama bottoms were damp . . . no . . . *nearly frozen.* It took every bit of effort she could muster to throw off the quilt and pull the lamp chain. What was happening was impossible. She knew this had to be some kind of crazy dream. Oh, great. All she needed, right. Moments passed during which Abby stood in icy silence before she let her hand travel over her clothing. Her soaked, frigid t-shirt had a ridge of ice along the bottom edge. She could feel the same lines of ice at her pajama bottoms. *This is crazy. This makes no sense. I'm a sensible person. Things like this don't happen to me.*

Forcing herself to calm, and since her shivers had lessened, Abby reached into a drawer and pulled out dry clothes. Mechanically, she slipped out of her sopping pajamas, kicked the troubled remnants across the wood floor, and then changed. There was nothing to do here but get back in bed, then wait to get out of bed, and then go take her finals. She might sleep in between. She'd no idea. The luxury of putting any thought to what she'd just experienced would have to wait for later. She needed to be clear-headed for the day upcoming. No time for strange events to throw shade on her already uncertain situation.

When Abby got up, her phone read *7:00.* Sheer focus helped her sleep, and sheer focus helped her get out of bed. Had she slept? Maybe. At least she woke up without further incident. No more ice in bed with her. She shrugged off the thought and slipped into her worn jeans and a hooded sweatshirt, the one with the big M for Mines. After that, she collected her thick charcoal braid of hair in a coil and shoved it inside her hood. Her hair had always been long and she never gave much thought to cutting it short. If she hurried, she could bypass the owners and any guests staying at the hostel. The owners were more than nice; that wasn't the point.

The Smiths had hired her to help with their hostel when others did not. Grateful didn't say it. Abby cared about the Smiths, but this morning she didn't have time for breakfast or any kind of chat. Mrs. Smith would want her to eat a good breakfast before her ten-minute walk to campus and finals. Abby'd never had a mother to cluck over her so. No matter. She didn't think about it most of the time except now, with Mrs. Smith being so kind to her. The grandfather clock in the parlor chimed seven-thirty. Abby slung her backpack over her shoulder and got out of there as fast as her Dickies work boots would take her.

"Hey, Einstein!"

Abby knew who called out but didn't want to turn around. She needed to get to the Lace House and her evening duties. Her last final was over, and grades would come out in a couple of days. Though not worried about them, still, she had to see for herself she'd done well enough to keep her scholarship status.

"Abby Gray, hold on!" Ebony yelled louder, hurrying to catch up. Raj Naidu did the same, keeping company with his classmate.

Abby didn't slow and kept walking at a fast pace. Ebony White had always been nothing but nice, and there was no good reason to ignore her. Abby just didn't want to talk to anybody at the moment, not even Ebony.

"Girl, you are lucky I get you and don't mind your weird self," Ebony said the moment she rounded in front of Abby.

Stopped in place, Abby shot a blank look at Ebony, aiming for annoyed but finding it hard to throw annoyance Ebony's way. Instead she saved her irritation for the guy standing next to her only friend on campus.

Raj stepped back, a little intimidated by the pretty girl in the hoodie. Apparently embarrassed by his reaction, he reclaimed his step.

Abby smiled, disarmed by his response.

"Well, I would have introduced you to Raj before if I'd known that's what it took to get a smile to crack that stone face of yours," Ebony teased.

"Sorry, but I have to get to work," Abby said, and tried to step around the two.

"Listen here, Einstein, finals are over and you should come with us to Starbucks at least, for a cup of celebratory coffee. Maybe even splurge on a grande mocha latte or something."

"You know I don't drink coffee, Ebony," Abby said, having been stopped again by conversation.

"Then how about the Red Onion and we'll force our fake IDs on the barkeep?"

The Red Onion resembled a miner's saloon. Abby loved to walk by and stare in the windows. You had to be twenty-one to drink alcohol in Colorado, so technically no one underage should go in. Still, college kids did, Abby knew. *The Red Onion in Skagway is haunted.* Where that thought came from, she'd no idea. It startled her.

"Well we can't just open another bottle of water and call it a day, Abby Gray, not after finals!" Ebony's shoulders sagged, frustrated by her friend's . . . unfriendliness. She should be used to it after a year of knowing Einstein, but she wasn't.

"You two go on," Abby encouraged and started to walk away.

"Not before I introduce Raj. C'mon, girlfriend."

"Hey, Raj," Abby mumbled, obviously uneasy. Even though she attended college with thousands of students, she could count on one hand those she didn't consider strangers. Now she looked at her boots and not him. This was normal for her. It kept people at a distance, and that's what she wanted.

"Uh, well, I guess, hello," Raj almost questioned.

Disarmed again by the boy's natural tone and innocent manner, Abby looked up. Raj stood inches taller than she.

"Sure, it's a hello," she said back.

"I'm Raj Naidu, a freshman here from California. I haven't seen you around before. What's your major?"

"Engineering physics," she answered.

"Okay, so that comes under applied science and mathematics, which is why maybe we haven't run into each other before," Raj said, more to himself than Abby. A geek giveaway, if noticed. A brilliant intellect at Mines, Raj kept his head in books most of the time. Social skills were not his forte.

"Let's don't leave humanities and social sciences out of this." Ebony lightheartedly inserted herself into the conversation. "Not everyone can be scientific brain trusts. Someone has to focus on economics and business at Mines."

"Geoscience and resource engineering are the keys to the future's renewable energy," Raj said, turning his focus to Ebony. "That's the most important business for our future."

Abby enjoyed this back-and-forth. Besides, it took attention off her. That was always a de-stressor.

"Why are you called, Einstein, Abby?" Raj asked.

Abby wasn't going to answer. She smiled and started to walk away.

"Not so fast, Miss Einstein." Ebony caught her arm, forcing Abby to stand still. "Raj, Abby is here on a President's Scholarship. Her composite GPA, SAT, and ACT scores merited a four-year ride. She's a Colorado Scholar, and the best of the best. And I know you know what that means, Raj, since you are here on scholarships, too. Two bests in one," Ebony joked.

Flushed and embarrassed, Abby regretted the day she opened up to Ebony about her scholarship status. No one else needed to know that. She should have stayed quiet from the start.

"And why I call her Einstein," Ebony kept on, still holding

onto Abby's arm, "is because she's weird, just like Einstein doubtless was. Genius will do that to you."

"I'm no genius," Abby gritted out and removed her arm from Ebony's grasp.

"What is it going to take to get you to come with us now and celebrate?" Ebony tried one last time.

"I have to go to work. Nice meeting you, Raj." Then Abby took off.

Ebony and Raj stood and watched Abby disappear down the street. Neither said another word.

Abby rubbed her hands together. She'd never get rid of calluses that left their imprint of a lifetime of hard work. Without realizing what she did, she had a habit of rubbing her hands red, trying to shake off the ugliness of her life. In the end, she'd find her hands in a ball and force her reluctant fingers open. So much for all the Lubriderm, she'd scoff. Today she had to pack up, and she'd best get it done before the campus shuttle to the ski areas left her behind.

Many college students used their summer break to work jobs in the mountain ski areas like Vail, Aspen, Copper Mountain, Steamboat Springs, and Winter Park, to name a few. The Rocky Mountains provided activities galore year-round, and ski areas depended on summer help to take care of the multitude of tourists who wanted to take scenic chairlift rides, hike, bike, slide, camp, attend outdoor concerts, utilize activity centers for children, and so on. Abby had another purpose, but she still had to make that shuttle. She didn't want to spend the money to go separately. The school shuttle was free.

"Are you almost ready?" Lucinda Smith stood in the doorway of Abby's room.

"Yes, thank you." Abby was all politeness with Mrs. Smith. It seemed the only way to be with the generous hostel proprietress.

Abby finished separating out what was to go and what was to stay and shot Mrs. Smith a bright smile, something she rarely gave anybody.

"Why are you so nice to me?" Abby was embarrassed and flushed the moment she said it, and now it was too late to take it back.

Lucinda chuckled.

"Uh, I mean why did you give me a job here, when I don't think you need me, really?"

"Don't need you? Such a thing to say," Lucinda retorted.

Abby watched Mrs. Smith's hazel eyes tear up.

Lucinda cleared her throat and caught a few errant strands of shoulder-length, graying hair back behind her ears.

"You remind me of the daughter I lost years ago to cancer. She was our only child, and we've never been able to have another. I'd be so proud of her if she'd grown up to be like you. You work hard and never complain. You're smart as a whip and don't brag about it. You're a native Coloradan with grit like the pioneers, I'd say. So, to answer your question about needing you . . . the answer is, you belong here. That's what I know. You belong here for as long as you need and as long as you want. This isn't charity, Abby. This is earned." Lucinda looked Abby in the eye, to make sure the girl understood her meaning.

Abby pulled her blue beanie cap down farther over her ears and stared at her work boots. She didn't know how to handle this emotion. No one ever said such things to her. No one had ever told her she *belonged* anywhere.

"Abby Gray, do not hide your beautiful face and your beautiful self. I've a mind to snatch that cap of yours away," Lucinda teased.

"I am no beauty," Abby mumbled, still not looking up.

"That's utter nonsense. Whoever told you such a thing?"

Abby stayed silent.

"All right," Lucinda gently began, as if understanding something else was going on. "Do you mind if I tell you otherwise?"

Abby dropped her shoulders and said nothing.

"Your beauty is timeless, with your long raven hair and eyes of blue that take you far away sometimes. Where that is, only you can know. Your angular cheekbones are perfect, your ears flat, your nose pert, and your shapely mouth has to be the envy of every girl at Mines. I haven't even talked about your figure, which also has to be the envy of all the girls and make them jealous that all the boys notice," Lucinda added pointedly. "So, don't hide all that you are, young lady."

"I'm sorry about your daughter." Abby looked at Lucinda Smith.

"The years have helped me heal, and having you here has helped me, too."

"The fall term begins August twenty-first. I'll be back just before then." Abby straightened to her full height of five-foot-three, and held Lucinda's tearful gaze.

Lucinda put her shoulders back and shook her head enough to clear away her sadness.

"You just have a good summer and try to have some fun at your internship in Alaska. I'll store what belongings you don't take, since this will be another rental until you return. We're nearly booked full for the summer as it is." The grandfather clock struck another hour. "You get going now, young lady, so you don't miss your ride." Lucinda rushed this last sentence, then turned on her heel and left.

Abby wondered if Lucinda had teared up again. She certainly had. Abby wiped her eyes with the sleeve of her sweatshirt. Humph. I don't cry. *I don't.* She needed to boot scoot across campus and had one more thing to do before leaving town.

★ ★ ★ ★ ★

"Girlfriend, this is sure a surprise," Ebony welcomed the moment she opened her dormitory door to Abby.

"I wanted to say goodbye."

"What? What goodbye? Just goodbye, or goodbye-goodbye?" Ebony ushered Abby inside, pulling on her arm as she often did, to hold Abby still long enough to finish a conversation.

"Just goodbye," Abby made clear. "For an English scholar, your words are interesting, Ebony. You could have written Shakespeare for Shakespeare, and here you're talking goodbye and goodbyes. Pretty funny."

"Whatever, Einstein," Ebony countered. "Where are you off to?"

Abby smiled at Ebony's choice of words again.

"Off to?" Abby underscored.

"If I choose to end a question with a preposition or an adverb, I will. Stay on subject," Ebony lectured.

Abby had memorized her narrative for Ebony.

"When I was in Alaska for spring break," Abby explained, "I saw the possibility for an internship as part of the Grand Challenges Scholar program here at Mines that gives freshman options for experience. Instead of 'unique experiences unified by challenges faced by our world today,' as the literature reads, I proposed an internship to 'identify challenges faced in our world in the past, in Klondike gold-rush days.' Gold-mining history, if you will."

Ebony listened to her friend, mouth agape.

"It's a three-tier internship out of Skagway and Dyea," Abby continued. "Both are prime archaeological and geological sites. I'll work alongside national park rangers with horseback tours, at mushers' camps, and hikes up the Chilkoot Trail. The National Academy of Engineering approved my test proposal. I'll be a student abroad of sorts; not really abroad but not in the lower forty-eight. The NAE has asked me to submit articles about each experience to them and also submit posts to the *Oredigger* for student consumption. My travel expenses are covered, thank heaven. I do have some funding left from my yearly stipend, but it really helps having the airfare to Seattle, and then passage on the Alaska Marine Highway to Skagway paid."

"I knew it. Gold-rush country, right?"

"Yep," Abby answered sheepishly.

Ebony wore a look of utter bewilderment.

"You were born in gold-rush country and go to college in gold-rush country. Why do you need to rush to another gold-rush country when there are enough digs in Colorado to keep a body going for this life and on into the next?"

"That's just it, Ebony. We're at the scene of the eighteen fifty-nine Pikes Peak Gold Rush. Before that, the first stampede was the eighteen forty-nine California Gold Rush. Alaska is the scene of the eighteen ninety-eight Klondike Gold Rush. Right after that, you have the Nome Gold Rush. These waves in history are so real to me, with thousands and thousands of gold-seekers stampeding across the West and then headed to the far-off North, a no-man's land, where surviving the day made for a good day. It's the idea to me, Ebony, of so much humanity doing the same thing at the same time in the same place and then, whoosh, all gone! The same for boomtowns: whoosh, gone!"

"There's that faraway look of yours again, Einstein," Ebony noticed. "What exactly do you hope to find?"

Abby's attention returned to her friend. Ebony got her. Ebony could tell she searched for something in these historic mining sites, but what? Abby didn't know herself, so she could hardly give a rational answer.

"Are you going ghost mining, girl?" Ebony suddenly asked. "If so, Buffalo Bill's buried just up the hill. You could start—"

"That's ridiculous." Abby didn't let Ebony finish. "Don't confuse a love of history and gold mining with any paranormal wacko hunt to *ghost* mine!"

"O . . . kay," Ebony said, and realized there was nothing more to say. If Einstein wanted to go ghost mining instead of gold mining, she wasn't about to stop her. Besides, Einstein was and is a genius. She'd figured a way to have her trip sanctioned by Mines. Who knew what she might turn up?

CHAPTER TWO

Abigail Grayce stood in line outside the Women's Exchange on Stout Street, a benevolent organization for needy women in the heart of Denver. The Women's Exchange took her in while another rescue mission, the People's Tabernacle, did not. They only accepted women and children who had been residents of Denver for at least sixty days. Abigail was disappointed to be turned away.

The rescue mission would have provided, "a free dispensary, winter clothing, a free bathhouse, classes in sewing, medical attention to prostitutes, and shelter to the homeless," so the sign posted outside read. Abigail needed shelter; not the rest. Admittedly, sufficient winter clothes would be nice. So would a bath. She refused to be embarrassed about needing help. It was a luxury she couldn't afford. Hunger and cold could do that.

Times were hard for everybody in the region, and had been since the silver collapse in 1893. Nationwide panic ensued. That was four years ago. Denver still suffered economic depression. Jobs remained hard for men to find, much less a woman. Earlier in the day, Abigail had slipped inside the doorway of the *Rocky Mountain News* for shelter, but then went indoors to read what news she could get her hands on. The statistics were not good.

The newspaper reported that 377 businesses had failed, 435 mines closed, and 45,000 people were out of work. When she read on, she learned train companies had been reducing their fares to encourage people to leave Denver. One company advertised a six-dollar ticket to Missouri, while other companies were flat-out free. The Union Pacific Railroad had gone bankrupt! She didn't want to keep reading bad news, but she did. The population had dropped from 106,000 to 90,000, with people taking the train companies up on their offer. From her reading Abigail knew miners who'd flooded to Denver found no jobs and little help.

In Creede, she'd read a little about such troubles in the *Creede Candle*. She always grabbed every newspaper she could to keep informed. Self-taught, she knew how to read and write well, while her brothers had never cared to learn. They disapproved of her "educating herself," and let her know it. In Cripple Creek, when they caught her with a copy of the *Spar City Spark* or the *Hinsdale Phonograph* from out of the county, they'd snatch the paper away and toss it in the fire. "You're not smart, and you're no beauty," they'd taunt, celebrating the ruined newspaper. They were bullies. How she wanted to answer back, but never did. They'd likely throw her a punch. She didn't need any more bruises.

A rush of boys broke into Abigail's melancholy when they burst inside the newspaper office, whisking right past her to get to their stacks for delivery. She put down the *Rocky Mountain News* and left, her heart heavy with the knowledge her brothers were nothing like these determined boys who wanted to work. Some even wore smiles.

It had snowed all day, and Abigail tired of scooting in and out of doorways to warm up. She knew she looked like a poor excuse for a gold miner but didn't care. As usual, her floppy-brimmed hat was pulled low. No one needed to see her face. Wearing skirts wasn't compatible with hard work. The look on people's faces as they walked or drove past in their fancy city clothes registered their disapproval of her, as if she were an incarnation of Calamity Jane. Humph. Denver's fine streets would be fortunate, indeed, to have the likes of the noted fron-tierswoman walking down them. Calamity Jane had lived a more colorful and adventurous life than any upstanding Denver citizen could ever imagine; at least according to the dime novels Abigail had read.

"All right, you can all file in now, but please, one at a time," an austere, middle-aged woman came outside the Exchange and announced.

Several women rushed in front of Abigail, and she let them. They were all cold and hungry. She'd wait her turn. When it came, she stepped to the small setup table just inside the Exchange door. The young woman sitting there didn't look up when she called out, "Next."

Abigail approached.

"Name?"

Abigail didn't like to give out details of her life to anybody; especially to this girl who didn't look any older than she.

"Your name, please?"

"Abigail Grayce. How old are you?" Abigail blurted before thinking.

"I'm nineteen. Your age, I'd guess," the girl said and smiled.

"Are you a nun?"

"Not exactly, but I work with the Episcopal Church, and we do charity work—"

Abigail unclenched her jaw and straightened her spine.

"I'm not here for charity," she interrupted. "I just want something to eat and a place to escape the cold for a bit. You can keep your charity."

"Yes, of course," the young woman said and returned to her list of questions. "Where are you from? How long have you been in Denver? Do you intend to look for work?"

"I'm from Creede. I've been in Denver two days. Yes, I intend to look for work."

The young woman looked up at Abigail now, not in scrutiny, but in wonderment.

"Creede must be an exciting place to live. A lot of famous people have been there, like Bat Masterson, Calamity Jane, and Poker Alice. Before he came back to make trouble in Denver, that's where Soapy Smith lived. And isn't Creede where Robert Ford was killed dead? He killed Jesse James and then he got killed."

Abigail started to respond but was cut off. She mentally noted Bat Masterson had resided in Denver for a time.

"Have you lived in Leadville?" The girl kept up her questions. "That's where Doc Holliday once was! He knew Wyatt Earp and was at the Gunfight at the O. K. Corral!"

Abigail sighed. Though she and this girl shared the same age, similarities stopped there. Abigail had never paid much attention to legendary outlaws and lawmen or the myths that lived on after them. She did recollect, however, Wyatt Earp and Calamity Jane hadn't died. She'd last heard of Jane Canary as a storyteller in *Buffalo Bill's Wild West and Congress of Rough Riders of the World* show four years ago. She was uncertain about Wyatt Earp's whereabouts and refused to admit to herself she read dime novels.

"I've lived in Leadville but never crossed paths with any of the names you mentioned. Are we done here?" Abigail intoned nicely, belying how she really felt. Long conversations were never a good idea.

"Of course. Sorry," the girl apologized. "Here's a meal ticket and your bed assignment. If you don't mind my saying, you are well-spoken. I mean, compared to most that come through here. You sound like you've had a lot of schooling."

"Homeschooling," Abigail answered when she didn't need to.

She accepted the tickets given and stepped farther into the welcome warmth.

Abigail needed to work. She knew a lot about gold and silver, since her family had migrated from mining town to mining town—gold mine to silver mine—in Colorado for as long as she could remember. She liked Cripple Creek and Victor the best. She loved the high country beyond Pikes Peak. Its heights rose to 10,000 feet. *Like living in the clouds,* she often thought. That's where she learned the most about mining, and where miners didn't treat her like a know-nothing girl, or run her out of the shafts when they discovered her presence. It was a pretty wild place, Cripple Creek. There was always fighting going on somewhere, which meant dying going on somewhere. Gunfire flew similar to blackbirds in the sky. Not much law and order. Her two brothers hated that she took to gold mining and hated her for shaming them. No decent girl should do what she was doing, they'd tell her.

She was decent all right. Her mother made sure of that. Abigail didn't hate her mother, but she didn't love her. Abigail didn't hate her father or her brothers, but she didn't feel any love for them, either. It was the oddest thing. None of them seemed to like her. She'd stay up nights trying to figure out why her parents bothered even to have her. It was hard for her to remember when her feelings died, the same as blackbirds in the sky, shot and falling to the ground in a dead heap.

A week ago Abigail sneaked out of the family cabin in Creede and meant never to return. She couldn't fight off all four of them, so she was relieved no one woke up when she left. Her father was likely sleeping off a drunk, anyway, and her brothers were fast asleep after a night of carousing. It was her mother she didn't want to encounter.

Her mother would scream and yell and shout to the heavens

Abigail was destined for *eternal damnation,* right before grabbing her sturdy switch and taking it to her daughter's back. A sensible mother would have maybe explained why she was damned, but then, Abigail's mother wasn't sensible. Something had made her go crazy a long time ago. Maybe someone told her mother, *"You're no beauty."* Maybe that's why Abigail grew up believing the same thing about herself.

Early on, Abigail found escape and a safe haven in books and newspapers. She didn't go to school on a regular basis, so couldn't count on school for her education. Bright by nature, her application to her studies paid off. She thrived on knowledge; that and hard work. Besides escaping in books, she escaped down into the mines when she could.

The darkness drew her in. The isolation from the rest of the world drew her in. The miners barely paid attention to her in the shaft house, except to tell her to be careful and not get in their way. Mostly the miners worked hard and ignored her. Amazingly, Abigail had managed to slip down shafts and wander here and there with her lantern. When discovered, the miners would hoist her topside. She'd ignored the danger of her actions. To her, the mine shafts were safer than the rowdy, dangerous boomtown streets. Day or night on the streets, you could be out walking and never see the bullet coming.

"Abigail Grayce, isn't it?"

Lump in her throat and flushed with nerves, Abigail hated to do this. She'd no choice. If she wanted to find any kind of decent work in Denver, she needed decent women's clothes for the task. Truth, she'd never owned a dress, always donning her brothers' leftovers. Her mother never saw fit to tell her otherwise and never made her any dresses. Abigail hadn't worried about this until now; until she needed a dress to get a city job. After filling her stomach, then setting her few belongings on her allocated bed, she went downstairs to the same girl who'd signed her in to the Women's Exchange. Abigail forced her hands apart. They'd been rubbed red with nerves. The gold nugget she clasped fell to the floor, and she hastily picked it up.

"I have this." Abigail showed the girl. "It's worth money. It's not much to some, but it's everything to me," she confessed. The tiny gold, heart-shaped nugget had been a gift from a stranger in Cripple Creek, a kind miner who must have taken pity on her. She couldn't imagine any other reason. His words, she remembered.

"You keep this, young'un, and someday when you need it, think of me. I don't have nobody in this world, and I'd like to count for somethin'. I'd be beholdin' to you if you'd take this."

Abigail had accepted the gift and thought of the aged miner every day since then. Her family never found out. She hadn't known much kindness in her life, so the little nugget held more than monetary value to her. She still regretted she'd never asked the miner his name when she should have.

"No, Abigail Grayce, it's your keepsake. We have a storeroom of donated clothing here. I think we can find you something." With that, the girl pushed her chair out and got up. "Follow me," she directed.

Abigail was mystified. How did the girl know about the nugget being a keepsake, and why didn't she accept it? Most others surely would have torn it out of her hand. The girl had to be a nun or somebody close to God to show such generosity to her. Abigail tucked the nugget deep in her palm, worried she didn't have a safe place to hide it in Denver. Public housing, tented or brick-built, couldn't be trusted.

"This way, Abigail Grayce," the girl said over her shoulder, continuing to walk down the hall to the storeroom.

"What's your name?" Abigail called after her.

"Mary," the girl said and didn't turn around.

Mary. I will remember.

The brisk March air greeted Abigail the moment she stepped outside the Women's Exchange in the center of Denver's commercial district. She determined to hold her head high no matter what or who she encountered. Besides, in her new, old clothes, she had no choice but to hold her head up, outfitted as she was in a gray shirtwaist dress with a high, stiff collar, tight waist, and seamed down her backside. Some sort of corseted contraption, too! Humph. She couldn't bend well. Odd, but necessary, she conceded.

More lighthearted than she'd expected to feel in this confining getup, she kept on down Stout Street in her black buckled shoes. It had stopped snowing. Abigail missed her reliable boots. Every few steps, she'd stop, pull her skirt from her ankle, and check her shoes to make sure of her raised step on the slushy sidewalk. A simple, black wool jacket covered her shirtwaist to hip level. The jacket had tight sleeves and a slight puffy flair at the shoulder. Her arms looked like muttonchops!

Her hair had been a problem. Mary said as much. She'd undone Abigail's braid and arranged her mass of raven hair into a bun at the top of her head, then plopped a black wool beret on top of that. Abigail was accustomed to a hat she could pull down for cover, not a circle of wool for decoration. Mary convinced her to let go of her floppy-brimmed hat, and Abigail regretted she'd let Mary win on this one. Abigail had never felt as exposed as she did at this moment. She allowed herself a quick look in the square of mirror in the storeroom.

Maybe she wasn't ugly, but she wasn't pretty, either. She took account of her ordinary blue eyes, her ordinary angular cheekbones, her ordinary turned-up nose, her ordinary flat ears, her ordinary, shapely mouth, and her mass of ordinary black hair. In truth, she had little use for mirrors and any study of her reflection. *Best leave it be,* she lectured herself. Too much study in the mirror, same as too much conversation, invited trouble. Abigail straightened her spine for the umpteenth time, and headed for the *Rocky Mountain News.* The newspaper office wasn't far. She'd had time to come up with an idea while the benevolent Mary helped stuff her into these confining clothes.

The editors at the *Rocky Mountain News* had been polite but did not hire her to report and write about the Colorado mining industry. They had their own journalists covering mining news, business news, banking news, social news, etc., and had no need for more staff. During her quick interview, when asked about her schooling and experience, she had nothing to say. Her spirits plummeted along with her idea of being a mining journalist. She didn't have a formal education. The *Rocky Mountain News* wanted a formal education.

Why didn't I speak up? She chastised herself. Why didn't I tell them about all my years living in most every mining town in Colorado? I know gold. I know silver. I know how to assay. I have the English skills needed for spelling and writing. I taught myself, but I have them. I'm schooled in math and science, too. *Why didn't I speak up?*

She found it hard to hold her head high now, despite the stiff, uncomfortable neck of her clothing. She felt dejected. Securing a job at the newspaper would mean security. She needed to take care of herself and not rely on some charitable center. Besides, she could stay a week at the center and no more. There were too many others in need. The western sun lowered, a grim reminder the day had been wasted.

"Say, Miss Grayce!" a man called out, and caught up with her at the front door of the *Rocky Mountain News.*

Abigail turned around, as much as she wanted to get out of

there. She eyed the man hard. His screech and his sudden swooping in reminded her of a predatory, red-tailed hawk. So did his appearance. His head looked too small for his thick body, and his arms and legs reminded her of blocky trees, sawed off. The shirt he wore could be mistaken for the white underbelly of the predator hawk, and his brown belt was identical to the brown band the hawk carried across its belly. Closer scrutiny revealed a short, hooked nose: a ringer for the predator bird!

"Miss Grayce," he said again.

Abigail heard, *"kreeeeear!"* easily imagining the screech of the opportunistic feeder. It took effort for her to stay put when she'd rather escape out the door. She didn't like unnecessary conversation, and she didn't like feeling so vulnerable.

"I, uh . . . wanted a moment more of your time, Miss Grayce."

Abigail waited while he huffed and puffed. He appeared closer in age to her than she'd noticed before, when he'd sat beside another editor during her interview. This editor had said nothing and let the other editor ask her questions. The longer she stood there, the more her suspicions grew.

"Maybe I can help you get a job at another paper," he said. "There's a weekly going to a daily paper that's setting up shop, and I could direct you there."

Uncomfortable at the man's leer, Abigail gave a polite nod and then turned to walk out. She'd seen that look on others' faces before and never liked it. She felt indecent. Her mother's words rang in her head. *You're indecent. You're no beauty. You're eternally damned.* Abigail always felt it was her fault when a man looked at her the way this editor did.

"No, wait, Miss Grayce," he implored. "*The Denver Examiner,* or I should say, the *Daily Journal,* is hiring. You might try there."

Abigail stopped and pivoted. His words, and the fact that his leer had disappeared, helped her relax.

"What's your name?" she asked quietly.

"Amos, Amos Garrett."

Amos. She would remember.

"Where is the *Daily Journal,* Amos? Is it nearby?"

"Sure is," Amos told her. "Go to Market and Fourteenth Streets, and you should run right into their brand-new sign." He grinned at her as if he were a boy scared to ask a girl to dance.

"Thank you, Amos. I'll let you know if I get hired at the paper," she offered when she didn't have to.

"I sure hope to see you again, Miss . . . Miss Grayce."

Abigail smiled inwardly at his innocent blush. He wasn't a predator after all.

Abigail took care in crossing Denver's teeming streets. She'd never been in a city so large with its busy trolleys, horse-drawn wagons and carriages, crowds of people on every corner, and a mesh of telephone and electrical lines as far as the eye could see. And city buildings; she'd never seen so many rising against the western scape. Still, none could block out the imposing view of the snowcapped Continental Divide rising from the foothills out of Denver. Abigail wondered what her grandparents must have thought when they first saw the Rocky Mountains, having pioneered west to join in the Pikes Peak Gold Rush. Relief maybe, Abigail speculated; relief to make it here to gold-rush country *alive.*

Abigail took the little gold nugget from her jacket pocket and turned the treasured heart over in her hand. The cool gold soothed her rough palm; not because of its monetary value but its emotional worth. A family gift to me, she thought, at the same time realizing she felt closer to the unknown stranger who'd given it to her than to her real kin. She turned the aged miner's words over in her mind, much as she'd done with the gold in her hand.

You keep this, young'un, and someday when you need it, think of me. I don't have nobody in this world, and I'd like to count for somethin'. I'd be beholdin' to you if you'd take this.

Abigail wanted to count for something, too. Feeling akin to the miner, she didn't have anybody in this world either. Never one to waste time on self-pity, she tucked the heart-shaped nugget back in her pocket and squared her shoulders, determined to get a job and make her life count for more than callused hands and empty pockets. She didn't need or want anybody to shout at her, punch at her, condemn her, or worse, forget about her. Bullied by her family all her life, she'd live alone and find peace. Family meant trouble. A husband meant trouble. Caring meant trouble. She was done with trouble.

CHAPTER THREE

Elias Colt hopped off the Northern Pacific Railway train in Seattle, out of money but never ideas. Success waited for no one, especially in these hard times with competition fierce for every dollar. He'd played out jobs along his path in Montana and wanted to forge a new one. Modern times called for modern ideas. It was 1897 now and Seattle waited for him. The gaming life but never a wife, he vowed. Success in business meant just that—no wife and no family life. His fortunes lay elsewhere.

Three o'clock. Elias checked his pocket watch and then his trusted sidearm, a Frontier Six-Shooter. The Gunfight at the O.K. Corral in '81 started at this exact hour, and some there carried the same sidearm he did. Elias ran a finger over the etched barrel of the branded Colt, noting the value of having a caliber that could fire both in a pistol and rifle. He'd been only eight years old at the time of the famous Tombstone gunfight, but news of it traveled fast to the Montana Territory and his home in Virginia City.

He'd been a kid, but kids grow up quick in the West; had to grow up fast around any mining boomtown. From an early age Elias knew about guns, gunfights, saloons, miners, prostitutes, and greed. Nevada City wasn't far from Virginia City, where one of the richest gold strikes in the Rocky Mountains was found. Tombstone wasn't the only boomtown to draw the lawless along with the law-abiding. Elias admired Wyatt Earp and determined early on to keep a Colt pistol handy. Born with the last name Cole, Elias changed it to Colt. His mother didn't care, and his father had died in a mining accident at Alder Gulch.

Elias accepted this. It hurt, but he'd learned to bury his feelings and close ties to family. He helped take care of his mother doing odd jobs in general stores, cleaning up in saloons, sweeping up in newspaper offices, digging mine shafts, cow punching, and working as a ranch hand when he could. When he was old enough, he liked being a barkeep in saloons. That job put more money in his pockets than most others. His mother had passed, and he left Virginia City soon as she lay in the ground. Then he bought his ticket out of town on the Great Northern Railway to Tacoma, with a connection on the Northern Pacific the rest of the way to Seattle.

The 1889 fire in Seattle had done a lot of damage to the port city, as Elias quickly learned when he asked at the train depot for directions to Yesler's Hall.

"You can't miss it," the stationmaster said. "Soon as you hit Skid Road, you'll see what's left of things." Elias didn't know how to take that and would find out for himself. He'd come to Seattle to get his own box house up and running. All in good time. At twenty-four, he wanted his own business, but he'd have to earn enough money first. News of Seattle's box houses had reached east, and Elias thought this would suit him since he'd been raised around *guns, gunfights, saloons, miners, prostitutes, and greed.*

Instead of what he'd imagined to see "south of the Deadline" he'd read about, the streets here were crowded with saloons and variety theaters with names like the Palace and the People's Theater, plastered with signs touting appearances by John L. Sullivan, Jim Jeffries, Jim Corbett, W. C. Fields, Eddie Foy, and Sarah Bernhardt. Elias had heard of the boxers but not the others. *Wait.* Maybe he'd read it wrong in the paper he'd grabbed up on the train. He pulled the rolled-up news from his pack and found the passage he remembered reading in the *Telegraph.*

"There is no law south of the Deadline. Anything goes," he read aloud.

What anything goes? He checked the date on the newspaper in his hands. It was four years old! Damn. He crumpled the paper and sent it flying. The "anything goes" Elias had counted on finding in Seattle meant bar brawls, knife fights, gunfire, whores cat-fighting, crowded faro tables, drunks, opium-eaters, lively piano playing, and unending calls from patrons. The *Telegraph* had described as much. It spoke of girls with painted cheeks, bare arms, necks exposed halfway to their waists, skirts just above the knee, giggling from behind closed curtains while their latest customer sipped his watered-down drink.

These surroundings today looked too fine for box house clientele. Customers in box houses wouldn't be waiting for entertainers like the John Jack Theatrical Company, the Fanny Morgan Phelps Dramatic Company, or lectures on matrimony and health posted here. Customers in box houses would be waiting for the show to start, but they'd also be waiting for their next drink, their next card game, and their next girl.

The box houses he'd heard tell of were connected to saloons, had a stage for variety shows, then two long rows of seating in front of the stage for men and boys to watch the show . . . the men smoking and chewing tobacco and the boys gorging on peanuts. In back and to the sides of the stage were small compartments made of thin boards, where customers could enjoy female company in private. Each compartment was outfitted with an electric-torch button. When time came for another drink, that button would be pressed, and a waiter would respond and take the order, and then hurry to the bar behind the stage. Good money for the barkeep, Elias always thought. Where in tarnation was the Theatre Comique on Washington Street he'd heard so much about?

Elias glanced up at all the signage again, looking for that theater. He had a headache. Too much reading always brought one on. He'd learned to read and write and cipher well enough, but he never liked to stay on any one of those things very long. Maybe he needed spectacles. Maybe he just needed answers.

March sleet rained down. Elias pulled his brown duster together in front of him, glad he had the reliable bushwhacker coat. It might snow any time. Snow would be preferable to this wet. Just then a large rat crossed his path. He watched it disappear down a flooded street. Instinct told Elias to follow the critter, so he did. People brushed past, but Elias barely noticed. He'd follow the rat, going down and dirty, already in the slums.

"Hey, good lookin', wanna come in?" A young woman stepped out in front of him, forcing Elias to stop his rat chase. Her rouged face, wicked eyebrows, tousled hair, and obvious clothing gave her away. She looked like she worked in a box house. Maybe he'd found what he'd been looking for.

"You should get out of the rain, darlin'," Elias said and smiled.

The girl looked bewildered. Sleet dripped across her smudged brow, and she'd begun to tremble from the cold, yet she didn't go inside. They both stood in icy water up to their ankles. Elias took hold of her elbow and guided her through the doorway. He had to bend his six-foot-three frame to clear it.

He'd guessed right. This must be her crib. The tin roof leaked onto the dirty sheets covering the rusted iron cot beneath. She couldn't sit there, but where? Except for the cot, a camp stove, and an unlit kerosene lamp, the ramshackle room looked empty. He took off his duster, wrapped it around the girl's shoulders, and eased her down to sit on her cot. At least she'd be dry with his coat on. Elias pulled out a match and lit the lamp. The moment he did, a closer look at the girl gave more of her away. She had to be an opium-eater at the end of the line, or damned near close.

"Thank you," she finally said.

"Sure," he said and smiled same as before. A hundred questions ran through his head, but he kept quiet. Besides, he had all the answers he needed right in front of him. He'd seen a lot of poor creatures like her, some at the end of the line before they hit twenty. This gal looked about that. He didn't have to ask how she'd ended up like this. Could be any of a dozen reasons; none of them a lie.

The girl slipped his coat from her shoulders.

"Mister, you want me?" she asked, her face unreadable.

Elias hated that blank look. He'd seen it too many times on too many whores, and he hated it.

"What's your name?"

The girl looked bewildered again, as if no one had ever asked her that.

"Nell," she whispered.

"That's a pretty name for a pretty girl," he complimented. He took a fin from his pocket and handed the five-dollar bill to her. "I don't have much on me or I'd give you more, Nell," he told her honestly, and started for the thin wood door.

"Your coat—"

Elias was out the door and down the alleyway before he let her finish. He'd get himself another duster as soon as he could come up with the money.

"That ordinance the city approved four years ago shut us all down," a former box-hustler told Elias. "When you can't be selling liquor in box houses, the whole shebang might as well shut, and that's exactly what happened; not just here on Washington Street but all up and down Skid Road. I guess we

45

got off easier than folks in Spokane. They couldn't even hire any gals to work in their box houses."

Elias rubbed his clean-shaven jaw, unsettled by this news. He knew times were bad all over, but this he hadn't expected—that the box house trade would come to a halt in Seattle. All his plans to own his own place went right out the window.

"Is business keeping up in saloons around here?"

"Sure is," the one-time box-hustler answered. "Ain't no way you can keep fellas from drinking and carousing 'round here. I miss the times when I'd fetch drinks to one box house compartment after another. The gals got a metal tab for each customer, and I got a piece of the take. Worked with a lot of decent barkeeps, I did."

"Any jobs open for barkeeps these days, mister?"

"Name's Gus, Gus Jacobs. I know the Merchant's Exchange Saloon lost their best barkeep. Got into the wrong fight and lost this time," Gus said, and shook his head. "Might be they'd take a look at you. You look like you could handle yourself. It's a pretty big place, lots of business."

"Do they serve liquor in all these theaters around here?" Elias still couldn't get past the loss of the box house trade.

Gus chuckled.

"No, sir. They serve up actresses and variety shows. Folks go, but it's a lot better with a shot of whiskey," he said and winked. "You can get a shot of whiskey or a five-cent beer at Merchant's. A fella can get a drink, a meal, a card game, and a room upstairs with a gal of his choice, all in good fun," Gus said, sending another wink and a nod Elias's way.

"Where is this saloon?" Elias returned to the conversation at hand, never one to look good fortune in the eye and refuse her.

"Now we're talkin'," Elias muttered the moment he set foot inside the busy Merchant's Exchange Saloon on Yesler Way.

Decent crowd, he acknowledged. The saloon's location drew a line between respectable business on Front Street and cathouse business on Commercial Street. Met with the smell of expensive cigars and spying expensive whiskey, Elias expected his fortunes to change in this fine saloon. The well-crafted rosewood bar with set-in mirrors, together with the shiny, hammered-tin ceiling overhead, told him as much.

"Hello, cowboy," one of the saloon's *ladies* greeted Elias. "I'm Evangeline. How can I help you?" she asked musically, all politeness.

The girl was a looker, Elias had to admit. Her voice sounded as sweet as the expensive rose perfume she wore. Soft brown hair escaped from her loose topknot; on purpose, he thought. He was suspicious of most every move until proven wrong. Her at-the-knee silver dress sparkled in the shadowy light, same as her mischievous eyes. A man could get lost in that lacy look; not him, not now. She liked him. He didn't miss that.

"Yes, you can, Evangeline. Who is the saloonkeeper here?" At the girl's approach he'd removed his hat, turning the Deadwood black westerner around in his hands. He waited for her to answer, all the while searching the crowded saloon for the man in charge.

"That would be me," said a stranger at Elias's back. "I've been called a lot of things, but never just a saloonkeeper."

Elias sized the gray-mustached stranger up. Yep, he looked the part in his white dress shirt with a bow-tied high-stand collar, black silk sleeve garters, brocade vest, and pocket watch, complete with derby and owner's inspecting smile. The vest was the only thing that threw Elias, since most vests he'd seen were cheap red and not expensive black.

"Name's Otto," the man said and offered his hand.

"Elias Colt." Elias gave a nod as well as a handshake.

"What's your business, son?"

"I'm a barkeep, and I need a job," Elias answered honestly. No point in beating around the bush.

"You look more like a cowpuncher than a bartender, Elias Colt."

Elias chuckled yet kept his eye on Otto.

"I reckon I do."

"C'mon to my office and we'll have ourselves a talk," Otto tossed over his shoulder, already headed that way.

Elias followed, leaving the beautiful girl in the beautiful silver dress behind.

"Tell you what," Otto said after they'd talked a few minutes. "You can keep the leather vest, the canvas trousers, and your worn Justin boots, but not the striped shirt, the neckerchief, or your holstered gun. That you can keep behind the bar, out of sight, but not on you. Were you ever a lawman?"

"No."

"It appears you've worked about every other job. Why not law, with that six-shooter of yours?"

The two men sat in Otto's office, Otto at his rolltop desk and Elias in a side chair. Elias shifted, a little uncomfortable with this conversation. Guns were a part of him, almost an extension. He knew how to use his Colt Frontier Six-Shooter and would if he had to. Same as always. The idea of not having his gun at his side bothered him. His black leather, unadorned holster fit his gun to the mark, and shouldn't bother anybody if he wore it. But Otto was boss. Elias had been around long enough to know what the boss's orders meant. Still, he didn't answer this boss's question.

"Understand me, son, about keeping your gun un-holstered?" Otto eyed Elias hard, without pressing him anymore about working for the law.

"Yeah." Elias shot back the same look.

"Good," Otto said after a long pause. "So I'll outfit you in a white shirt, black sleeve garters, and give you the use of a white barkeep's apron, as you call it."

Damn. Elias felt like he was in a dress shop, with all this fuss. *A job was a job,* he had to remind himself.

"We've got ground rules here. Have to, with all the money coming in and all the gals working for me. See this scale? It's to weigh gold dust when it's brought in. Miners come in with their pouch of dust and we trade, taking care of business. See this safe? It's our business, yours and mine, to keep it protected," Otto made clear. "If you need to take that six-shooter of yours and use it, do."

Elias settled in his chair. Now the job got more interesting. Otto didn't just want a barkeep but a good shot.

"We're a lot of things here," Otto kept on. "We run a restaurant, hotel, card room, and saloon on the first two floors. The top floor is a brothel."

Elias was familiar with this setup but not one so refined.

"You appear to me to have an even temperament, Elias. That's good. You can keep your head, and this job calls for it. With all the girls working here, all the card games going on, and all the liquor being served, sometimes things get out of hand. I don't want barroom brawls in my place. This isn't Tombstone or Deadwood or Dodge City. The law is the law here. I expect my customers and my employees to abide by it. Understand me, son?"

"Yeah."

"Let me explain our brothel setup. There are pictures of our *ladies* on the saloon walls. If a gentleman comes up to you and then points to one of our lady's pictures, you need to direct the customer to the right room on the third floor." Otto reached for a stack of papers from a far drawer, causing his leather swivel to creak on its hinges. "I'll go through all the names with you and make sure you meet each one and can put the right lady with the right picture. While we're on the subject, Elias," Otto said, his focus back on Elias. "No mixing with any of the ladies here. That's my rule, and if you break it, you're gone."

Elias nodded.

"You're a handsome young man," Otto said, his tone more fatherly than boss-like. "Most of my ladies will be after you some time or another. They know the rules here but might try to buck them. With your looks and their eye for a strapping westerner . . . it's trouble waiting to happen."

"Show me the list," Elias said and nodded toward the papers in Otto's hand. *The gaming life but no wife,* Elias mentally repeated. No wife, no family life. Accustomed to gals fawning over him, he'd take it in stride and deal with things fine. His fortunes lay elsewhere.

CHAPTER FOUR

Abby looked out the shuttle window, staring at the swift waters of Clear Creek but thinking about her upcoming visit with her father. She hadn't seen him since last fall, when she'd started school at Mines. Their parting had been awkward, and she didn't think this meet and greet would be an improvement. Meet and greet. Not the best way a child should think about a parent. It sounded cold and distant . . . an exact definition of her relationship with her father. She shifted in her seat and pulled her North Face beanie down farther, her fingers lingering a moment on her security cap.

She'd spent a hefty twenty dollars on it but got payback in gold every day. When she pulled the reliable acrylic, fleece-lined beanie over her brow and ears, she felt hidden. The logo cap was shadowy blue, similar to her eyes. This fact didn't play into her decision to buy it, she rationalized, even though she found it a pretty color. Humph. She switched her thoughts back out the window and back onto the beauty of Clear Creek Canyon. They'd be in Idaho Springs soon, then Empire—her stop.

The crowded shuttle bustled with conversation and college-kid antics, but Abby paid little mind, same as always. Overstuffed backpacks, tied-on hiking boots, and biking gear overflowed. She'd been lucky to find an empty window seat where no one could force her into any annoying conversation. That no one tried didn't bother her. She had Ebony White and Lucinda Smith in her life, where this time last year, she did not. Abby wouldn't mind if either one sat next to her. No forced, annoying conversation there.

Clear Creek wound through its namesake canyon, never missing a rapid twist or whitewater turn carved out by the rock-sheeted walls above. Any open spot on their stony surface was covered over in scrub brush. The canyon signaled the Continental Divide lie ahead. Abby wondered if any pioneers thought twice about going into the formidable Rocky Mountains once here. No, gold seekers wouldn't have turned back, unlike what she wanted to do this instant. She didn't want her visit with her father to end in an argument. Maybe he'd moved on to another mine like the Climax and had left the area. The thought brightened her spirits.

The shuttle came to a stop.

"Idaho Springs," the driver called out. "If you're headed for Central City or Black Hawk, this is also your stop."

Located in the heart of Colorado's historic mining district and mineral belt, these one-time boomtowns beckoned tourists year-round. Today, Idaho Springs was known for its hot springs, good eats, gold panning at the Argo Mill, a seat at the Buffalo Bar, or a chance to don Old West apparel at one of the shops lining Main Street. Black Hawk and Central City—connected not only by mining history but by Gregory Street, winding up the hill from Black Hawk—were known jointly for slot machines and a good game of blackjack. Both semi-ghost towns had legalized gambling. The drive from Idaho Springs up to these heights didn't take long. If a body fancied a thrill ride, leave Idaho Springs via Russell Gulch, then up the Oh My God Road to Black Hawk and Central City. The infamous trail earned its name early on. "Oh, My God!" was the most-heard cry when daring the steep, scary trail. Four-wheel drive did little to dissipate fear.

Abby let this modern-day description play out in her head

just as a tour brochure might extol if picked up at any one of the myriad of stacks supplied to ready tourists. She'd been to all three one-time boomtowns, tried their four-wheel roads, explored their old mine shafts, hiked their ridges, traversed unsure train trestles, and crossed bridges over their historic gold-panning creeks. The once touted "Richest Square Mile on Earth" wasn't anything new to her. Her father hadn't struck it rich in Central City—or any of the other boomtowns, for that matter. She had, Abby thought; rich in the sense of gold-mining history—her first love.

"We're pulling out in five minutes," the shuttle driver called back to his passengers. They were parked in a public lot behind the popular Buffalo Bar. Some had run in for pizza-to-go, but Abby stayed behind. Empire was just ten miles up Route 40. She'd get a snack at the Conoco there before she'd head for her father's cabin, buried in the woods.

"Empire!" the driver shouted the moment he pulled into the Conoco.

Abby had to laugh. You'd think he drove a stage to Empire, needing to call to his passengers tucked inside, instead of calling to a bunch of college kids in a shuttle van. Empire had been a supply stop for those continuing west in gold-rush days, but Abby's seatmates headed to ski areas now. The next stops were Copper Mountain and Steamboat Springs, for Pete's sake. They headed to ski country, not gold country. *That's where we part ways*, Abby thought. She always chose gold country.

Abby let everyone file out before she got out of the van, her backpack in tow. No one else would stay here, she'd overheard. They all wanted to grab lunch at the Hard Rock Café. "It's dope," she'd heard one say. *Dope* in today's culture was defined as super cool and relevant, she mentally repeated. Well, dope or no dope, she wasn't going to follow the summer job-seekers inside the Hard Rock. She really didn't care they likely all thought her a *mouse potato* and a *noob*—basic, boring, and unaware of what's hip. "I'm as aware as I need to be," Abby mumbled to no one, as she was left standing alone at the Conoco.

She walked the needed steps for a good view of the Peck House Hotel and Restaurant. Built in 1860, it was the oldest hotel in Colorado, though it didn't appear open and the parking lot was empty. For long minutes Abby stared at the two-story, white clapboard building with its red trim and spanning front deck, easily holding multiple rocking chairs, planters, and room to roam. She'd never stayed there herself and couldn't afford the expense, but she had been inside, upstairs and down. The uneven flooring creaked, and she remembered every step. Each cozy room's decor fit the Old West right down to the iron beds, patchwork quilts, and pitcher and washbasin sets. Tombstone, Deadwood, Dawson, Dodge City . . . their hotels couldn't have differed much from this one in Empire. Abby thought it a magical place, but then she thought better of it. She believed in science and mathematics and fact, not magic and mysticism and myth.

Afternoon sunshine poured down. Abby had to shield her eyes for a better look at the historic hotel. Last year the Peck House had been open. She wondered if the owners were on vacation or if the hotel had closed permanently. It shouldn't matter so much to her, but it did. No reason, at least none she could come up with. Lace curtains veiled the windows from view, except for one. Abby looked closer at the second-story panes and thought she saw movement. The curtains were pulled aside for a time and then fell back in place.

At first, she didn't react, but when the hairs on the back of her neck stood on end, she thought of ghosts and paid closer attention to the window in question. She saw something white, maybe a sleeve, maybe a dress front. This defied belief, so she kept her stare fixed on the feminine picture. She certainly didn't believe in ghosts and didn't think this apparition anything but her poor vision in the nuisance sunlight at work. A level-headed person, Abby would collect facts first and theorize later.

But someone *was* looking back at her. She felt drawn in, suddenly more curious than she'd been in a long time about such things. She was a gold miner, not a ghost miner. Such things usually didn't interest her, but this apparition's gaze on her did. Could be the owner, but the owner wouldn't be dressed in Victorian sleeves and billowy white. Hard to make out a face or details, but Abby could feel eyes on her and *did* see a woman in white. Then Abby had to laugh at herself. Every ghost story from every mining ghost town had a lady in white or a young girl playing on stairs in it. Likely, she'd made this up in her head based on these stories and the offsetting sunlight.

Relieved to bring this exercise to an end, Abby ran her hands over her face to rub off all the nonsense. Hah. She remembered an 1898 archive from the *Rocky Mountain News* on the subject, where the paper declared it "refused to print any more ghost stories since they were too many in number." Too many ladies in white and too many young girls playing on stairs being reported, Abby concluded as the reason for such an editorial directive.

The moment she took her hands from her face, she couldn't resist another look at the same window. It appeared as all the rest. Nothing there and never was. *No lady in white. No girl in white, and no sea captain,* she added. The sea captain's ghost had been written about in a recent *Denver Post* Sunday magazine piece. The gossip section, no doubt. She never believed in such stories and had forgotten about the sea captain until this moment. All nonsense, she knew . . . all fodder for newspapers and the latest scary thriller.

Clouds moved in overhead, and Abby welcomed the afternoon threat of a storm, typical for the mountains in summer. The only time an afternoon storm could be a real problem was if she were hiking above the tree line, where'd she'd be an easy target for a lightning strike. The mountains had rules about survival, and if you didn't pay attention to them, you could pay with your life. A sobering thought that brought her back to the moment at hand: surviving her visit with her father . . . if she found him.

She pivoted around to look across Route 40 to the Hard Rock Café, to see if everyone had gone inside. The moment she did, a strange feeling came over her. Time passed in slow motion as if she were underwater—*ice water*! Her bones all at once ached under the cold, paralyzing effect. She shut her eyes, wary of her growing confusion and sudden trembles.

"Abigail . . . Abigail . . ."

It was the same voice she'd heard in the Slide Cemetery in Dyea! She didn't want to see who called out in dreams or in person. She didn't want to acknowledge the garbled male rasps, which were surely meant for somebody else. She called herself Abby, *not* Abigail! She never called herself Abigail and had to be getting sick again. Her brain chemistry had to be off, creating this hallucinogenic nonsense in her head. Worthless flu shots!

"Abigail . . . Abigail . . ."

The voice charged at her as if electric, its edges all static and faraway. If she had her finger in a light socket and could hear the sound of the shock, the spark, that was the sound she heard. Held within this cold energy bubble, Abby fought increasing anxiety over this bizarre phenomenon. If she kept her eyes shut and waited, it would pass, just as it had before when she'd first returned from Alaska.

"Abigail . . ."

Go away, you . . . you EVP recording! That's it: Electronic

Voice Phenomena! She didn't watch any of the paranormal, ghost-hunting shows on TV, but she knew about EVPs all the same. Ghost hunters claimed they electronically captured sounds that resembled human speech from dead people. All a bunch of bunk, Abby knew. The static noise she imagined was not coming from a dead guy or any guy. *I am no beauty.* That thought opened Abby's eyes.

The pair stood frozen in time, their gazes locked.

Abby fixed on the tall, good-looking stranger dressed in a long-sleeved white shirt with black sleeve garters, wearing a classic bartender's apron and the warmest smile she'd ever seen.

Eli Cole fixed on the beautiful tom-girl who kept herself hidden behind whatever she could find to keep him away. His whole existence in this life depended on her. She didn't realize it. She'd never accept the truth of the danger ahead. He had no way of warning her, barely able to stay in her time and unable to fully connect with her. They had one chance at this. He checked his pocket watch; it never lied. Time was running out for them. Eli gave an acknowledging nod to the figure in the second-story window across the street, then looked again to Abby.

I'm going to stay with you as long as I can, darlin', he silently promised her, before he disappeared inside the Empire saloon.

Abby watched the phantom stranger go inside. Her first instinct told her to follow him, but her next said don't. If she did, she'd be playing right into her wild daydreams or her night terrors. At this moment she couldn't decide which. She'd never assigned any terror to all of this nonsense; an element of fear, yes. For long moments she stood at the side of Route 40, sandwiched between the supposed lady in white behind her at the Peck House and the drop-dead, handsome stranger who'd disappeared inside the Hard Rock Café. She swallowed hard, trying to deny her descriptive choice of *drop-dead*.

How was she going to shrug this off? She knew she had to for her own peace of mind. How silly she must look to anybody driving through Empire, where the enforced thirty-mile-an-hour speed limit would give gawkers plenty of time to . . . *gawk*. The thought that anybody might have any window into her soul upset her, ghost or human. The impossibly handsome stranger's penetrating stare left her exposed. This was turning out to be a bad day. Here she was, standing on the side of the road conjuring ghosts, when she needed to find her father and get this obligatory visit over with.

She started across the road, hesitating in front of a green-crossed sign. Two such posted signs bookended the small town of Empire. If she thought marijuana would help her in any way, she'd go inside one of the pot stores. She didn't think it would. She needed to chase her confusion away and let logic return. Her father worked at the Henderson Mine, nine miles west of Empire. *Henderson is a molybdenum mine,* she right away lectured herself, to keep her thoughts off ghosts. The chemical element for molybdenum is Mo. Its atomic number is forty-two. It's the fifty-fourth most abundant element in the earth's crust and the forty-second in the universe. Molybdenum is not a free metal, but found only in varied oxidation states in minerals. To recover molybdenum from ores, flotation remains the primary isolation process. Molybdenum was first isolated in 1781. Molybdenum can also be recovered as a byproduct in copper and tungsten mining. Molybdenum—

"It's about time you decided to show," her father sarcastically greeted, leaning against the doorway of his rundown cabin.

Abby stared at her boots and not him.

"You just gonna stand there, or are you too good to come inside and visit your old dad?"

58

His iron voice grated at her, same as always. And he looked the same as always—unshaven, eyes drooped, graying hair uncombed, frayed flannel shirt untucked, in dirt-streaked work denims with a lit cigarette hanging from one corner of his mouth. Had he ever worn a different expression or a different outfit? She thought not. He always greeted her with the same sour expression, the same unkind words, and wearing the same tired clothes. She walked past him and went inside.

Abby looked around the untidy cabin. That was the same, too. Metal dishes piled in the sink, a rusted percolator coffee pot hissing on the stove, cobwebs framing the windows, the linoleum floor unswept, with today's breakfast crumbs spattering the room's only serviceable table.

"You should take better care of yourself," she told her father, staring at her feet instead of him.

"Huh," he snorted and dropped his finished cigarette in the dirt outside.

Abby watched the tiny embers die at the doorstep. That's how she felt around her father: dead.

"Where's your pickup?"

"Broke down on me in the Jones Pass parking lot by the mine," he answered, talking more to himself than her. "Damn transmission is going," he grumbled.

"I have some money to help toward fixing it," Abby offered. She couldn't say *Dad,* and hadn't for years. In actuality, she didn't have a dime extra to spare at this point. He was still her father and she would find a way to get by, same as always.

"I don't need anything from you, girl," her father declared and pulled one of the two kitchen chairs out to sit.

The scraping sound bumped down Abby's backbone like nails jutting at her. She forced herself to sit down across from him and face him. This obligatory father-daughter visit needed to be quick. She reached for her nearby backpack and unzipped the most secure pocket, where she kept her plane tickets and her money.

"Here." She slid fifty dollars across the table, half her money to last the summer in Alaska.

"Well, *college girl*," he snarled, "I don't want it."

Abby scooped up the fifty. She wouldn't offer a second time.

"Why are you here, girl?" he said in an accusatory voice.

She blew out the breath she'd been holding.

"I'm taking a job in Alaska this summer, in Dyea and Skagway." She thought it best to say job, knowing her father would take added issue with the word internship.

"What? You quittin' college?"

Abby didn't miss the satisfaction in his tone.

"No. I'm taking a mining assignment." A mistake to add, she knew. Her father wanted her to fail—to fail in school, to fail in work, and to fail in life. At this moment she wondered how she ever grew up around this sad old man.

"Oh, a mining *assignment*," he jeered. "You think you're better or something, going all the way north to find mining work when you could look for something in Colorado, if anybody'd be stupid enough to hire you. And to do what? You're a girl, a snot-nosed, know-nothing brat, still wet behind the ears."

Abby sat facing her father. She knew he had more to say. Her stiffened back ached from the effort of paying attention.

"Your whole life, all you done is scoot outa here every chance you had, to run off to this school or that, thinking you could learn more than your old dad and beat me at my job," he said, his jaw tensed.

Abby sat there, knowing it would do no good to come back at him with any reply on this subject. She'd tried to explain her every move to him all of her life, since he was her only father, and she had no mother. It was just always the same. He didn't want her to get a decent education and never stepped up to make sure she was settled in school. Social Services had stepped in, however, and worked with her to enroll her in school and help her with college counseling. "You're a smart young lady," they'd told her. "You need to stay in school and not in mine shafts."

Local churches had stepped in, too, to help her with donated food and clothing. While her father made enough money for food, the churches and school district wanted to support her in any way they could. Abby accepted the help of strangers, much as she hadn't wanted to. They were kind and well-intended, but she kept everybody at a distance. Safer that way, since trust was not a word in her vocabulary. Mistrust certainly was. This, she'd learned from her father. Still, she didn't want Social Services to snoop around much regarding her father. She didn't want him jailed because of child neglect or related charges. He didn't hit her. He didn't make her feel unsafe. He just didn't seem to care about her. How could you jail him for that?

"Tell me about my mother," Abby suddenly blurted, surprised at her own question. This was the first time she'd confronted him about her mother. *And it may be the last time I see my father for a long time,* Abby realized. At this point, she had a right to ask and a right to know. She squared her shoulders and faced her father down.

"Your mother?" he repeated; his voice suddenly frail and pained. He stared at his hands, rubbing them together hard as if to rub away any memory of the word *mother.* "She was no beauty," he mumbled, shaking his head in support of this. "She was no wife and no mother."

Abby sat stunned at his words, at the fact he was actually answering her question. She'd imagined him yelling or storming out of the cabin, but not this uncomfortable calm. From her father's faraway look, Abby could tell he wasn't talking to her anymore but rather to himself.

"My *wife*," he spat on the word, "ran off on me. Just up and took off on me and our baby girl, like we was so much trash. Ran off with some guy she met at a bar. Just took off," he repeated, his voice faint.

Spellbound, yet desperate to leave, Abby stayed put and listened. She wanted to hear him out, yet she didn't. "Those times were hard, me with a baby and tryin' to make a living in the mines. I was that worried we weren't gonna make it, but we did." The corners of his hard mouth broke into a slight smile. "I had me a good job in the mines and had me a beautiful baby girl." He lost his smile. "That's what brought all this on, my wife thinking herself a beauty. Thinking her too good for me. Just because she had the blackest of hair and the bluest of eyes didn't make her any beauty. Just because her face could light up any room and get the attention of any man taking a look didn't make her any beauty . . ." His voice trailed.

Abby watched a tear fall down her father's weathered cheek. Then she wiped her own away. She couldn't decide which hurt worse: that her father blamed her for the sins of her mother, or that her mother had abandoned her. Either way, it was lose-lose. She pitied her father, carrying this sadness around for so many years. That was some form of caring, she supposed.

"I'll be leaving," Abby quietly told him the moment he looked at her again.

He nodded her way and then at the door.

"I'll visit when I can," she added when she didn't need to.

He nodded again, this time looking at his rubbed-raw hands and not his daughter.

Abby grabbed up her backpack and pushed out from the table, then got up and left her father's rundown cabin and rundown life. She didn't feel dead inside. That was something she could take away this time, where she hadn't before.

CHAPTER FIVE

"Abigail Grayce, is it?" James Lomery greeted and ushered her inside his newspaper office at the *Daily Journal*.

She cringed for no reason other than close proximity to this stranger made her nervous. She hated her confining getup and longed to put her brother's hand-me-down miner's clothes back on. Behind an outfit all miners wore, she felt anonymous and unrecognized and less exposed. But she needed work, and she needed to get a job here. It was just that gold mining was what she knew; not journalism. She felt defeated already, and her spirits slumped.

I'm a woman and that's against me, she believed. I'm young and that's against me. I don't look like a refined Denver citizen, and that's against me. I don't have a formal school education and that's against me. I don't have any newspaper experience and that's against—

"Miss Grayce." The newspaper publisher interrupted her thoughts. "We're not going to get anywhere in this interview if you don't pay attention."

Abigail couldn't feel any more wretched and stared at her feet, at least at the hem of her skirt around her ankles. Her buckled boots peeped out, and this embarrassed her even more than she already felt for letting her mind wander at this important time.

"Have a seat, Miss Grayce," James Lomery offered.

She sat down in the straight-back wood chair and forced her

63

gaze up to meet the publisher's. She tried to smile but failed miserably.

"All right, young lady, tell me why you're here."

Shouldn't it be obvious? I need a job; any job here. Her anxiety got the better of her. Maybe I could offer to clean or do some kind of women's work? Or men's? I could drive newspaper wagons and deliver papers to mining towns, or tend to horses utilized here, or anything else related to mining and gold; especially reporting and writing on the subject. No. She was a woman and wouldn't be hired to do a man's job. *If I were a man, this newspaper would consider my skills.* This sad fact dispirited her. She should go.

"Thank you, Mr. Lomery, for your time," Abigail said and stood. "I'll just leave—"

"Not so fast and not before you tell me why you're here in the first place," the publisher insisted.

Abigail sat back down and fought for composure.

"I need a job."

"Yes? Go on," he encouraged.

"I never quit until the job is done. I know how to clean and mend. I know horses, dogs, and mines—gold and silver. I was hoping you might need help and would give me a job."

"An interesting paradox, Miss Grayce, offering to do women's work and men's work in the same breath," he said.

"Yes." She couldn't think of anything else to say.

"Do you have any newspaper skills, Miss Grayce?"

"What do you mean?" She edged to the front of her seat, ready to leave.

"I mean just what I said. I mean, do you know anything about newspapers and journalism and what goes on the printed page?"

This conversation had already gone on too long. If she stayed, she'd have to come up with answers to Mr. Lomery's questions; answers she didn't want to give and answers he might not want to hear. She lost her nerve, yet needed to say something.

"I've followed newspapers in most every mining town in Colorado all my life. I've been educated on newspapers. Self-educated, that is."

"So, no formal schooling then?" he asked, cocking an eyebrow.

Her heart sank to her buckle-booted feet. *Here we go.* She started to rise from her chair.

"Please sit, Miss Grayce. You're the first woman who's applied for a job here, and I'm interested in what you have to say."

"But that's just it, Mr. Lomery. I'm a woman. I don't know why you're giving me the time of day." There; she'd said it. Now he'd show her the door, fast.

"I'm giving you the time of day *because* you're a woman, and a well-spoken one, at that. As much as you've kept up with Colorado news, I don't think you've read how modern we are here in Denver, when it comes to women."

Abigail sat still. No, she didn't know this.

"Women have the vote here and have since eighteen ninety-three, same year as the financial crash. At least something good came out of it, with suffrage succeeding in Colorado. In the next year, we elected three women to the Colorado House of Representatives, the first women to hold office anywhere in the United States. Denver has proud roots in mining and pioneer resolve. Now that I see I have your full attention," he quipped, "I'll continue. Most jobs for women at this time, in most of the country, are in domestic service or factories or piecework sewing, as salesclerks, typists, and telephonists. Then there are teachers, nurses, librarians, and some doctors and lawyers, even journalists. Which is why I'm interested in your knowledge of newspapers," he said, his expression serious.

Abigail couldn't believe her ears. Her whole life, she'd thought, foretold the rest of her life. Women were relegated to women's work. Women in mining towns were kept out of mines and assay offices. Women in the mining towns she'd known didn't work as journalists.

"I don't have journalism experience," she confessed.

"You said you know horses and gold and silver mines. Tell me about that," he prodded.

"All . . . right," she answered hesitantly. Long conversations were never a good idea, but she did need a job. "I know about mines because I grew up in mining towns and have been in more shafts than you can count. I've lived everywhere from Creede to Central City to Leadville, and have been around ranching, too, since much of mining country is ranch country. I know horses and dogs, growing up in this part of the West. I have an education because I educated myself on newspapers and what books and libraries I could find."

Abigail exhaled and looked down at her hands in her lap. She'd been rubbing them together, self-conscious about talking to the publisher. She forced her hands apart and looked to Mr. Lomery, expecting a critical expression, not a friendly one.

"I don't suppose there are female miners or assayers you've heard of in Colorado?" she asked reservedly.

"Not in any numbers yet, but the time might be coming sooner than you think. At the School of Mines in Golden, their first female student will graduate next year in mining engineering. I don't know much about the program, but it would be interesting to find out and put in my paper. I think this would be of interest to our female readers, don't you think?"

She stared at Mr. Lomery in stunned silence. *A female mining engineer!* Her pulse picked up. This was the first time in a long time she felt excited about something. Oh, yes, she wanted to know about such a school that would admit women—women with a formal education and the means to pay for such a school. *She* would never have such means, Abigail knew.

"Why the glum look, Miss Grayce? You should be glad for

such an advance for women in the mining field," the publisher told her.

"Yes, of course," she replied. "I was just giving this news some thought."

"Well, good. Then I will give you a job at the *Daily Journal* to chronicle your noteworthy thoughts," he said and chuckled. "Let's make your first assignment a story on the first female to enroll in the Colorado School of Mines. How's that?" he asked, as he leaned back in his chair and folded his arms across his chest.

For the second time in the same conversation, Abigail couldn't believe her ears. She had a job! She could afford to eat and get a place to live. Well, maybe not both at once. Maybe the Women's Exchange and the *kind* Mary would house her a bit longer. She could help out at the Exchange and contribute what money she could for food. It would be a good place to lie low, so no one in her family could find her should they wander into town. Her brothers would go to saloons and carouse all night with shady women and end up in drunken brawls in the bad part of Denver before they'd go searching for the sister they didn't like in the first place. Still, at the Exchange she felt safe. She'd ask to stay.

"I'll pay you the same as I'd pay a man, but it's not much to start. If you work out and our paper sales pick up, your wage will go up accordingly. Is that a deal?" he asked.

"Deal," she agreed. "Can I wear what I want here? I mean, do I have to dress up like this all the time?" she pressed him, gesturing to her female garb. She thought, since Mr. Lomery was so "modern" in his thinking about women, he might let her dress how she wanted.

"As long as you're neat in appearance and get the job done, that's fine with me. If you're going to report mining news you might as well look the part," he said with a wink.

Abigail reached into the pocket of her jacket and found her heart-shaped nugget, squeezing the treasured gold, grateful for her good fortune.

"How about that," Elias remarked to one of his customers at the Merchant's Exchange Saloon bar, and poured another drink in hopes of getting more news about the 1889 fire that had left Seattle in ashes. The three-story brick building they were in at this moment had burned down along with much of the city. "This one's on me," he told his customer, who had lost his Dietz and Mayer Liquor Store in the great fire. His customer and the city, as far as Elias could tell, looked like they had come back all right from the destruction. Still, Elias wanted to know more and listened attentively while the customer went on.

"When the fire reached us, whiskey barrels in the basement exploded and showered the walls. Alcohol flamed everywhere. We all took off in time. Too late for any fire hose trucks to do anything, and too much smoke to even try. Right after us, the nearby Crystal Palace Saloon and the Opera House Saloon went up in flames from all the alcohol on site. The Frye Opera House went up and . . . hell, everything around here on Skid Road went up. The business district and heart of Seattle— doomed. Whores, pimps, and white-aproned barkeeps like you fled," the man gritted, and then swallowed his whiskey in one gulp.

Elias wouldn't press further. The man looked too upset.

Mr. Dietz motioned for another pour.

Elias complied.

"Damn fire started in a cabinetmaker's basement on Front Street. It was a paint store and a woodshop that went up in flames when glue was heated over a gasoline stove and boiled over, for God's sake! Gobs of glue splashed onto the floor and lit up the wood shavings and turpentine spills. Stupid, careless!

Of course, every wood building where the fire caught on went up in flames, including my business." Mr. Dietz took a swallow of whiskey and set the glass down hard on the bar, spilling the rest of its contents.

By now, Elias could feel the heat of the fire.

"The fire died out sometime in the early morning, when there was nothing more to burn. Every wharf and every mill from Union Street to Jackson Street . . . gone. Even the toughs on the waterfront couldn't wade in and retrieve the hundred barrels of whiskey a saloon had rolled into the water, trying to save their store. Two barrels were saved—only two. Scores of businesses and fifty-eight city blocks, all gone up in smoke. People were left homeless and hungry and without any kind of roof over their head. Skid Road didn't have one tumbledown building left for one pimp or one whore. We were left with nothing, Elias. Nothing," Mr. Dietz finished.

Elias thought Mr. Dietz had fared well since the fire, judging by his expensive appearance. He wouldn't ask for details now. Elias had been a barkeep long enough to know when to keep quiet. Best to let the customer do the talking. This was the customer's dime, not his.

Mr. Dietz looked at Elias, his expression easier. He picked up his empty glass and turned it upside down on the bar, but didn't push away to leave.

"Did you know Chief Seattle himself had his photo taken right over where we're standing? E. M. Sammis had a photography studio on the second floor. Don't know what happened to Sammis after that. Chief Seattle and the Suquamish tribe are settled on a reservation across the Sound. I think the chief is still alive. Not sure. The variety store here burned away along with everything else. Now this place is brick, and so is the rest of the city. Fireproof this time, and about time," Mr. Dietz added, then pushed away from the bar. "Good talking with you,

Elias. See you again."

Elias watched Mr. Dietz exit the Merchant's Exchange Saloon. It struck him how much it must have taken for people in Seattle to pull together and rebuild their city. All of Skid Road and the business district needed to be put back together. Elias doubted whether pimps and whores had waited for new brick buildings, and instead erected tents where they could set up trade. The business of gambling, gaming, and whoring wouldn't stop for any fire, no matter how widespread.

A fine saloon, complete with gaming tables, a restaurant, and a brothel on the top floor, all built in brick, now took the place of what had been a variety store and photography studio built out of wood. Elias shuffled his feet, testing the floor behind the bar to ensure its hardihood. He thought of the basement floor below, housing all the whiskey barrels and alcohol, relieved the walls were brick and not wood. Out of habit, he checked his Frontier Six-Shooter resting in its holster on a shelf beneath the bar. It felt like brick to him, the power and clean shot of his Colt pistol.

"Ahem."

Elias looked up from his gun. Another well-dressed customer stood at the bar, this one gesturing to one of the ladies pictured overhead. Elias followed the direction of the customer's hand and saw he wanted Flavia, an attractive blonde.

"She's in room six on the third floor. Knock and wait for her to open the door."

The customer nodded in understanding and tipped his derby to Elias before he headed upstairs. Elias watched him and fought his impulse to follow. He felt protective of all the ladies and always worried something might go wrong, despite this being a fine brothel. He wanted to protect the ladies as much as the gold in the office safe. For a moment, he took himself back in time to Virginia City, Montana, and the same worries.

Nothing changed for him in leaving Virginia City and coming to Seattle in terms of his same worries whenever gambling, liquor, saloon girls, and ladies on the line mixed. The ladies at the Merchant's Exchange Saloon were at the top of the line now, but Elias knew they had a downward path from here. He had no power to change the path they'd chosen for themselves. He'd grown up seeing too many women head up, then down, the same path. From an early age he'd understood this was none of his business. Still, he worried. He'd bedded whores but he never wanted to let them get too close; it was safer that way. Boss's orders or not, he wouldn't take any of the ladies here to his bed.

His interests lay elsewhere. This saloon was a success. He wanted the same success, whether in his own box house or a similar setup of his own. What he needed was the capital to do it. Money in his pocket; that's what he needed. For the next year he planned on staying here and earning every penny he could to put toward his own establishment. There was money in liquor. There was money in cards. There was money in brothels. It would be hard for him to turn down any opportunity to make good money, dangerous or not.

"Afternoon, Elias." The girl with shadowy eyes and a sultry look came up to the bar.

Elias watched Evangeline approach. Today she wore the same expensive rose perfume and the same silver-sparkly-to-the-knee dress she had on when they'd first met. She also wore the same look meant for him, to bed him. A rare beauty, with her soft brown hair and soft cream complexion and a body that drew men in as a fly to a spiderweb, Elias grabbed up his bar towel and set to work polishing glasses. Her picture over the bar in back of him burned through him same as her standing in front of him.

The smoke-filled saloon was crowded with customers coming

in after their workday to play cards, have a few drinks, have dinner, and maybe a lady, too. The room buzzed with conversation and, at the moment, no one else stood at the bar but Evangeline.

"Elias Colt, put down that glass and look at me," she said with a pout. "You have time for everybody else around here, so I know you can make time for me."

"I'm busy, Evangeline," he said and kept to his task.

"Room number one is my room, Elias."

He knew that. She was, in fact, the *number-one lady* in the house.

"I always get what I want, Elias Colt. If you don't make time for me, I can go to Otto and get you fired," she threatened in a silky tone.

Elias blew out a breath and slapped his towel down on the bar.

"Sweet Evangeline, you're about the prettiest gal I ever did see, and I would like nothing better than to feel your soft curves, every one of them, against me. I'll be fired if I do, and then I'll be out of here. Won't be any need to talk to Otto. I'll be long gone," he drawled slowly, then gently chucked her under the chin.

Evangeline furrowed her brow and moved out of his reach. She tried to fake tears.

"I care about you, Elias. I love you. I want you. You have to love me and want me, too," she said with a sniff.

"Course I want you," he told her. "That has nothing to do with anything while we both work here. I can't quit this job. I don't think you want to quit yours, either."

"Humph," she fretted. "I'm going back up to my room and wait for a paying customer to tell me he wants me and loves me. You just think about that—me being with another man. I hope you stay up nights, alone in your bed, and think about that, Elias Colt," she taunted, and then turned on her heel and walked to the stairs.

I won't and I won't, he thought. I won't stay up nights and I won't think about that, Evangeline. Fact is, I won't always be alone in my bed. It just won't be you in my bed or any of the ladies here.

CHAPTER SIX

"Zone Two, we are now boarding Zone Two," the agent announced to the passengers waiting at the Frontier Airlines gate in Denver.

Abby grabbed her backpack and checked to make sure she'd left nothing behind on her seat. Though she kept the compartments of her pack zipped tight, she had to check. Riding the School of Mines shuttle from Empire to Denver International Airport the day before, she'd slept in the terminal, waiting for her flight to Seattle this morning. The carpet worked fine for a bed. She'd tucked herself and her gear along a wall outside the security area, and managed to catch a little sleep. No dreams. No nightmares. *No ghosts.*

A sudden shudder ran down her spine, making her hurry to the plane. The boarding pass in her hand tingled, and she wanted to let it go but had to hand it to the gate agent. The eerie sensation aggravated her already frayed nerves. *Abby Gray, get on the plane and leave your stupid nerves behind! That's all this is—nerves over seeing my father and not over seeing any ghost.* Once she handed her pass to the agent, she hooked her thumbs inside the straps of her backpack and continued down the jetway to board. She had a window seat in row fifteen and kept her eyes on that row, anxious to stow her pack in the overhead and curl up, away from passengers with searching eyes and unwanted conversation. She'd feign sleep the entire flight if she had to.

Walking down the aisle of the aircraft, Abby couldn't help but check the face of every passenger boarded so far to make sure *he* wasn't on the plane with her. Ridiculous, she knew. She was being utterly ridiculous to imagine any ghost would appear, and even more ridiculous to conjure such a thought. *I'm a gold miner and not a ghost miner.* Ebony's words came back to haunt her. Abby shoved her backpack in the overhead bin and quickly sat in her seat, buckled herself in, pulled her cap down over her brow, then curled up as planned. Luckily she found her row empty and could do this easily. If others sat down, she'd keep her back to them as if she were asleep.

"The cabin doors have been closed. Please turn off all cell phones unless they're in the airplane mode," the flight attendant announced over the speaker system. These were the last words Abby heard before shutting down her senses for the flight to Seattle.

Abby felt a nudge at her arm and woke with a start.

"We've landed," the passenger seated next to her said.

Abby couldn't believe she'd just slept for three-plus hours, and soundly. She nodded her thanks to the woman who'd awakened her, then saw her row was about to exit the plane. Her sweatshirt had fallen to the floor of the aircraft and entangled her feet. After grabbing her still-full water bottle from the seat pocket, she scooped up her sweatshirt and stood to take her turn off the Frontier flight. When she did, she thought she recognized someone . . . *someone she knew.* She only glimpsed him from behind, but an odd sense of familiarity struck her. Her pulse quickened. She stared hard at the brown cattleman's duster and the black-brimmed hat, trying to place the tall westerner. She wished he would turn around so she could see his face. For an instant, she imagined him to be the handsome stranger in front of the Hard Rock Café in Empire. Before she knew it, he'd disappeared out the cabin door.

By this time, Abby had her sweatshirt tied to her backpack and the straps secured at her shoulders, a little short of breath at the effort. She ignored the jumbles inside her since she was busy trying to walk off the plane and, at the same time, search for something on her person. The action felt automatic, but she had no idea why she did it. Her money was safe and buried deep in a zipped compartment in her backpack. She wasn't missing anything. The urge to throw down her pack and search every nook and cranny nearly overwhelmed her, yet she headed off the plane and onto the jetway at Sea-Tac International Airport.

Something else didn't make sense. The westerner had on a cattleman's duster, but it was summer and the warm weather didn't call for such a heavy coat. His black-brimmed hat she understood, since many ranchers and cowboys in Colorado always wore them, no matter the season or the weather. She thought the westerner she'd spotted must have held his hat in his lap during the whole flight to Seattle. The more she thought about this and the stranger, the stronger her urge to search for something she surely had on her. What could it be? This didn't make sense, any of it. She hurried down the jetway to see if she could spot the stranger again. She wanted to see his face. Her heart raced.

Disappointed when she didn't see him in the gate area, she hurried into the central terminal causeway and looked in all directions for a cattleman's coat. She stopped short, realizing what she was doing—following ghost dreams. The westerner had been another passenger on the plane and that's all. *I'm being ridiculous!* Everyone had to be gawking at her. She stared self-consciously at her feet and needed to find a restroom. She didn't have to go to the bathroom, but she wanted to check her backpack in private. No one needed to see. She'd wait for a handicapped stall. The urge to find something in her belongings spurred her on, as phantom pain might have done. She had no control over the unwanted sensation.

Abby turned into the first women's room she came across to check her pack and her mental status.

Elias went upstairs to the second-floor restaurant kitchen to make himself a cup of Chase and Sanborn's. Today was July seventeenth, and the summer was half over, he calculated. He'd slept well last night, a busy night, a money-making night at the Merchant's Exchange Saloon. His agreement with Otto to take a room off the office for his sleeping quarters had worked well so far. Otto was happy because Elias could better guard the safe, and Elias was happy because he didn't have to rent a room. With the kitchen right overhead, he never worried over his next meal, at least about cooking his own food. So far this setup worked, but Elias still wanted his own box house business.

The front doors of the Merchant's Exchange stayed locked until the restaurant opened later in the morning. The same went for the card room, bar, and brothel. Elias hadn't heard much going on in the kitchen above his room and looked forward to enjoying his coffee alone. The ladies usually slept late, and he didn't think he'd have to deal with Evangeline this early. He'd buckled his gun belt on and never left it behind. Anything could happen any time, especially in this part of town. His job here meant protecting the money, the ladies, and himself. He thought of Wyatt Earp and chuckled to himself. Elias wasn't exactly bringing law and order to Tombstone, but he liked his responsibilities here, helping keep the peace behind "the Deadline."

"Gold! Gold! Gold! Gold!"

Elias heard shouts from newspaper hawkers and looked out a front window to the street below. He pushed up the window to better hear the news. His pocket watch read *8:30.*

"Sixty-eight rich men on the steamer, Portland*! Stacks of yellow metal! Gold! Gold! Gold! Gold!"*

The boys hawking newspapers went up Skid Road, but folks were streaming down and headed for the wharf. Had to be a gold strike in the far north, Elias thought right away. He'd heard chatter in this very saloon for months now about veteran prospectors—hundreds of 'em—panning along the Yukon River; whether in Canada or Alaska, he didn't know. The ports in Seattle had begun to see more gold-mining business coming and going, but not like this: not reporting sixty-eight rich men coming in on the same steamer!

The idea of gold dust filling his own pockets hurried Elias on. He forgot about his coffee and hustled downstairs to grab his black frock coat before going to the wharf to see for himself what was going on. His three-quarter wool coat covered his holstered Colt. He never went outside with his gun in view. Not a good idea to invite any trouble, but a bad idea to be in a large crowd without his Frontier Six-Shooter.

Otto wouldn't arrive to start his business day until ten.

Elias measured his every move. He'd grown up in mining country and knew about gold fever. He knew a body could make fool decisions at the drop of a hat and end up dead. At this point, he took care to lock the office door, then the heavy front door of the Merchant's Exchange Saloon before joining the throng of people in a rush to Schwabacher's Wharf.

He took the morning's *Seattle Post-Intelligencer* from one of the newsboys selling papers along the way, and then stepped aside to have a look. The banner headline read much as the boys had shouted. *Latest News From Klondike. Nine o'clock Edition.* The Klondike is it? Elias noted. *Some have $5,000. Many have more. A few bring out $100,000 each. The steamer carries $700,000.* We'll see, Elias said to himself. He'd have to see it to believe that much gold just docked at Schwabacher's Wharf. He tossed the newspaper away and stepped back into the moving sea of gold-hungry men. Most had been down on their luck for too long. People didn't have enough money for food and shelter, and jobs were hard to come by. Elias understood this rush of humanity pouring to the wharf. He couldn't blame a one of 'em for wanting gold dust in their pockets.

"I'll be damned," Elias muttered, when he spotted the single-mast steamer, *Portland,* still belching smoke into the misty morning air. Bumped in all directions by the crowd around him, all trying to get as close as they could to this treasure ship of gold, Elias put his hand over his holstered gun to make sure of it. *There must be thousands of people here!*

When gray-haired passengers came down the gangplank, hoisting their sacks of gold overhead, the crowd broke out in whoops and cheers. Elias had trouble believing his eyes. Suitcases bulged with the men's stashes of Klondike gold. Sack after sack of gold dust came off the ship in the grateful hands of their owners. Excitement shot like electricity through the throng gathered at the wharf. Elias felt it, too.

The fervor lasted all day and into the night for Elias and the rest of Seattle's excited citizens. Steamship tickets were bought up fast. It took over an hour for most even to get inside one of the ticket offices of companies running steamers between Seattle and Alaska. All available berths were snapped up by noon. The public clamored for goods. Stores emptied their supplies out front for customers to buy, and buy they did. Clerks and teachers and loggers and lawyers and a good number of police quit their jobs that very day. Even Seattle's mayor resigned to head far north. Despite some men off the *Portland* admitting claims in the gold fields were all taken, they declared every river in Alaska spilled over with the yellow metal!

So many who had suffered misfortune for so long had hope now—hope to change misfortune to good fortune. People didn't care that they had no idea where they were going or what they'd need, so energized were they to have a chance for riches beyond their wildest dreams.

The Klondike Gold Rush was on!

Abigail re-read page one of a rival paper, the *Denver Rocky Mountain News,* dated today—July 20, 1897—to make sure of the details. She'd picked up a copy from a newsboy hawking papers nearby the *Daily Journal* office where she worked. The article reprinted a page out of a Seattle newspaper, dated yesterday:

SEATTLE, Wash., July 19—The people of this town have gone wild over the Clondyke discoveries. Not in the history of the town has there been such excitement. Everybody who can raise the money is going north. Steamer accommodations have all been taken.

The statement that the new fields would output $10,000,000 worth of Gold this year has made the excitement greater and tonight everybody is burning the wires with telegrams to friends in the East to send them money to invest in the fields.

Yesterday this news would have spurred Abigail to find a way to get to the Klondike gold fields but not today. Her heart pounded with the same excitement everyone must be feeling at the news, but she needed to follow her head, not her heart. A chance of a lifetime isn't easy to turn down. That's why she'd followed her head at this life-changing moment and decided to stay in Denver.

News of the gold strike in the far north had already turned

Denver upside down, with a flurry of activity from people who had the means, and who planned to leave for the Klondike. Those without means scraped and scratched to get backing and the money to leave. Abigail had grown up in mining country and knew what it took to mine here in Colorado. Alaska was a far-off, unknown place where she instinctively knew life, even for experienced miners, would be uncertain at best. Was the risk worth it? *Yes.* Yesterday she would have somehow, someway, joined in the rush to Alaska and the Klondike. But that was before she'd met and interviewed Florence Caldwell, the first female student enrolled at the Colorado School of Mines.

Abigail had to pinch herself, so much had changed in the months she'd lived in Denver at the Women's Exchange. So much had changed, yet some things stayed the same. She still dressed like a boy and kept the girl inside hidden. Old habits died hard. She had no reason to try, she thought. Why should she want to attract any man? She didn't. She didn't want marriage, family, or love. Love wasn't something she'd known in her lifetime. The very word made her cringe, she feared it so. Her family taught her well. *Old habits died hard.*

Now she had an opportunity for a formal education, laid out for her with the help of Florence Caldwell. Florence had earned a college degree before being admitted to the School of Mines. A bachelor of science degree, she'd told Abigail. Florence had had to leave the first college she attended, since they'd repealed their coeducation status and forced her out. Undeterred, Florence went on to get her degree from Ohio Wesleyan University, then got accepted at Mines where she stayed, despite being disrespected by the male students. This changed over time, and now she was considered a fellow miner.

Abigail admired Florence from the start. She felt akin to Florence, being a female interested in mining but not taken seriously by men. Abigail knew gold and gold mining and assaying, but that didn't matter to many men. At Mines, the focus was on gold and gold mining and assaying, and Abigail wanted to be accepted at the same school as Florence. Without any college degree or formal schooling, Abigail knew she didn't have any chance for this dream to come true. She didn't need money, since she'd found out that tuition was free. She needed a degree behind her name. For a school of men to accept a second female, Abigail had to have something besides hands-on mining knowledge.

Florence Caldwell, in getting to know Abigail, had come up with some ideas on how to help her realize her dream. There might be a chance for Abigail to take proficiency tests at Mines, and this might satisfy their board of directors enough to allow them to admit her to the school. If not right away, then perhaps Abigail could attend school in Denver and earn the credits she needed. Florence would help her the entire way, she'd promised. "You're smart as a whip, Abigail," Florence had said. "I have no doubt you'll have your degree from Mines if you set your mind to it. We women must stick together," she'd lamented.

Abigail put the *Denver Rocky Mountain News* article out of Seattle on her desk. No, she wouldn't act on the overwhelming urge to head far north for gold "beyond wildest dreams." She'd stay in Denver and realize her dreams twelve miles away in Golden, at the School of Mines. Her dream was to get accepted there, no matter how long it might take. Tired after two long days of gold-rush news, she knew Mr. Lomery wouldn't mind if she left work early. She always turned in her work in a timely manner, and he let her keep her own schedule to get it done— other than making deadline that is. Full of genuine hope for the first time in her life, Abigail hurried out the front door of the *Daily Journal.*

"Thought we'd find you at one of these-here newspapers. Ma and Pa sent us to fetch you back to Creede, where you belong.

You need to take care of 'em like always. If we have to slap sense into you, gal, we will and you know it," the elder of her two brothers said.

Their threats and impassable arms held Abigail to the spot.

Chapter Seven

It would be a two-hour shuttle ride to Bellingham, Washington, where Abby would board the ferry taking her up the Inside Passage to Skagway. She had tickets for the shuttle and then for her trip on the *Columbia,* the flagship of the Alaska Marine Highway fleet. Most stampeders 120 years ago didn't have easy tickets in hand, Abby realized. First they had to have money to purchase tickets and then they had to actually find an available berth on the multitude of not-so-seaworthy steamers heading north. It couldn't have been easy for stampeders forced to take the rusted-steamer-poor-man's-route up the Alaska Panhandle, instead of steam-lining the rich-man's-route all the way to St. Michael—located across the Norton Sound from Nome, Alaska—and then navigating down the Yukon River to Dawson and the gold fields.

Guilt tugged at Abby. College had paid for this trip of a lifetime into Klondike gold-rush country; she hadn't. This route couldn't exactly be called a poor man's route today in comparison to times past, since you didn't need to have 40,000 dollars for your cache, but you did need deep pockets for a ferry ticket, a berth, food, and a reservation well ahead. Skagway remained a popular destination, with tours often booked a year ahead. A cruise line would charge much more than the ferry, she knew.

Abby was in good shape, since she didn't need a berth to camp on one of the ferry decks. She preferred to be outdoors rather than cooped up in a cabin, rustic or otherwise. An experienced backpacker, she'd slept on the ferry on her way to and from Skagway spring break. It was another expense she was relieved not to have to worry about this trip.

"Thanks," Abby told the shuttle driver, when he hoisted her backpack and gear onto the luggage rack. In truth, she didn't like ever to be separated from her pack, but the crowded shuttle didn't allow her to keep her things with her. At least she had a window seat and could focus her attention outside rather than inside, and avoid unwanted conversation. Her spirits sank at the possibility of needless chatter.

Her summer internship meant inside attention and unwanted conversation. She could hardly work alongside park rangers and deal with the public without paying attention to people and exchanging conversation. She'd chosen to do this and needed to work on her social skills, she reminded herself again. No excuses. Lucky for this opportunity in all other ways, Abby resolved to make the most of it and straightened her spine against her seat for the rest of the seventy-mile drive to Bellingham, and the four days it would take once on the ferry to reach Skagway.

With all passengers loaded, the van pulled out of the airport parking lot. Abby stared hard out the window, then caught what she was doing and brought her gaze back inside. She stared at her hands, rubbing them hard. The tall stranger in the brown cattleman's duster and black western hat was nowhere to be seen. She tried to push his image away. It didn't work. No matter how hard she tried not to, all she could envision was the handsome stranger standing in front of the Hard Rock Café in Empire. *He might be the one on the plane.* If she turned around at this moment and looked behind her, she knew she'd see the woman in white peering at her through the veiled second-story window of the Peck House. This ghostly image didn't scare Abby.

The idea she conjured ghosts, did.

"Looks like we're getting quite a little neighborhood together on this deck," a fellow passenger on the *Columbia* called over to Abby from his already setup tent.

Abby hadn't unpacked her gear or tried to set up her sleeping area, but still sat cross-legged and stone-cold still. She thought someone spoke to her but couldn't make out what was said. The Inside Passage unnerved her on this trip, where it hadn't before. Her bones ached with . . . what? *A fine time for me to get cold feet for my internship,* she lectured herself. Her feet were cold, actually, and so was the rest of her. The day had stayed warm. This didn't make sense. Why couldn't she hear? A rumble built in her head and the sensation nearly overwhelmed her.

She'd experienced noise like this before, in a mine shaft right before it collapsed. She'd gotten out in time, unhurt. *Get a grip on yourself, Abby Gray.* This is a 600-person-ferry headed to Skagway and not down any mine shaft. There are no swells coming at you, either, even though the Lynn Channel is famous for them. Abby sighed uncomfortably and regarded the blurred images across from her on the second-story deck of the *Columbia.* Edges; all she could see were edges of figures and tents but no faces and nothing clear. If anyone tried to speak to her, she doubted she could hear them over the crush of noise in her head. She might be going deaf, and this was a first sign.

Abby struggled for calm and to piece this puzzle together in some kind of scientific manner. She'd carefully planned out her trip and her whole summer. The jobs ahead would satisfy her, without question. Yes, she would need to bump up her social skills and interact with park rangers and tourists in gold-rush country. That made her like people in the North already. They'd chosen to be in gold-rush country, just as she had. This shouldn't cause the odd feelings assaulting her now.

She'd jumped at the opportunity to work with horses and sled dogs, as she'd done much of her life, growing up in mountain mining towns across Colorado. Summer meant ranching jobs and horses, while winter meant helping with sled dog teams. In between she'd go to school when she could. Colorado was cowboy country and ski country, and she found work where teens were hired. Now she headed to Alaska for similar work and shouldn't be experiencing this kind of upset. For Pete's sake, she'd grown up in gold-rush country! No logical reason for any of this distress, she concluded. No reason for her blurred vision and all this noise in her head.

Then everything went silent. No rumbles. No crushing charge of noise jamming her ears. Dead silence. Abby swallowed hard, suddenly convinced she *had* gone deaf.

"I said, it looks like we're getting quite a little neighborhood together on this deck, young lady."

Abby focused on the man speaking to her from across the deck. She not only heard him; she could see him clearly. Relief shot through her and helped her stand. The man appeared friendly enough, and so did the woman at his side. They weren't gawking as she'd expected, given her actions moments before. Either they hadn't been looking at her, or everything happened in a split second, a sudden blur in time. Abby didn't believe in blurs in time and pseudoscience.

"Yes, it does," she said to the older couple, wanting to be polite and brushing aside the odd feelings she'd just experienced. "Do you need any help with your tent or your stove setup?"

"That's very kind of you, dear, but we're old hands at this," the woman responded. "I think Sam and I were born under the

87

stars, the way we both have trouble sleeping indoors instead of out camping. If I can't make our meals on a collapsible stove, we don't eat," she joked.

Abby smiled and warmed to her new deck neighbors, forgetting all about any blur-in-time absurdity.

Dead on his feet, Elias looked forward to catching a little sleep the moment the saloon cleared. His workdays had turned to all-night work from the moment the *Portland* docked in July with its ton of gold on board. Leastways, that's what it felt like to Elias. Lately there seemed no stop to it. Good for business but bad for a body's health. Unlike most men around here, Elias didn't over-drink or over-smoke. He enjoyed a good glass of whiskey and a draw on an Old Gold as much as the rest of them, but he never established habitual use of either one. Didn't need either to start his day or end it. Better that way, Elias thought. His business in life was business. Too much alcohol, too many cigarettes, or too many women were distractions that interfered with his business of making money.

Elias couldn't complain about making decent money these days, not with all the gold-rush customers coming in day and night from all parts of the country. Hell, he'd had customers from all parts of the world, it seemed. The Merchant's Exchange Saloon was a gold mine for Otto. No need for his boss to head to the Klondike gold fields to find gold. He had plenty here. *This is Otto's place, not mine,* Elias acknowledged. *I want my own place, my own gold mine.* It gnawed at Elias that he didn't have his own place, despite making good money as barkeep and sheriff here, so to speak.

One after another cheechako—greenhorn miner—came into the Merchant's Exchange behind one after another sourdough—seasoned miner—enough to signal to Elias his fortunes might lie in the far north after all. Steamer after steamer offloaded passengers in Seattle and then reloaded more to head for St. Michael and the Yukon River, or up the Inside Passage to Skagway and Dyea. An idea struck him. Hell, if greenhorn miners were willing to pay up for liquor and cards and women here at this saloon and spend money they didn't have before they even headed north to the gold fields, then what am I waiting for? I could have my own gold mine in Dyea or Skagway, my own place. The way I hear the towns are starting to boom, it's a sure bet.

Elias caught himself.

Nothing was ever a sure bet, but a smart card-player knew which hand to play.

"Sorry, pard," Elias said to the man he'd bumped shoulders with outside the crowded Cooper and Levy Pioneer Outfitters on the corner of First Avenue and Yesler. The man quickly disappeared inside the busy store that advertised it would outfit all gold-seekers who entered with what they'd need in Alaska. A wall of supplies fronted the store, where men sat atop the sacks of goods and equipment waiting for freight carts to take them to the wharf and load the supplies onto the next steamer. Cooper and Levy Pioneer Outfitters marked the center of Seattle's gold-rush booming business district. There were other stores like this one but not as big. Elias went inside for a closer look, more interested in the numbers of customers than the goods offered for sale.

Satisfied to see so many people ready to give up their money to be outfitted for the gold fields, Elias sized up the customers. Most looked like cheechakos, greenhorns for sure. Only a few women mixed with the sea of men. Made sense, Elias thought. From what he'd learned about the far north, it wasn't any place for a female, except in saloons. Maybe not even there, he thought further. Elias didn't believe he saw one real miner in the crowd. He'd been around miners most of his life, and these greenhorns looked more like clerks, teachers, and trolley drivers, all of them city folk wet behind the ears, than they did sourdoughs digging for gold. They didn't know what was coming, and Elias knew it. He wondered how many people in this store would survive the journey to the gold fields, much less find any gold once they arrived.

"I'll be," Elias mused aloud when he spotted a sign posting all the goods needed for gold-seekers to outfit themselves for Alaska. These lists of outfits were in stores and on storefronts all over town, so customers could purchase them in a package deal. Elias hadn't scanned any of the lists in person until he stopped in this store. From what he saw, the cost would be anywhere from 250 dollars to 500 dollars per person, to be outfitted with over 2,000 pounds of goods. It takes a *ton of gold* to go for that ton of goods, Elias couldn't help thinking. Something on a nearby counter caught his eye, and he went over to the stack of forms and read the sign posted next to it.

"Well, if that doesn't beat all," he muttered. The form he'd picked up listed every possible item folks might need to fill out their ton of goods. If they had the money, all they had to do was check off what they wanted and get it in a packaged purchase. Seeing the form, he believed it.

The list was divided into three sections: equipment, clothing, and provisions. His eye went to provisions first, hardly believing the numbers: 800 pounds of flour, 300 pounds of bacon, 50 pounds of coffee, 40 pounds of condensed milk, 12 pounds of matches, and two boxes of candles holding 240 in each box. Everything from baking powder, beans, evaporated potatoes, apples, peaches, and vinegar was on the long list of provisions supplied for one person. It already sounded heavy, and that was just the start.

Equipment covered items such as gold scales, handled axes,

bread pans, cartridge belts, picks, snow glasses, galvanized pails, shovels, frying pans, coffee pots, gold-dust bags, a medicine case, and on and on. Elias noted the snow glasses and realized what this meant. They'd be needed to protect a person's eyes from the weather and snow glare. Did anyone in the store realize they were headed into unknown snow country? He doubted they'd given the matter this much thought. Elias scanned the clothing list and decided what he'd buy right away: the Mackinaw overshirt, jacket, and pants; flannel shirts; extra heavy underwear; waterproof seal mittens; and knit socks. The boots he had, but he'd probably pick up rubber shoes and anything else waterproof.

"Help you, son?" a store clerk asked.

"No, thanks," Elias said, then made a quick exit out of Cooper and Levy's. He needed fresh air and room to think over all this. When outside, he still traveled crowded streets, past horse-drawn delivery carts carrying goods to the waterfront, past sleds leaning against outside walls of buildings, past the Mosquito Proof Tent Company; then past McSorley and Company Hardware, the Northern Pacific Ticket Office, Bon Marché, Pioneer Alaska Clothing and Blanket Manufacturers, the Bartell Drug Company, the Columbia Grocery Company, the Seattle Trading Company, and Fischer Brothers, ending up at Schwabacher Brothers and Company and Wharf, at the water's edge.

Elias saw right away that Seattle's shipping industry and waterfront business boomed along with the rest of the city. Steamers docked in every direction with goods and passengers being offloaded and reloaded. Decks were crowded with both. It had been two months since the *Portland* docked here, and Elias guessed thousands and thousands of stampeders—gold-seekers to the Klondike—had already left this port for Alaska. He had trouble getting his mind around the tons of freight that must have left with them.

When he turned away from the harbor, Elias had to laugh at what he saw. Portable aluminum houses were advertised. These collapsible houses were guaranteed to keep a body safe from air, frost, and fire. Each house weighed 150 pounds. Elias's shoulders sank at the thought of more weight on a stampeder's back. He couldn't laugh at that.

Here it was September, and newly arrived stampeders already had to wait weeks for tickets on steamers heading north. During their wait, they needed food, shelter, and amusement. That's exactly why Elias would wait those same weeks before he'd head north to start his own business in Dyea or Skagway. The stampeders here who needed food, shelter, and amusement would surely need the same along their journey to the gold fields. *Money in my pocket,* he reckoned.

Elias couldn't leave until he had enough to outfit his own venture, and working with Otto would help him get there pretty fast. The Merchant's Saloon was a prime destination for stampeders waiting for passage north. Skid Road and Pioneer Square offered amusements, good meals, gambling halls, variety theaters, and saloons. The area might be rough and tumble, but that didn't stop stampeders from frequenting the Merchant's Exchange or nearby saloons and eateries. Hotel rooms and boarding houses filled up, making it hard to find a place to flop.

Word on the street was every spare room, basement, and attic had been rented out. Elias welcomed this news, knowing customers would continue to pour into the Merchant's Exchange Saloon, and money would continue to pour into his pockets. This pleasing thought spurred him to leave Schwabacher's Wharf and get back to work.

"Don't turn your back on us, girl," Abigail's eldest brother threatened, and gripped her arm tighter. "Don't even try."

"Let . . . me . . . go, Jasper," she said through a clenched jaw.

"That ain't happening, girl. You're gittin' back to Creede with us."

Her other brother stood by and smirked. His help wasn't needed yet.

"Both of you get and leave me be!" Abigail yelled this time.

The front door of the *Daily Journal* opened and the publisher, James Lomery, stepped outside.

"What's all the ruckus?" He calmly folded his arms across his chest and held his ground.

"This ain't none of your business. Abigail is our sister, and she ain't none of your business," Jasper blurted.

"In any case, let her go," Mr. Lomery insisted, at the same time lowering his arms and putting one hand inside the breast pocket of his jacket, as if a gun might lurk there.

Jasper slowly released his sister's arm, all the while keeping watch on the unwanted intruder's gun hand.

"Jasp—"

"Leave it be, Ike," Jasper said, not taking his eyes off the newspaper publisher.

Abigail stepped away from her brother and stood at her boss's side.

"Thank you," she managed to tell the newspaper publisher. The wheels inside her head turned violently, as she tried to figure out what her next move should be. All she knew for certain was that she had to get away from Denver and from her brothers any way she could! No time now to think about what she might be leaving behind—her one chance to realize life-changing dreams and count for something besides work-worn hands and hollow purpose.

"Abigail," Mr. Lomery said, keeping his voice measured and his eye on her two brothers, "go on inside and get back to work. You need to make today's deadline, and then you can come back out and talk with your brothers. It shouldn't take you long. I'll just wait here with them while you do."

"Yes, Mr. Lomery," she answered him, knowing full well she didn't have any more work to do or any deadline to meet. Mr. Lomery was giving her time to get out the back door of the newspaper, and he'd keep her brothers occupied long enough for her to do so. She put her hand to his arm for the briefest of moments, before she slipped inside the *Daily Journal*.

No sooner was she inside the front door than she was out the back door, racing toward the Women's Exchange to grab up her things and get out of town. Her heart pounded and her head ached and she agonized over the need to do this, to escape her brothers again. Where could she go to be sure they wouldn't follow and drag her back?

They didn't love her. They didn't even like her. Her brothers wanted her back to keep whiskey in her father's glass and her mother from her crazy fits. Her mother always calmed down a little after she'd switched Abigail long enough. Abigail's back ached from old wounds and the fear of new ones. She didn't believe for a second, "Ma and Pa wanted her back" as much as her brothers did. They wouldn't leave her be until they'd killed her, one way or the other.

She didn't stop to take a breath until she rounded the corner on Stout Street and could see the Women's Exchange. Then she couldn't take another step until she made sure of the heart-shaped nugget tucked deep in her jacket pocket. There it was, safe, hidden away. Her brothers would *never* find it and snatch it away. She hurried to the women's center, knowing she had little time to collect her meager belongings, then tell Mary goodbye.

Abigail had everything she owned in her newly purchased leather satchel. She'd saved to buy the luxury item, wanting to have it for all her school work and college supplies. Believing she'd one day go to college and maybe even the School of Mines, she'd bought the satchel, already taking pride in her anticipated studies. Well, there was no pride in what she was doing at this moment—running away from her family and the switch.

She looked up and down Stout Street, searching for any sign of her brothers. Mary told her they'd already come to the Women's Exchange to try and find her. Mary had told them nothing, but still, her brothers could come back. Clearly they'd figured something was up at this point, and had charged past Mr. Lomery to go inside the newspaper office. Yet her brothers were cowards. They might have just left. Too late to think about that now; her brothers knew her general whereabouts. She had to get out of sight and out of Denver.

The busy afternoon traffic of horse-drawn carts, trolleys, and scores of people going this way and that would give her cover, Abigail hoped—or at least enough time to make some kind of plan of where to go and what to do. She had twenty dollars saved, and she needed to make it stretch as far as she could. The money wouldn't get her very far out of Denver on the train and wasn't enough to get her own horse. When afternoon shadows struck her face, her heart jumped to her throat, thinking her brothers had found her. She had to get out of sight and decide what to do.

So intent was she on heading down the first alley she found, Abigail didn't see the horse-drawn caravan of travelers until she bumped into them.

"Look out there!" a woman shouted from her wagon perch. "No need to run us poor music-hall entertainers into the ground!" Then the woman, clad in a gray wool traveling dress and western hat, climbed down from the driver's seat, while at the same time, another woman pushed open the back of the theatrical-looking wagon.

"We're *actresses,* Maud," the second woman corrected and came around front. She wore a white, long-sleeved blouse, dark wool skirt to the ankles, wide leather belt at the waist, and a black-brimmed hat.

Abigail moved away from the horse nuzzling her hands. No doubt the bay mare was looking for some kind of treat that might be hidden there. The other horse reared its head at this action, probably wanting a treat, too. Abigail stared at her booted feet and not at the women approaching. Panic built. She couldn't afford to be held up by this acting troupe or anybody else.

She needed to get out of town, fast.

CHAPTER EIGHT

If Abby had to experience this same dull drone of isolation, shortness of breath, queasiness, and fear that had taken hold of her during the entire four days up the Inside Passage to Skagway, she might jump ship first! Everything had calmed after her initial upset once she'd boarded the *Columbia* ferry, but things didn't stay that way. Something wreaked havoc with her emotions, and she couldn't put her finger on what that might be. Emotions; she didn't really have any, she thought. Her birthday numerology number was four, and fours were not emotional people. More, fours don't necessarily understand the emotional realm.

Abby didn't think she could feel any worse, but she did as she espoused numerological nonsense that had no scientific basis. She did not hold any "belief in the divine, mystical relationship between a number and one or more coinciding events," as the dictionary defined numerology. That was for paranormal ghost hunters and astrologists to speculate about; not her. The idea she'd draw any pseudoscientific numerology reference from the number four—which she'd done with *four* days on the ferry and her birthday numerology number *four*— went against everything that had been in her heretofore. Yet she did have a bad habit of delving into numerology, since so many numbers in her life and studies repeated themselves.

"The Alexander Archipelago is a group of eleven-hundred

islands, three-hundred miles long, which rise steeply from the Pacific Ocean," the park ranger informed his group of rapt listeners on the uppermost deck of the *Columbia*. "This archipelago shelters the northern portion of the Inside Passage we now travel."

Abby fought for concentration—away from her intrusive numerology habit and to the park ranger on board. If her whole summer went like this, she'd be in trouble. The School of Mines would never accept any articles for the student *Oredigger* or proposals for any Grand Challenges Scholar's internship if she didn't get this pseudoscientific nonsense out of her head.

"The Lynn Channel we're ferrying is over two thousand feet deep, the deepest fjord in North America and one of the deepest and longest in the world," the ranger continued. "The width ranges from three to twelve miles in this narrow passage and runs ninety miles in length. Strong, semi-diurnal tides occur in these waters, where there can be thirty-foot differences between high and low tides, and underwater obstacles to navigate away from. For those who have not heard the term *diurnal tides* before, this refers to two high waters and two low waters each day. So the two highs are not the same and the two lows are not the same, but are unequal."

Daily duality. Abby thought about the descriptive term and more. The number four in Pythagorean theory spoke to two plus two and daily duality. Diurnal tides in relation to daily duality. There were four parts of organic chemistry, four states of matter, and four known physical forces. This last comprised nuclear, radiate, electromagnetic, and the force of gravitation. The Bible referred to the earth being created on day four; not according to Pythagoras, but God. Her thoughts detoured back to electromagnetic force, and she couldn't pull her mind away from the ghostly sense. The static voice she'd been hearing, and the current shooting through her each time she did, unnerved her to the point of phantom pain.

"Abigail . . . Abigail . . ."

Abby stared hard at the park ranger, mentally accusing him of calling her out. How could he stand there so casually and speak to everyone now as if he'd done nothing wrong? Covered in goose bumps, she hugged her arms to get away from the unwanted eerie sensation and get away from whatever or whoever tried to cause her such a scare. She hated to admit she was scared, but she feared something.

An electrical storm could force these kinds of bizarre charges. But it wasn't storming. A powerful mine collapse might, too, she thought. Any powerful act of nature might create disturbances, upheavals and blurs in time and space. Abby dropped her arms to her sides, not believing what she'd just pondered. That she tried to connect powerful acts of nature rationalized by scientific study . . . with blurs in time rationalized by nothing . . . unnerved her more than hearing a strange male voice calling out to her. Besides, *I am no beauty.* She kicked herself for this last misstep in thought.

"Abigail . . . Abigail . . ."

"What!" she shouted back before she could control the impulse.

The park ranger stopped talking. The group listening to him stepped away from Abby, doubtless startled by her sudden outburst.

"I'm sorry. I just couldn't hear you. I get frustrated sometimes," Abby said and knew she sounded like an idiot. "I'm sorry," she said again to the park ranger. She couldn't explain any of this craziness to herself, much less to anybody else. Being hard of hearing was a poor excuse, but the only one she could come up with on short notice.

"No worries, young lady," the ranger said, then went to stand next to her. "This should work better," he reassured her with a smile.

The group returned to their closer circle to hear the rest of the naturalist's talk.

Relieved they all accepted her lousy excuse for her poor behavior, Abby forced herself to remain and listen along with everybody else. If she left before the ranger finished, it would add insult to injury and call more attention to her. She didn't want that.

Abby lay down on her rolled-out sleeping bag, glad to be alone on the *Columbia* second deck for the moment. Most of the passengers were inside eating, taking photos from various vantage points, or using one of the lounges on board. After thirty-eight hours of sailing, they'd docked in Ketchikan, where many stepped off the *Columbia* to see all the totems and local art of the native Tlingit, Haiku, and Tsimshian peoples. A good plate of salmon filled the bill here, especially since Ketchikan was the salmon capital of the world. Abby had seen Ketchikan, and she wasn't hungry; two good reasons to stay on board. A third reason held her on board: to try and explain the unexplained.

What happened earlier during the naturalist's presentation shook her confidence in getting through the summer with her wits and her internship intact. She had four years of "normal" behavior and good scholarship at Mines to complete, and that's all that mattered. None of this pseudoscientific nonsense mattered. *There's that number four again.* Numerology got her nowhere, and she should throw the habit away like so much trash. She couldn't put her finger on when the habit started; maybe something related to gold mining and assaying and numbers of nuggets, bars, or bags of gold dust. Repeating numbers had become a habit. She should leave it at that.

Gold-rush numbers came to mind often; enough to repeat

events in historical context and even tie them together. Abby loved gold-mining history and, of course, loved the history of the major gold rushes in America. They always stirred the numerology pot with so many coincidences to explain away . . . if you could.

She settled deeper onto her zipped-up sleeping bag and determined to puzzle this out. *I'm not crazy.* I just keep most of my thoughts to myself. Call me antisocial, and you'd be right. Call me eccentric, and you'd be right. Call me a gold miner, and you'd be right. Call me a ghost miner and you'd be wrong! With that, Abby sat up.

This circular argument was getting her nowhere. *Puzzle out the problem,* Abby Gray. She laid back down and forced herself to stay emotionally even. No emotion, just facts. Numerical facts marched across her line of vision; gold-rush facts.

The number 100,000 repeated itself with each of America's great gold rushes. It had started with the California Gold Rush in 1849. In the two years of this first rush to find promised gold, 100,000 Native Americans were killed. The push of progress had a terrible price, and Native Americans paid with their lives. Abby didn't know about the other side: how many gold-seekers died, or how many had joined in the gold rush in the first place. It broke her heart . . . the loss of life to find gold. Her tears would never dry.

In the Colorado Gold Rush of 1859, where *Pikes Peak or Bust* became the catchword slogan, 100,000 participated in the rush. Then, with the Klondike Gold Rush in 1897, the same number—100,000—of stampeding gold-seekers came from all over America, and all over the world, to find the promised yellow metal.

In numerology, the number 100,000 refers to Day of Judgment. To have the same number repeat itself three times in the same type of event in American history, and to have this extraordinary number of people facing judgment at the same time, sparked Abby's interest. When she considered the Klondike Gold Rush in particular, the number 1,500 stood out: 1,500 was the number of women determined to reach the gold fields, and the number of ice steps an entrepreneur carved out at a time to reach the Chilkoot summit. That the exact number of ice steps—the Golden Stairs—carved out amid the innumerable steps needed to ascend the treacherous trail matched the exact number of 1,500 women out of 100,000 male stampeders, stood out to Abby. The meaning of the number, in biblical terms, was light. Abby warmed to the idea of this biblical interpretation.

She forgot there was another reference to the number 1,500 in Klondike gold-rush history. After the horrific Palm Sunday Avalanche, 1,500 stampeders had rushed up from Sheep Camp to help dig for survivors.

Coincidences or clues? she wondered. If clues, then to what? Time is not absolute; therefore these numbers could represent clues to any time—to the past, the present, or the future. Was there something in the coincidence and intersection of the same numbers at the same time performing the same task? Could events coincide and connect the past, the present, and the future? Abby didn't know if she were onto something or off the rails in her thinking.

It had been 119 years since the Klondike Gold Rush. She'd looked up the numerological definition and ran its meaning over in her thoughts; particularly since she traveled to the same gold-rush country now. Most definitions of 119 were written in terms of guardian spirits and angel numbers; a mystic and religious arena, she realized. While Abby didn't practice Christianity, she had formed her own beliefs. Mysticism and religion might have a place in there somewhere, especially since service to others figured prominently in the definition. Another defined association indicated the number 119 would lead a person to "fulfilling your life path—your mission to find your soul's destiny."

Abby bolted upright.

Could this be a clue to what was going on? Was she searching for her soul's destiny?

The wind in the alleyway picked up. Abigail set her floppy-brimmed hat firmly on her brow and wanted to get away from these actresses and out of Denver. She gripped her satchel harder and turned to head out the way she'd come. Should she go down Market Street or Larimer? Should she try for the train depot and see where twenty dollars could take her? Her brothers would be combing the streets by this time. If they caught her, she'd pay for running away. The punches they'd inflict already smarted. Tired of being bullied and made to feel ashamed, she couldn't let her brothers find her.

"Wait up!" One of the women behind her called out.

Abigail didn't want to cause a scene with this group of performers. She grudgingly turned around and shot the woman a wary look.

"I think I know you," the woman said as she approached Abigail. "Aren't you that entertainer from the burlesque show back east? Are you in a show here, or are you in between shows? We gals could use some new blood in our troupe. We're heading out of Denver, and I don't suppose you'd consider coming with us? You already have your travel satchel in hand, so I see you might be headed out yourself. I didn't see any harm in stopping you to see if you'd consider traveling as part of our stock company."

"Ye-yes, I am . . . headed out of town." Abigail fumbled with her answer. "And yes . . . I'll travel with you."

"Girls!" Maud called back to the three women waiting by the

horses. "We have a new member in our group. This is Belle Bingham, the burlesque star who dresses like a man and draws in crowds big-time. Girls, come and greet Belle."

Abigail braced herself at Maud's introduction and her new role as a burlesque star—her ticket out of Denver.

After three tense days of wagon travel, Abigail could relax a little about her brothers following her, but not about her role in the stock company troupe. Maud, Lilly, Francesca, and Simone questioned Abigail daily about her skills, where she'd learned them, and how she'd come to star in burlesque. The women were music hall entertainers primarily, and not theater actresses, despite calling themselves such. Turned out they'd entertained in mining boomtowns all over, and Denver had been a decent stop for them. The biggest news for Abigail was that these entertainers wanted to head for Seattle and the stampede to the Klondike. The women talked about box houses and variety theaters in Seattle, but all Abigail heard was *Klondike Gold Rush*.

Abigail had grown up in mining boomtowns and had seen enough of saloons and read enough newspaper ads about music halls and entertainers to at least have a basic knowledge of what she'd got herself into. If she needed to be somebody named Belle Bingham to reach the Klondike gold fields, she'd be a burlesque star. None of her fellow troupe picked up on this ruse, at least not so far. The troupe hadn't stopped to entertain anywhere yet. At every chance, Abigail fished for information about her taken-on identity. What did they like best about her showmanship? How would she best fit in with their music hall performances? Abigail had never talked so much in her life—or lied so much.

In truth, Abigail did feel like a different person since she'd left Denver with this devil-may-care group of women. The worry about her brothers finding her lifted. She felt akin to this ragtag band of women. They had stories she could relate to in some ways, but not to their relationships with men. Abigail didn't have any relationships with men and didn't want any. Men were bullies. Men were liars. Men were only nice if they wanted something. Men didn't know the meaning of love. She didn't either. Besides, *I am no beauty.*

Dejected about leaving her opportunity to attend college and the School of Mines behind, Abigail forced herself to look ahead for a likely prospect. Joining the rush of stampeders to find gold in Alaska and the Yukon gave her renewed purpose in becoming a miner herself. She'd never traveled out of Colorado and never dreamed she'd be on her way to the far north. Abigail knew Seattle was similar to San Francisco, a port from which gold-seekers departed for Alaska. She'd stay in Seattle as long as it took to find her own way to the Yukon gold fields.

"So, tell me again how you learned to shoot and ride horses, Belle," Lilly asked, wide-eyed, for the umpteenth time.

Lilly was the newest member of the group and the youngest, at nineteen, the same as Abigail. She'd run off from her family at a young age, and Abigail related to this, too. She felt compassion for the happy-go-lucky brunette, and glad Lilly could be happy-go-lucky at this point. Abigail didn't ask why Lilly had run, and Lilly never offered the information. Some things were best left alone. Long conversations and revealed secrets were never a good idea, Abigail reminded herself. A twinge of guilt hit her when she thought of all the lies she'd told these women in too-long conversations. But Abigail needed to survive, and she saw this her only way: to lie herself out of Denver and away from the bullies who claimed to have raised her.

The women, all speaking of the men they'd known, sounded as though they were speaking a foreign language to Abigail— talking about *giving* this one the mitten or *getting* the mitten from another. The idea of rejecting a lover or being rejected by one didn't resonate with Abigail in any kind of romantic sense. She didn't have a romantic sense.

The women might as well be speaking French or German. For the life of her, Abigail couldn't understand why they all seemed to like men so much and sound all soft inside when they talked about this handsome one with muscles aplenty, or that good-looking one with sandy hair. It turned Abigail's stomach, listening to all four gush about men as though they were any saloon girl or female working the line. Yet none of the women had said they ever worked as prostitutes but were music hall performers. Abigail didn't think they'd lied, but that was for them to know, not her.

Abigail had talked herself and her fellow travelers into believing her role as Belle Bingham. She wasn't a singer or dancer, but she did prefer men's clothes to women's. That wasn't a lie. She might mirror herself after Calamity Jane, the famous westerner. Only Abigail would have a gold-mining talk to give about how a woman can do the same as a man in the same job. She could shoot and knew horses and all about ranch life in the pioneer west, and could maybe take off her hat or something as she spoke. That thought bothered her—removing her hat and opening herself to scrutiny—but she needed to pull off this ruse.

She supposed she'd have to undo her braid, too, and show her long hair to the men in the audience. Hurdy-gurdy gals did this sometimes. Men would whoop and hoot when dance hall girls took off any item of clothing or undid their hair. Much as it turned her stomach to do such a thing in front of men, she'd no choice. *I'm not an entertainer. I have another purpose, to get to the gold fields. If I have to take off my hat and undo my hair to get there, I will.*

Abigail needed to work on her story. Gloom weighed on her heavily. She needed to practice what she'd say and how she'd say it. The women around her would figure her out if she asked to rehearse in front of them, so she had to keep her real story to herself. She'd talk mining and using a six-shooter and about being a determined pioneer woman. Actually, that storyline wouldn't be a complete lie. The lie would be in her using some kind of sugary voice and moving like molasses dripped over hotcakes to win men's attention. Bile rose at the image and she emptied her stomach while no one could see her.

An inspiration struck the moment she wiped her mouth dry. She put her fingers back to her lips, as if willing them to talk. Mentally, she whispered the lines of something she'd read in a local newspaper reprint from the *Brooklyn Daily Union* back east. The "anonymous poem" stood out enough for her to remember the lines, word for word. They resonated with her. She knew about winners and losers and dying for gold. If she spoke these anonymous words on stage, she could be anyone, an unknown. If being some kind of actress would get her to the gold fields, she'd do it. She'd pretend to be someone else.

But I am no actress. I have another purpose.

In the next town Maud and company decided to get on the train for Seattle instead of staying for a possible performance at the music hall. Seattle beckoned. Boomtowns beckoned. After selling their wagon and horses, they had enough money among them to get their belongings and themselves on board the Union Pacific. Abigail didn't protest this welcome reprieve from her dreaded music hall debut.

Seattle and box houses and variety theaters would come soon enough.

CHAPTER NINE

"I'm your huckleberry," Elias said to the upset card-player who'd just pulled a pistol on another man at the crowded faro table. Elias shot out from behind the bar at the Merchant's Exchange, the moment he saw what was going on. He kept his Colt Six-Shooter at his side, and not pointed. These arguments always went fast and always meant trouble.

"No, you ain't!" the red-faced card-player spat out, not looking at Elias. "You ain't the one for this job, I am. I'm putting a bullet right between this lily-livered, petticoat pensioner's eyes for cheatin' me," he threatened and cocked his pistol.

The men at the table didn't say a word and didn't move. Everyone knew the danger they faced, the accused cheater especially. Sweat trickled down his brow, and his hands, placed flat on the faro table, held a tremor.

"I didn't cheat," the accused said in a monotone.

In the next instant Elias knocked the gun from the heeled card-player, then knocked him out.

"Wally," Elias called to one of the waiters. "Get some help and get this one outa here."

The waiter started from across the room where he'd been watching the action. Another waiter joined him.

"Fellas, take him to the precinct jail, and we'll let the police deal with him," Elias instructed.

Both employees put an arm under the still-out card-player

and dragged him through the front door of the Merchant's Exchange.

"For your sake, I hope you're not a cheater," Elias said to the seated faro player in question. "This is a tough neighborhood, and you might not be so lucky next time. Clear out for tonight. Game's over for you."

Once the man left, the rest of the players settled back into their game. Two men quickly took the vacated seats and the overflowing saloon buzzed alive when things returned to normal. Elias went behind the bar and stored his pistol in its holster on the shelf below. There were police in town, but Otto and Elias both knew it was up to the two of them to patrol here. Things could easily happen before any lawman might show, particularly with so many new faces in town. Gold brought business and trouble. No one got killed in here tonight, and that was a good thing. Out on the streets and in alleyways, it might be another story. Like he'd said before, Skid Road was a rough and tumble neighborhood.

Elias scanned the full crowd at the Merchant's Exchange. There'd be little sleep for him tonight. He had help at the bar with drinks but not with security. At the thought, he turned around and scanned all the painted pictures of the ladies on the third floor. It was still crowded up there, too, with all the ladies bought and paid for; some for an hour, some for the night. A fine brothel might be good business, but it had a bad side to it, Elias knew. Too many ladies could end up at the end of the line.

Elias studied each picture, remembering each one's turnover time. He stopped at Evangeline's picture. Her turnover time was way past. Her customer hadn't paid for the night. Elias reached under the bar and took up his Colt pistol again, this time to head up to the third floor.

"Gideon, watch things here," he said to the junior barkeep, then found the pair of stairs. This might be a brothel, but it was a good one; not any hook shop where ladies were nothing more than pieces of calico. Elias had room number one in his sights and worried over Evangeline. He tried to picture her last customer and couldn't, other than his being older and carrying more weight than most. That should have struck him as odd from the first—being older than most regulars, sourdoughs, or greenhorns around here. Elias put the customer at about fifty-five.

All appeared fine when he stepped to the third floor. Electric-charged sconces lit the thickly carpeted hallway. He heard quiet chatter and giggles from most rooms, but not room number one. Elias put his ear to the door. Silence, *dead* silence. He went cold, thinking of Evangeline and what might be going on. Always risky, being a prostitute, no matter how fine the brothel. Part of his job was to protect all the ladies, and he'd fallen down on the job with Evangeline.

Dammit!

He cocked his pistol and busted through the door.

Evangeline lay tied to the iron bed, and her customer lay in a pool of blood next to her.

"It's all right, sweetheart," Elias reassured Evangeline, who stared as if in a trance and didn't respond. She had blood on her dress, but she was alive. A quick exam showed no bullet wounds. She'd been struck with fear, he could see. "Let's get you outa here," Elias crooned softly. The bastard lying dead next to her must have taken his own life, and wanted to do it in front of Evangeline. *Sick.* No other way to say it.

Elias hadn't heard any shot, and he knew why. The noisy first floor gave cover to any goings-on, on the third floor. He needed to remember that. He needed to remember the stampede to the Klondike brought a lot of desperate people in these hard times, and not everyone had good intentions. *Like this poor son of a bitch here.*

Elias had just served his last drink and thrown out the last troublemaker on his last watch at the Merchant's Exchange Saloon. Tomorrow he'd leave on a steamer out of Seattle, bound for Skagway and Dyea. He wouldn't leave anybody he cared about behind here; all of his Seattle ties could easily be broken.

Always best that way.

He'd booked passage weeks ago with room for his cargo of whiskey, tobacco, and faro gaming materials. It was past time for him to leave. Business already boomed in Skagway and Dyea, and he didn't want to miss out any longer. He had enough money in his pockets to start up business but still hadn't decided in which boomtown. He'd make that decision once he arrived in the area and could size things up.

Elias chose the route that made the most sense for his business, and decided to travel along the Alaska Panhandle, up the Inside Passage to Skagway and Dyea. His intent wasn't to reach Dawson and the gold fields, but one of the boomtowns—*his* gold fields; so he wouldn't steam to St. Michael, then boat down the Yukon to Dawson. Any building supplies he'd need he would secure on arrival. Maybe he could find an empty place to buy. He'd have to wait and see. He ran his fingers over his holstered Colt, knowing he'd need the six-shooter in the days ahead. Ready ammunition was a must. From everything he'd heard, the law in Alaska was no law that could help him much. He'd watch his own back and his own business.

Always best that way.

He strolled along Skid Road and breathed in the salty air, going over his plans for tomorrow. The streets were still thick with people going to saloons, variety theaters, restaurants, or searching for hotels. Places to rest your head were hard to come by.

Any flophouse would do for most. Elias stopped and pulled out his pack of Old Golds. He felt like a smoke. In the time it took to strike a match and take a draw, he heard music and whoops and laughter coming from the variety theater across from him. Maybe he'd allow himself this simple pleasure before he turned in for the night. It could be a while before he'd have another opportunity to enjoy variety entertainment. The idea of a soft-curved gal wearing a silky gown and singing bawdy songs appealed to him. He stamped out his lit tobacco and went inside the raucous theater.

Once he'd sat down, the whoops and applause turned to boos and shouts to *"leave the stage!"* the moment the next performer appeared.

Abby was downright anxious, asked by one of the rangers on board the *Columbia* to talk about gold panning and assaying and mining during gold-rush days. Ever since she'd interrupted the naturalist's talk, the ranger didn't leave her alone, seemingly curious about her. She'd brought this on herself, she knew. Now she'd no choice but to suffer through giving a lecture to strangers and do her best to remain anonymous at the same time! The challenge nearly overwhelmed her and she rubbed her cold, sweaty hands raw with nerves. She had two more days on this ferry. Defeated before she started, Abby stepped warily to the front of the group gathered on the top deck for her talk. Her mouth filled with cotton and her heart beat out of her chest.

"We don't need any actor *on this stage! We came here to see actresses!"* a man shouted.

"I want my money back!" another member of the audience yelled.

Elias felt for the poor thing on the stage whom he sensed

right away was female. She had to be a greenhorn at this; he could see from the start. He'd heard of females wearing men's clothes to perform, but this gal looked out of place for this variety entertainment. He couldn't see her face that well, but he could easily imagine her slender shape beneath the mining getup she wore.

Just then one of the other female performers took center stage. This one looked as he'd expected: like all females in musical variety with their rouged lips, ribbons in their piled hair, in curvy-to-the-knee dresses, with near-bare bosoms.

"Now all you men just hush," Maud chastised in a musical voice. "You've never seen burlesque, so you're in for a treat. This is Belle Bingham, and you need to let her perform."

"Her? That's a her?" one man jeered loudly. Others laughed at his remark.

More curious by the moment, Elias didn't laugh. He'd heard the word *burlesque*, but never seen the entertainment. At least he didn't think he had. One thing he did know: the gal onstage in that getup must be something special. He'd never thought that about too many females, and this one was a stranger to him. Yet wild horses couldn't drag him from his seat.

"That's better. You don't sound like Rocky Mountain canaries that's been slipped rotgut whiskey anymore," Maud joked to the quieting crowd. To her they did sound like a bunch of burros, just like miners in the Rockies used for hauling, the way they heehawed from their seats in the audience.

Silenced by her joking, the room went quiet, and Maud left the stage. She gave Belle a wink for courage before she did. This would be the first time she'd see her perform, and she prayed Belle lived up to her press and would be a moneymaker for their troupe.

The piano player struck up Abigail's intro music, and she stepped forward on the stage, stopping at her mark; her floppy-brim hat square on her brow, a gold pan in one hand, and a pick shovel in the other. She couldn't afford to fail. That's what this was all about: being able to afford reaching the Klondike gold fields. *Remember,* she told herself, *you're an anonymous writer of poetry, your identity unknown. You're not an actress or a music hall entertainer wanting any man's attention, but a gold miner needing to get to the mines.* The piano introduction ended and Abigail looked up, then over the crowd of men seated. She looked into the unknown, to her fortune.

Success

Success is counted sweetest
By those who ne'er succeed.
To comprehend a Nectar
Requires sorest need.

Not one of all the Purple Host
Who took the flag today,
Can tell the definition,
So plain, of victory.

As he defeated, dying,
On whose forbidden ear
The distant strains of triumph
Break, agonizing clear.

Reciting these words in slow rhyme picked up Abigail's flagging spirits when she considered their meaning. Only those who knew defeat could know success, she'd interpreted the poem to mean. She'd had a lifetime of defeat, mostly at the hands of her own family. Gold fever is a strong desire. Even nearing death and hearing heavenly music, it was hard to kill a miner's desire.

114

Gold was a man's world, but she had her place in it. She'd find her fortune or die trying. She had to count for something besides callused hands and empty pockets.

Caught up in her own thoughts, Abigail almost forgot the rest of her performance. She swallowed hard and then set her gold pan and pick shovel on the chair provided. When the piano music started again, she straightened her spine and slowly removed her hat. The moment she did, her lustrous raven hair tumbled down her back and across her shoulders. She gave her head a slight shake to un-tousle it, then moistened her lips.

Honestly, at this moment she didn't think she had a drop of water in her! Then she slowly and purposely removed her jacket and let it slip to the same chair, ignoring her nausea. Careful not to make eye contact with any of the men gawking at her, she looked straight ahead before she tucked her white, blousy, long-sleeved shirt farther into the waistband of her wide leather belt. She forced a smile past the bile rising in her gorge, then moved her feet apart and put her hands on her hips, enough to take on a man's powerful stance.

The piano music stopped. The room stayed silent. Abigail feared failure. Hands started to clap, building to all-out applause. Men whooped and cheered. Abigail forced a bow and then quickly exited the stage.

"She's a real actress," Elias heard men say as they filed out of the theater.

"Yessir . . . we saw ourselves a real back-east actress with all those fancy words. A pretty thing, too, turns out," another quipped as he passed by Elias.

If they felt anything like he did now, all of 'em were in trouble. Seeing a female dressed as a man was more seductive than any thin-veiled, brothel-gown a fellow could imagine. Belle Bingham didn't need to strip down to attract men to her. All she had to do was open that sweet, soft mouth of hers with the promise of "success" in a voice that cut through him. It almost hurt, she sounded so melodic yet melancholy at the same time. He'd never heard a female so pleasant-sounding. Whew. He let out the breath he'd been holding and got up from his seat. He'd intended to leave the theater but went backstage instead.

"Don't," Elias said in a hoarse voice the moment he spotted the lady in question trying to shove all her lush hair back inside her western hat.

"Don't what, you good-looking man." Maud answered for Belle, then turned and gave her friend another wink in understanding. "Looks like you have your first admirer, Belle," Maud said with a knowing smile, and disappeared behind the dressing curtain. The rest of the troupe had changed and waited in the dressing area for Maud and Belle, their loud chatter easily picked up.

Abigail turned and looked behind her, thinking this stranger had to be talking to someone else. No one who looked like him would want to talk to somebody like her. The light here was dim, but she could see every detail of his handsome expression.

"No, darlin', I'm talking to you," Elias said, chuckling.

She held onto her hat and, instead of putting it on, looked behind her a second time. Every single nerve she had stood on end. This wasn't real. No one in the whole of her life had called her *darlin'*.

"Listen, mister," she said, fighting the blush heating her. When she looked at him, it made things worse, but she couldn't look away. Her insides tangled at his hooded brown eyes and cropped-at-the-neck, tawny brown hair that reminded her of smooth, tanned leather. Its edges curled against his skin. He didn't wear a mustache or beard like most men in these parts, and she took pleasure in his appearance—in his chiseled jaw, sculpted mouth, and white, even smile. His imposing height and well-muscled frame filled the stage doorway. She kept up her scrutiny. His black frock coat, brimmed western hat, and cowboy boots drew her in farther. The smell of new tobacco and musk flared her senses. "Mister, you have me mistaken with somebody else," she managed to get out through her nerves, and looked at her booted feet instead of him.

"Darlin'," Elias repeated and moved in to lift her chin to him. "I don't make mistakes."

Thrown off balance by his words and his touch, Abigail stepped away and nearly fell.

Elias held onto her arms to steady her.

"You *are* Belle Bingham, right? The performer who just entertained on the stage?" he gently asked.

His warm breath teased her frayed nerves. She quickly pushed his hands from her arms. Touching him sparked her insides and mixed her all up. Her unexpected response to this stranger scared and confused her.

"Yes . . . I am Belle Bingham," she managed, and kept up her lie.

"I was hoping you'd come out with me and have a drink so we can talk," Elias invited. He could be a schoolboy, the way he felt in front of this beauty. Her complexion wasn't painted, but natural and radiant. She had the bluest eyes and the blackest hair he'd ever seen and soft, sensual lips that waited for his kiss. Wildflowers rained down. His body woke to hers. She hid her beauty behind men's clothes, but she couldn't hide from him.

He hadn't been looking to meet someone like her, but he had.

He wasn't looking for any gal he'd regret leaving behind tomorrow, but he already regretted leaving this one.

"I don't drink, and I don't talk," Abigail clipped and then felt foolish. She sounded ridiculous and she knew it. "I mean I don't go out and talk." Tarnation! Her inexperience with the opposite sex showed. Why should she care? *I don't!*

Elias liked Belle Bingham a lot. He didn't know if she were putting on an act. If she was, he'd fallen for it.

"Then we'll stay here and talk," he said.

"No. I have to go, mister," Abigail blurted and abruptly disappeared behind the dressing curtain.

"Name's Elias Colt," he called through the curtain. "Not mister. I'll be right here waiting for you so we can . . . not talk and not go out," he teased.

Abby's eyes opened wide at the apparition coming at her on the top deck of the *Columbia,* then turned her back and shut her eyes against what she saw. In her defense, she pulled her North Face cap down farther over her brow to better hide from the formidable image approaching. He looked out of place in his western frock coat and black-brimmed hat, but he looked *real,* and she knew he couldn't be. She feared she'd gone completely batty! She didn't have time to go batty. She didn't have time to conjure ghosts, either.

Abby opened her eyes but didn't turn around. She'd wait to see who might pass by. No one did, ghost or human. She pivoted. The apparition had vanished. Good. *Good,* she told herself a second time, then made her way down the stairs to her camp area on deck two. She'd wanted to clear her head, and she had. No more ghosts. She could sort this out if given time. There had to be a reason her imagination had taken control of her good sense. Something had hold of her, but what? Who?

"Abigail . . . Abigail . . ."

She recognized the voice . . . the same rasped whisper she'd heard in the Slide Cemetery.

Chapter Ten

"Belle, what is wrong with you?" Lilly whispered hard, the moment Abigail came inside the stage dressing area. "That man is about the best-looking thing I've seen in Seattle—maybe anywhere, dang it! What is wrong with you, not staying out there and spooning with him?"

"Spooning? What's that?" Abigail genuinely wanted to know.

"Shhh. Don't let him hear," Lilly cautioned. "You know, like going out sparking with a boy."

"She means flirting and love-play, Belle," Simone interjected with a wry smile.

"You gals hush and leave Belle be," Maud warned. "She might not be new to the world of entertainment, but she's sure as shootin' new to the world of men. Give her time to make her own way."

Abigail thought she'd die of embarrassment. If she did, she wouldn't have to deal with any of this—with the girls inside the dressing room or the man outside.

"Can't you just see what he wants?" Lilly begged her.

"I know exactly what he wants," Simone insinuated.

"That's enough, both of you," Maud lectured, then turned to Abigail. "Belle, go back out there and give that man five minutes of your time. You owe him that much for coming backstage to find you." Maud crossed her arms over her chest to underscore her point.

Abigail's shoulders slumped along with her already flagging

spirits. With little choice, she stepped back through the curtain, hat still in hand.

"So, I have five minutes, do I?"

Abigail stared at her boots. That would help these five minutes go by. She mentally repeated the lines of the poem, *Success,* to shut everything else out; especially this masculine assault on her feminine soul! Any girl inside her had died long ago. She'd no will to resurrect her feminine soul or acknowledge her feminine side. *I am no beauty.* Her mother had made sure of that.

"Take this, please," Elias quietly asked of her and put a slip of paper in front of her.

Abigail looked up from her feet, at the offered note. She didn't reach for it.

"I know life has hurt you," Elias said straight out. "I can see it in your eyes. I don't want to hurt you; I want to know you. Tomorrow I leave Seattle, and it hurts me to leave you behind," he admitted openly. The shock of his own words jarred him.

Abigail looked at Elias Colt and listened hard to every word he said, believing and disbelieving at the same time. This had to be a dream. Nothing else could explain how a complete stranger, handsome or not, saw through her . . . and still wanted to *know* her.

Upturned sapphire eyes shone at Elias and colored his world in smoke and mist blue. His chest tightened. She didn't run from him as he expected she might after he'd said what he just had.

"I'll be opening my own place in Dyea, a saloon. Might be I'll have musical entertainment same as yours tonight. If you and your friends come my way, might be I can give you jobs. I'll need time to get my place going. What's on this paper," Elias said and pressed his note into her hand, "is my name and where you can find me."

Abigail unwittingly let him hold her hand in his. She felt the paper but also his warmth, his genuine nature, his strength, and the safety she sensed at his touch. How could such an unnatural reaction feel so natural, even familiar?

Elias gave her fingers a gentle squeeze and reluctantly let go of her, then touched his hat brim in goodbye.

"I'm that pleasured to meet you, Belle," he said in a strained voice, and then turned to leave. He needed to get out of there. *The gaming life and no wife;* he couldn't forget. Still, he left the note; the decision to go to Dyea made the moment he'd put pencil to paper.

"It's Abigail," she called quietly to his back.

Elias turned around to her.

"Abigail Grayce is my true name," she said, when she didn't need to.

"I'll remember," he said, and then left before he changed his mind and his booked passage on tomorrow's steamer.

Abigail clutched his note in her hand. *I'll remember you, too, Elias Colt.*

The push of stampeders didn't let up in the weeks that followed since Abigail had met Elias Colt. The Klondike Gold Rush connected from Seattle to the Yukon, Abigail understood, with the crush of humanity pressed the entire length of the set-upon gold trail. A fast and wide-sweeping current carried stampeders along the dangerous trail, point to point. Abigail knew enough about gold mining to know the dangers to be faced, but she knew nothing about the far north—she knew nothing about gold-mining conditions in the far north. September turned into October in Seattle, and Abigail realized she'd little time left to leave, with winter coming.

Maud and Company were already tired of Seattle and ready to move on. Everyone seemed to be headed north, so why shouldn't they? At least that's what Maud, Simone, Francesca, and Lilly proposed to Abigail. Abigail quickly agreed. She'd tired of her ruse as some kind of variety entertainer and was anxious to head north herself, to the gold fields and not the next music hall. She'd wait to tell her companions the truth until they'd reached the North. Guilt over her lies tugged at her. The women had been nice, and she had not been nice in lying to them. But traveling alone would draw attention she didn't want. Admittedly, not only was she reluctant to part with her newfound companions, but she didn't have the means to purchase the ton of goods she'd need for the Yukon.

By this time Abigail knew what it took for any gold-seeker to head north—money to secure the goods necessary to last out a year in the Yukon. Royal Canadian Mounted Police posted checkpoints at the summit of the Chilkoot Pass out of Dyea, and the summit of White Pass out of Skagway. No one without sufficient supplies got through. Abigail had seen the prices posted on Seattle windows of outfitting stores, hardware stores, and steamship companies and knew the expenses involved. She knew she didn't have forty dollars for a cabin on any steamer or five-hundred dollars for the ton of goods required. All the greenhorn miners flowing into Seattle, bent on gold mining in the Yukon, probably didn't have the required money, either. If they somehow got supplied, then so could she!

No matter how hard she tried *not* to think about running into Elias Colt in Dyea, the more she thought about doing just that. Then she'd convince herself thousands of people populated Dyea nowadays, and the chances of seeing him again were slim; especially since she'd be in Skagway and miles from him. That's what she wanted: never to see him again. Unknowingly, she wrapped her heart-shaped gold nugget inside his note, then tucked the treasured bundle in a deep pocket. When she discovered this, instead of ripping up the note, she kept it as cover for her keepsake treasure. No harm in this, she thought.

Besides, she couldn't bring herself to toss it away.

When she thought of Elias Colt, she thought of the unnamed miner in Cripple Creek who'd gifted her with the gold nugget—a piece of his heart, as she'd come to think of it. Abigail supposed she wanted to keep a piece of Elias Colt's heart with her, all the same. *No harm in this,* she thought again.

"Who?" Elias asked the veteran miner standing at the bar of his Dyea saloon, the Trail.

"Jefferson Randolph Smith, that's who! Soapy Smith, himself," the miner spat, as if he'd suffered at the hands of the man he'd called out.

Elias didn't know the name and hadn't heard of Soapy Smith in Montana or Seattle. He knew names out of Virginia City, Tombstone, Deadwood, and the like. No matter; the sound of this name went down the wrong way.

"I got gold dust in my poke for this here whiskey and that's about it," the miner gritted out, then swallowed his pour in a last gulp. "Soapy Smith done got my goods for the trail and my last bit of dust. Dust from my grave, more like. It's dug now!"

Elias listened to the miner's words and the pain in his voice. He'd been fleeced by this Soapy Smith, and to say the miner was bitter didn't even make a cut. The poor sourdough was at the end of his rope, Elias could see.

"Have another on me," Elias offered and poured from his best opened bottle. He could do little more than listen, having seen down-on-their-luck miners before. It never ended well. Whoever this son of a bitch, Soapy Smith, was, he deserved to pay for killing a man's hopes and dreams in one card game or throw of the dice. Had to be a gambler, Elias figured . . . a cheating one, at that. He determined to ask around about Soapy

Smith after this last customer, and instinctively put his hand to his holstered gun.

When Elias arrived in Dyea in September, the town was still being mapped out. At this time Dyea comprised a trading post, several wood buildings and saloons, a motley cluster of tents dotting the site, and a Tlingit encampment. The one-time seasonal fishing village and staging area for trading between the coast and the interior—between the Chilkoot Tlingit people and First Nation's people—buzzed with humanity, despite the lack of structures or any wharf for offloaded goods. This wouldn't stop gold-rush stampeders from arriving with their ton of goods, nor would it stop Tlingit guides from charging a steep price for their help in this endeavor.

The Tlingits had first allowed prospectors into the Yukon over Chilkoot Pass some twenty years before, when an agreement had been made that prospectors wouldn't interfere with the Tlingits' regular trade. Tlingit guides went with the first prospectors and helped move their goods, for a fee. Their packing business proved a success from the start; thus, the Tlingit name of Dayéi, which translates, *"to pack."*

The first stop Elias made in Dyea was the Healy and Wilson Trading Post, established years ago, and the supply and information stop prospectors made before heading into the Yukon. Alaska Natives and First Nation's people gathered here every spring, at this same trading stop, to help prospectors pack for their climb over the pass. Elias didn't head for the Yukon but needed to get any information he could about starting up his own place in Dyea. The wood-frame trading post was crowded with sourdoughs, greenhorns, and Alaska Natives, making it hard for Elias to get his foot in the door. This reminded him of trying to get in the door at Cooper and Levy Pioneer Outfitters in Seattle, where he'd had to elbow his way in, same as here.

He'd had a good parley with the owners and got what information and supplies he needed from the trade store to start building along the main street of the growing downtown district. One of the owners hailed from the Montana Territory. *Like home,* Elias thought. Then he thought again. No, Dyea wasn't like any boomtown he'd been in. This gateway to the Yukon gold fields was more isolated and harder to reach, and was set at the foot of unknown mountains, with unknown weather ahead for anybody faced north.

"Two more steamers just come in!" the next customer who entered the Trail shouted out. "Like always, there's a passel of folks on 'em," the man threw in, then sat down at the only available seat at one of the six rough-planed saloon tables.

The Trail filled up quickly every day, and every day Elias waited to hear about new steamships arriving . . . thinking Abigail Grayce might be on one of them. If she showed up, he'd damned sure offer her a job, any one she might want with him. It would be dangerous to have her close, but he'd risk it. He didn't have saloon gals, ladies on the line, or variety entertainers in his place and still thought about it; Dyea was growing so fast. He did have a brisk restaurant business going.

Stampeders had empty bellies and dreamed-up gold dust itching in their pockets to spend. Elias had two good cooks to fill the bill; a married couple who decided early on against heading to the gold fields. Their old bones couldn't take it. The Farleys sold their goods at the Dyea wharf, where plenty of stampeders wanted to buy them.

In the time it took for Elias to put his own place together, supply it, then open for business, Dyea had grown from several saloons and businesses to over a hundred restaurants, hotels, supply houses, and other saloons. The mapped-out town measured five blocks wide and eight blocks long—overnight, it seemed to Elias. Freight companies popped up, along with two wharfs, steamship agents, real estate agents, doctors, undertakers, a dentist, and even two newspapers, the *Dyea Trail* and the *Dyea Press.*

Elias had never seen anything like it, the way Dyea sprang up out of the Taiya River Valley at the head of the Lynn Canal, where the Taiya River and the Taiya Inlet converged. Two telephone companies served the town, with one line running up the Chilkoot Trail to Bennett and the other to Skagway. The promise of gold was a powerful thing, Elias knew. It could lead a man to fortune or to the end of his rope. He thought of the veteran miner at the end of his, after being taken by the con man, Soapy Smith. Elias hadn't seen the miner again and feared the worst.

"Soapy Smith's been run off the White Pass trail and out of Skagway, Elias," Nate Farley told his boss. "He was run out for operating three-card monte and pea-and-shell games on the trail. I heard when I was serving supper yesterday that Soapy's cleared out, but they say the crook will be back. He was a big crime boss in Denver and in Creede, Colorado, they say. He had the politicians tied around his little finger and ran things in both places." Nate shook his head at sharing this bad news with Elias Colt, but he should know when Jefferson Randolph Smith and his gang came to any town, they came to take over. "If Soapy gets hold of Skagway, you know he's headed another ten miles here."

"I reckon I need to be ready for him," Elias answered Nate, his stony expression unchanged. Things could get bad, real bad. Law and order in Dyea didn't amount to much, and couldn't be counted on to keep Soapy Smith from running the table in both Dyea and Skagway. Elias had asked around about Soapy Smith and got an earful, none of it good. The name, Soapy, came from the con he ran on folks, peddling five-dollar bars of soap with the promise of finding a hundred dollars inside the wrapping if you were lucky. All it took was a plant to shout he found a hundred dollars and wave the bill high, for the soap to sell out. The son of a bitch was a no-account robber and a cheat who could work his way up in a town and then run the table.

Elias watched the front door of his crowded saloon and started scrutinizing each customer even closer than he already did. He'd been waiting for Abigail to grace the doorway, and now he waited for Soapy Smith. If Abigail showed, he'd invite her in. If Soapy did, he'd order the con man out. Elias made sure of his holstered Colt pistol, mentally counting each cartridge in his gun belt.

Jolted awake, Abigail shook all over. Numbing cold penetrated her to the bone. Everything went dark. Her lungs felt caved in and she couldn't breathe. A heart-stopping headache pounded at her. Was she dead? She had to be dead, killed in a mine accident and buried in some forgotten shaft! Icy fingers crept over her, pushing her farther into her grave. Her frozen clothes thwarted any attempt to escape. Knives poked into her and turned life to death.

"Abigail . . . Abigail . . ."

She strained to make out the voice coming from above the layers of crushing rock, knowing it would be the last she'd—

"Belle . . . Belle! Wake up!" Maud cried and took hold of Abigail's arms to shake her awake and to shake some sense back into her. Maud didn't think Belle was hooked on opium, but she couldn't be sure, the way Belle behaved in this moment. The little brown bottles were easy to come by but hard to leave behind. The first ten cents spent could ruin the rest of a body's life. Maud thought Belle had more sense than to be an opium-eater.

Abigail swallowed hard, realizing she'd had a bad dream;

only that. *Dead and buried in some mine shaft . . .* what was wrong with her? She hadn't known a sick day in her life and couldn't afford to have one now, on her way to the Yukon gold fields on this steamer. Her spirit waned at the idea of getting sick. She might have caught something on this ship. Typhus and cholera came to mind, the way bad food, poor water, and unclean conditions could bring on the dreaded ailments. She'd seen enough disease in mining towns, and this steamer held nothing but miners. The far north would offer up its fair share of typhus, cholera, and whatever else, she'd little doubt.

"Belle, are you all right?" Maud asked and let go of her charge.

"Yes. Only a bad dream, Maud."

"It's no wonder we're all not having bad dreams, having to sleep outside on this overcrowded deck in this wind and weather," Maud complained. "We bought tickets for berths, and all we got was this! I'm going to the captain of this rusted-out excuse for a boat and see what I can do first thing in the morning," the veteran music hall performer fumed.

"Here, take my sleeping blanket," Abigail said and wrapped the thick canvas around her companion. "It should keep out the weather well enough. I have another in my gear."

Maud heaved an appreciative sigh, accepted the welcome gift, and then did her best to settle down next to Francesca, Simone, and Lilly; all asleep and tucked in at their assigned camping spot on the *Bald Eagle* steamer.

Abigail sat upright and stared at what stars she could find in the northern sky. She'd had enough so-called sleep for this night. If she found any star to make a wish upon, she'd wish they'd left Seattle before now—before winter had set in.

CHAPTER ELEVEN

Abby lay awake all night, but at least she didn't see any ghosts coming at her. She bolted upright. Is that what kept me awake . . . looking for *him*? Since she hadn't zipped her sleeping bag, she easily climbed out and stood. Other deck passengers, camped around her on board the *Columbia,* stayed asleep. Abby slipped to the railing and stared out over the water into the dark seascape. A mild breeze brushed her cheeks. Few stars lit the sky. No storms brewed, and the temperate forty-degree night made no serious trouble for passengers. Still, she wished for stars on this mysterious passage.

Two days and two more stops before she'd arrive in Skagway, with Juneau and Haines to go. Had she made a mistake in coming here? Should she have stayed in Golden where she felt safer? She'd thought she knew what she was getting into—creating this internship opportunity—but right now she wasn't certain. Her whole life had been about certain steps taken to achieve certain results, with her studies and with gold mining. She'd thought of herself as a gold-mining geek. Research, formulate a plan, implement said plan, evaluate said plan, and then make changes needed to achieve a desired result. This worked as a simple way for Abby to solve the most complex of problems.

She stared at the night sky, intent on finding a way to handle the immediate problem she faced: a sudden conjuring of ghosts from Colorado to Alaska. Where to start, she'd no idea—or did she? These pseudoscientific events started happening after she got back from spring break, after spending time . . . *here.* Abby let go of the ferry's railing as if it had burned her hands. Like it or not, she had to follow this unwanted mystery through and look for answers. She had to *conduct research, formulate a plan, implement said plan, evaluate said plan, and then make changes accordingly, to achieve a desired result.* Relieved to have come up with this defense against the unexplained, Abby put her hands back on the railing and straightened her spine. Centering her problem in a scientific framework eased her nerves, for the moment anyway.

She deftly made her way past sleeping passengers, back to her own sleeping bag and gear. She sat down and pulled her backpack close, unzipping its safest compartment where she kept her tickets and money, and pulled out the list of addresses she'd need for the summer. She shone her flashlight on the list, mentally repeating every detail. Her first stop was the Klondike Gold Rush National Park Ranger Station, located at 291 Broadway, Skagway, Alaska, 98840, where she needed to report in to begin work. Her research would begin there.

Abby had time to catch a little sleep. She curled up in her sleeping bag and zipped it shut this time, to better keep ghosts away. A familiar ache gnawed at her, and she did her best to ignore the discomfort in her tight chest.

I am no beauty.

"Ten cents for a cup of coffee!" Maud complained. "It's robbery on this steamer, pure robbery!"

The winds along the Alaska Panhandle had cooled, but Maud's temperament heated up with each passing day. Eight days left on board the *Bald Eagle* were eight too many for her! She'd had little success with the captain, who gave no answer about their purchased sleeping berths having been taken. Hah, Maud told her troupe. He'd likely sold their berths away for more money. "*Criminal,* I say," she fumed.

Abigail could have predicted as much, with the rush of so many gold-seekers, all reaching deep into their pockets for anything they could find to help them get to the Yukon gold fields. There was little anyone could do but keep their head down and keep moving onward through the thick of ships and humanity. The *Bald Eagle* headed for Skagway and not Dyea, and this fact eased her mind. Elias Colt would be ten miles away in Dyea. Some steamers headed for Dyea. And Abigail relaxed, knowing she wasn't headed there. She'd do without ten-cent coffee and a berth on this steamer, to *not* chance seeing Elias Colt again.

"*Blechhh! Blechhh!*"

Abigail rushed to the railing to help Lilly retch over the side. If Lilly leaned any farther over the rusty rail, she could fall into the sudden, heavy seas. These waters were treacherous and added to the uncertainty of the journey ahead. Abigail realized all on board faced the same dangers and the same unknown. We're all greenhorns here, she thought. More passengers took to the rail, succumbing to seasickness. Abigail didn't feel queasy from the turbulent waters, but from thoughts of Elias Colt. He upset her in a different way.

She'd never felt more like a greenhorn. She knew nothing of men and how they could touch a woman's insides, *without touching.* Agitated at such a revelation, she wanted the female inside her to be dead. That way she wouldn't have to endure another moment of pain from bullying fathers, mothers, brothers, or lovers.

Lovers!

This thought unnerved her more than any rough seas beneath any falling-apart steamer ever could.

"Did you see that man, Belle? Did you see what he just did?"

Francesca exclaimed and poked Abigail's arm for attention to the scene along Ketchikan's port. A man jumped back on board the *Bald Eagle* with a dog in his arms he'd just stolen from a nearby yard. *"Look!"* Francesca yelled. "There's a boy trying to catch up! We have to do something!" She yanked harder on Abigail's arm.

Abigail's heart went out to the boy, who stood on the shore in tears, watching their ship pick up steam and pull away from the dock. A child's valued treasure, his forever friend and companion, had just been taken from him; all for gold! Dogs were valuable to stampeders since they could haul supplies. It was unforgivable, what just happened. Gold fever was a poor excuse. She would remember the image of the child in tears, and wish every day for his tears to dry. Gold fever could bring out the worst in a person. To wound this child and steal his dog was sinful. *There will be a price to pay,* she believed, *in this life or the next.*

Winter rain started to pour, forcing Abigail and her companions to seek shelter under whatever cover they could find. The weather matched her sorry mood. She felt sorry for the little boy left behind, sorry for the dog that had been brought on board, and sorry for every single animal being dragged, carted, and shipped north, all to haul a ton of goods for stampeders. The greenhorn miners headed north on this steamer wouldn't remember the little boy and his lost dog, or think ahead to how many animals freighted north with them would lose their lives in the rush ahead.

Abigail fought the urge to toss every sled she could see overboard, along with every would-be miner who intended to purchase dogs, mules, or horses on arrival in Skagway. Business had to be booming for any kind of dog or any kind of freight animal. No doubt there were plenty for lease or sale, by this time in both Alaska boomtowns ahead. She imagined the poor animals stood in this same icy downpour, waiting to head into worse conditions under heavy burdens. An idea struck.

There might be a job waiting for her along Skagway's beaches, tending those animals . . . *to help dry their tears.* She had to try and make it up to that little boy. Her own purpose for making this journey could wait. She'd grown up with animals in the Rocky Mountains, in boomtowns and ranchlands, and could be of use. Reaching deep in her pocket she wrapped her fingers around her treasured heart-shaped nugget, and thought of the little boy. The moment she did, she thought of Elias Colt and felt his note wrapped around the gold piece. Her fingers heated. She withdrew her hand from her pocket as fast as she could.

I am no beauty.

The *Columbia* pulled into Skagway in the afternoon sun, and tied up to the ferry mooring. Two cruise ships already docked in the same waters at the farthermost point of the deep Lynn Canal. Tourists dotted the town, going to and from ships, and roaming Skagway's historic streets; nestled between ridges of green with rocky snowcaps guiding the mountainous route out of town.

Abby had her gear ready to leave the ferry and, after she'd said polite goodbyes to her fellow deck travelers, she disembarked the *Columbia* and headed downtown. Skagway bustled with cruisers, campers, hikers, canoers, and some locals. Abby knew the town didn't have more than a few hundred residents. They had to be the ones running the multitude of shops, outfitters, tour companies, hotels, and restaurants open for summer trade. Everyone wanted to go back in time, just as she did. Abby chuckled to herself. We're all searching for nuggets in gold-rush history.

The White Pass and Yukon Railroad Station at the front of

town carried tourists back in time over White Pass, and the narrow-gauge train brochure told of prospectors' hard times through Dead Horse Gulch, Tormented Valley, and Pitchfork Falls. Abby tucked the picked-up copy in her backpack and kept on down the busy main street. She was far more interested in Chilkoot Pass and its Golden Stairs than White Pass and its Yukon narrow-gauge train. Fifteen-hundred women had ascended those Golden Stairs during the Klondike rush, and she often imagined herself one of them, and *not* anyone using animals to bear all the burden of the journey to find gold. Abby carried her own burdens in life and didn't ask others, man or beast, to do it for her.

Skagwayans, the townspeople here used to call themselves. Abby imagined they still did. She also thought Skagwayans in gold-rush days couldn't have imagined a well-established train station, a busy airstrip, jewelry stores where you could buy gold, loaded jeeps and vans ready for camping adventures, kids running across streets with candy and store-bought knickknacks in hand, or hundreds of tourists wearing Skagway sweatshirts milling about looking for the next restaurant or saloon to satisfy their appetites and wet their whistles . . . instead of thousands of stampeders crowded together on the same muddy thoroughfares, risking their lives for a place in line to travel up unknown, treacherous trails to reach promised gold.

Abby brought herself back to the present. She needed to locate the ranger station, where she'd report for her summer internship. The address was on Broadway, where she walked now. Her eye went to Jeff Smith's Parlor, and she forgot about the ranger station, thinking about the trail of corruption laid down by the notorious Soapy Smith here in Skagway in gold-rush days. Then she spotted the famed Red Onion Saloon across the avenue from where she stood. Abby knew the history of this saloon. Something . . . *someone* . . . stared out at her through a second-story window, similar to what she'd experienced at the Peck House in Empire. The image startled her and covered her in goose bumps! Her imagination took over. *This could be Lydia's ghost!*

The female figure didn't move. Neither did Abby; she couldn't, immediately fixed to the spot in her mind's eye. That's all this was: her imagination at work. Lydia was one of ten prostitutes who'd worked in one of the ten cribs on the second floor of the Red Onion Saloon, a one-time brothel, casino, and classy dance hall in gold-rush Skagway. Ten lookalike dolls were visible to customers in the saloon. If a doll were placed flat on her back, that prostitute was busy. If a doll was upright, that prostitute was available. Abby thought of Lydia's doll at this moment and imagined the figure in the window was Lydia, until she caught herself conjuring ghosts again and shut her eyes against such nonsense.

When she opened her eyes, the figure still appeared in the window! She seemed to want Abby's attention, the way the apparition didn't move and kept up her stare. A cold breeze blew past, ruffling the curtained window as well as Abby's nerves.

Abby turned away from this impossible-to-explain situation and headed straight for 291 Broadway and the Klondike Gold Rush National Park Ranger Station, needing to shake off the ghost she'd just imagined. Time for common sense to outwit nonsense! The hair at her neck rose on end, and she felt the pair of female eyes following her.

After two weeks of travel on the heavily trafficked Inside Passage, aboard a crowded, falling-apart steamer, sleeping on an overrun-with-stampeders deck, grabbing little sleep and even less to eat, steaming into winter and the great unknown, Abigail's mouth dropped open when the *Bald Eagle* finally docked at Moore's Wharf in Skagway Bay. She was so surprised at the sight in front of her; she felt as though they'd landed in the middle of a nest of ants instead of a frontier boomtown, the way people stirred in all directions, climbing over each other to get to the steamer first. More like a swarm of bees. As if stung, Abigail unwittingly rubbed the sleeves of her jacket to ward off the sensation of being assaulted, then checked her deepest pocket to make sure of her treasured bundle.

"Maud, all of you!" Abigail shouted over the din. "Keep your satchels close, and don't let anybody threaten you with paying a fee to get off this steamer! Stay behind me and we'll offload together!"

The bewildered women followed along behind Abigail and let her carve a way out of the unexpected mayhem. Their excitement over arriving in Skagway quickly turned to fear. This place was lawless; they all could see as much. A frontier boomtown with no law and order meant music and dance hall jobs aplenty, but it also meant gunfire in the streets every day—fighting over gold and ladies on the line.

Abigail wanted to lead her companions off the steamer to safety, but where?

"Captain, my ticket's for Dyea!*"* A man shouted.

"Ours are, too!" another man, standing beside his wife shouted. "We paid for Dyea, not Skagway!"

Abigail caught sight of the disinterested captain. He took something from his pocket and gave it to two bearded men who'd come aboard. A payoff, she thought right away. The captain's getting fleeced like everybody else on board. But then, he fleeced his passengers, taking their paid tickets for Dyea, when he knew he wasn't sailing there. The undercurrent of corruption slithered down Abigail's back and made her stiffen. Skagway wouldn't be easy. The gold fields lay over the mountains beyond. It wouldn't be easy reaching them, either. Nothing to do but put her shoulder to the crowd and bump her way through, all the way to the Yukon.

The dock and packed beaches were overrun with goods, piles of them in grouped stacks, some with men sitting on top of their caches. The warehouses in view spilled over with their cargoes, leaving seemingly uneasy stampeders standing around in dismay over what to do. Abigail guessed some slept with their cache over fear of being robbed of their ton of goods.

"You can buy a ferry ticket to Dyea, here!" a street hawker yelled out to stampeders still offloading. "Get your goods on board and get to Dyea!"

"Need a hotel? Come with me!" another called.

"Follow me and get a decent meal!" rang out along the dock.

"The Klondike Outfitters is right this way!"

"Want directions to the Post Office?"

"Don't matter if you're a Catholic or a Methodist or an Episcopalian, the Union Church is up this way!"

"The Pack Train Restaurant is open night and day!"

"I'll tell you where you can get the best faro or blackjack game in town!"

"The Red Onion is the best brothel around. Right this way, gents!"

Abigail tried to shut her ears to the commotion and lead her companions away from the noisy beaches and into town. Throngs combed the mud-and-slush streets, where random, planked sidewalks appeared to do little good. Oxen, horses, mules, and dogs, harnessed in pack trains or in front of sleds, littered the thick streets. Signs posted everywhere on framed buildings advertised merchandise stores, restaurants, meat markets, saloons, lumberyards, pack trains, hotels, lawyers, variety theaters, and the *Skagway News*. Town proved no better than the dock—both a nest of ants.

"Belle, stop!" Maud cried out. "I'm done in. We're all done in!"

Abigail halted, and then turned to her companions. Maud was right. Abigail looked up and down Broadway and saw a sign for the Gold Nugget Hotel. It looked like all the others, and they'd little choice at this point for shelter tonight.

"Let's try this hotel," she said and motioned to the Gold Nugget.

"Oh, yes." Lilly almost cried in relief.

"Remember, keep your satchels close. We don't know anything about this town, and we'd best learn, for our safety and for our own good," Abigail lamented. The women rushed past her the moment she'd finished. Abigail started to follow but felt held to the spot. She rubbed the hair at the back of her neck; it stood on end and the eerie feeling puzzled her. She hadn't walked over anybody's grave.

Pivoting in a circle, Abigail stopped the moment she saw the Red Onion Saloon on the corner of Broadway and Second Street. Her gaze moved up to a second-story window where someone, a female, stared down at her. Lace curtains billowed outside the open window and a female hand pulled them inside. "The Red Onion is the best brothel around!" the man had shouted. This woman must be a prostitute, Abigail thought. The hair at the back of her neck still stood on end, unnerving Abigail to the point of pain. The figure in the window is staring at me *as if she knows me.* Abigail felt so uneasy, she had to find out.

The instant she started for the Red Onion Saloon, the second-story window shut with a bang, and the mysterious figure disappeared from view. This chilly action turned Abigail around toward the Gold Nugget Hotel. Her neck felt fine now and she dismissed any idea of ghosts. She quickly lost all interest in the stranger in the window.

Once Abigail turned her back on the Red Onion Saloon, the figure reappeared at the window and pushed it open. Cold breezes brought the lace curtains back outside, and this time the mysterious female let them stay.

CHAPTER TWELVE

Elias caught himself watching the front door of his saloon too often, waiting for Abigail and not Soapy Smith. He should have got up from his seat at the variety theater in Seattle the moment Abigail Grayce came onstage. Now he even regretted giving her that note with his name and whereabouts on it. He should have made a clean break from the start; then he wouldn't have his gut torn every time he looked for her to come through the door. Damn, he felt like she'd given him the mitten and rejected him, when he'd never started anything up with her.

That was the problem: he wanted to start something with her.

That he'd fallen for a Miss Nancy–dressed gal surprised him the most. He liked women, pure and simple; not men with female airs. Abigail dressed like a man but was all woman underneath. Something must have turned her away from being the beauty he saw. He wanted to know what . . . who . . . could have hurt her badly enough to cause this. His anger flared at the thought. Elias wanted to meet the son of a bitch who did this to her.

But maybe she didn't like men, but liked—

He shut this thinking down, remembering the expression in Abigail's bluest of blue eyes—for him. Something in her had reached out to him in that moment. And what did he do? Left her in Seattle while he went to Dyea!

Maybe he was the son of a bitch.

Elias took a shot of his own whiskey, something he rarely did. If he didn't get his head on straight and get on with business, he could lose the Trail. If he didn't stay focused on running a good saloon and restaurant, others could come in here and take over. Any day he expected to hear Soapy Smith had returned to Skagway. With the Yukon River freeze-up and storms on the trails, the logjam of stampeders in Skagway and here in Dyea meant more suckers for the notorious crime boss. Elias welcomed the money he earned from so many customers— sourdoughs and greenhorns alike—but he didn't try to con them out of an honest faro game or a decent meal. Elias delivered what he promised. His business was no false front, like Soapy Smith's evidently was.

Elias took one more shot of whiskey, then firmly set his empty glass upside down on the bar. Who was he kidding? Abigail wasn't going to come waltzing into his saloon, to judge by the way she shied from him in Seattle. Even if she were to come to Dyea, she'd steer clear of him. That would be best anyway, he thought—the gaming life and no wife. If he wanted female companionship, he'd find a dance hall gal or a lady on the line; but none with raven hair and eyes of blue.

By this time, Elias wondered how long he'd stay in Dyea and make this good living. Long as the Klondike gold held out or as long as it took for Abigail to show. Fool's gold, he knew, think-ing any woman in any boomtown should matter. He was a damned fool for thinking of Abigail.

Soon as he shut down his place for the night, he'd find the nearest brothel and forget he'd ever met anybody named Belle Bingham. Like all the rest, Abigail pretended to be something she wasn't. He didn't need the distraction. Long nights with ladies on the line would take care of his itch. That and finding the next gold-rush town when this one played out.

★ ★ ★ ★ ★

"Next time, you're a dead man," Elias warned and returned his Colt to its holster.

"You done shot me. I'm gettin' the law after you."

"I'd get to the doc first, you son-of-a-bitch-speeler," Elias advised the gambler he'd just winged in the arm. "You want to cheat at cards and pull a gun over it, do it in somebody else's place, not mine."

The man holstered his gun, then held onto his bloody arm and spat out his tobacco chew at Elias's feet.

"Whatcha gonna do about that, E-l-i-a-s C-o-l-t. You think yer a big operator, but yer a nuthin'. The boss man is comin' soon. He'll do more'n spit on yer mud pipes. You'll see, Mr. Big Shot," the half-drunk speeler threatened.

"You can get the marshal, the Mounties, or the whole gall-danged army in here, but you'd better not be with 'em," Elias warned before he shoved the cheater out the front door of the Trail. Others followed and stood behind Elias.

The man landed in a heap on the muddy, slushy street. He cursed under his breath and then managed to stand. A crowd quickly formed a circle around the action, but left a path open between the two men.

Elias readied his gun hand. He knew the man was heeled. If the bastard went for his pistol again, it would be his last move. Light snow fell, and the street seemed eerily quiet.

"You'll see, Mr. Big Shot," the man said again and spat at the ground.

Elias watched while the wounded bastard broke through the crowd and lumbered away in the direction of the doc. Waste of time to patch the son of a bitch up. A cheating speeler like him wouldn't last long in this boomtown, or any other, Elias knew from experience. High-graders, either. If a miner stole big nuggets from a sluice box, he'd be found out and dealt with. It wasn't any different here in the North than in Colorado or Montana or Arizona. A cheater at cards or gold panning ended up on Boot Hill. That was the law Elias lived by: the law of the West.

Elias turned around and went back inside his place. Those who'd come outside followed suit, while the crowd in the snowy street bundled against the cold and kept on their way. Elias stood behind the bar and surveyed his saloon and restaurant for any more signs of trouble. He gave his piano player a nod to start the music back up. The three dance hall gals working for him circulated among the faro and blackjack tables, smiling at customers and ready to take drink orders. A lively mood returned. It was a packed night at the Trail—Christmas Eve, in fact.

"Merry Christmas, Elias Colt."

Ever suspicious, Elias eyed the man clad in black broadcloth who stood at his bar. Both of the man's hands were visible, so Elias relaxed his gun hand, but never his guard. Soapy Smith was more on his mind than this preacher-man.

"Yeah, Merry Christmas," Elias said and gave his customer a half-smile. He hadn't remembered the holiday, and never celebrated it in any traditional way, having grown up in rough mining boomtowns. It was always busy in saloons. Holidays didn't make any difference. "What can I get you?"

"A glass of whiskey will do me fine."

Elias served his customer, then turned to the next one standing in wait.

"The wife doesn't know I have a glass of spirits every year at Christmas, Elias Colt."

Elias returned to the preacher-man after he served the new customer, realizing the preacher-man wanted to talk. Just like holding a gun, Elias had to hold a conversation when such action was called for.

"Spirits, is it?" Elias joined in.

"Name's Zebulon Pike, Elias Colt; same as Pikes Peak," he chuckled. "I wasn't in Colorado for that gold rush, but I'm here for this one."

"Is that so?" Elias kept his eye on Preacher Pike and his ear to the room; understandably curious, since the preacher called him by his full name.

"Names mean a lot, don't you agree, Elias Colt?" Zebulon downed his whiskey and set his glass on the shiny bar in celebration. "Ah. Fine and dandy, that was."

"Get you another?" Elias watched more customers come inside the Trail, milling about for seats at one of the card tables. If seats didn't open up, he'd set up one of the restaurant tables if waiting customers got unruly. Elias caught the eye of Nate Farley in the restaurant area and his dance hall girls in the saloon, to note the customers and keep watch. His piano player would keep the tunes coming and the mood festive. It was, after all, Christmas.

"Take yours, for instance, Elias Colt," Zebulon kept on. "Elias is after the Hebrew, Eleazar, which is also Lazarus. Do you know the story of Lazarus, Elias Colt?"

"I guess you'll tell me," Elias joked, still with his eye fixed on the room and not Zebulon Pike.

Zebulon laughed.

"I'm a man of the Bible, son. Except for this one time a year, I live by the word of God. I've come all the way from Missouri to bring the word of God to the last frontier. It's our mission to save others."

"Our?" Elias was halfway interested in hearing what Zebulon had to say by this time.

"My wife and my church group travel with me. There are ten of us here, five men and five women, all good people of God, all believing in life after death."

144

"Wait . . . there are five women in your party?" Elias knew women followed their husbands, but he hadn't run across so many women in one Klondike gold-rush party. Actresses traveled together, he knew, but they headed for boomtowns; not over treacherous passes. This made him think of Abigail Grayce, when he wished he hadn't. He pictured her dead on one of the passes. She might dress like a man, but she was a woman under all that canvas and corduroy. This was no place for a woman, he believed. He wondered if Abigail had left Seattle and come north. Right now he hoped she'd stayed put.

Dammit.

Elias realized all the nights with all the ladies on the line hadn't made a difference in helping him forget about a slip of a female he'd met one time on one night. Why couldn't he forget the look in her bluest of blue eyes, reaching out to him for something, but what? No female had ever touched him like that, as if she didn't want him to leave and was desperate to tell him something. Well, he'd left her all right. He'd given her his note, but she'd likely tossed it away.

Dammit.

He wasn't responsible for her. She was a stranger, really; just one female in a sea of females. He'd always wanted to do right by females, no matter their temperament or profession. That's what got to him—that he hadn't done right by Abigail. Maybe he should listen to Preacher Pike and the word of God to help make up for his mistake.

"Elias, Eleazar means 'God is my help.' "

Preacher Pike's words brought Elias back to the moment. Evidently the one-drink-a-year man of God hadn't stopped his Christmas Eve sermon.

"Elias, Eleazar and Lazarus are one in the same. The story of Lazarus of Bethany is the story of a miracle of Jesus. You do know of Jesus Christ, don't you, Elias Colt?" Preacher Pike raised a judging eyebrow at Elias.

"Yes." Elias might not live the gospel life, but he knew the story of Christmas.

"The story of Lazarus is found in the Gospel of John, Chapter Eleven in the Bible. Lazarus died, and Jesus raised him from the dead four days later. Death is our final enemy, and Jesus showed His power over life and death, resurrecting Lazarus from the dead. Lazarus was a follower of Jesus and believed in him. Many others followed Jesus after witnessing that miracle.

"Jesus said, 'I am the resurrection and the life: he that believeth in me, though he were dead, yet shall he live: And whosoever liveth and believeth in me shall never die.' This is according to John, Chapter Eleven, Verse Twenty-five, the King James Version of the Bible.

"Then, 'Jesus wept.' This is according to John, Chapter Eleven, Verse Thirty-five, the King James Version."

"I can't say as I've ever been a Bible person, preacher," Elias explained, "but it sounds like a miracle to me, bringing someone back from the dead." Elias didn't really believe in miracles, but he wanted to show respect to Preacher Pike.

"And the Christmas miracle, Elias Colt; we must not forget the birth of Jesus in Bethlehem on this fateful winter night."

Elias nodded his agreement.

"I'll be leaving now. Don't want the wife to worry," Zebulon said with a twinkle in his eye.

Elias felt strangely removed from the constant bellow and roar of Klondike gold-rushers after hearing Preacher Pike's words. He might not be a believer like the preacher, but he felt better about himself for the brief talk. It made up a little for him deserting Abigail in Seattle.

Christmas Eve found Abigail hunkered down in a livery stable shared by the pack trains in Skagway. Oxen, horses, and mules were quartered here, until hired or sold to stampeders going over White Pass. Abigail cried for them all, knowing what their cruel fate would probably be. Animals suffered on the narrow, slippery, steep trail, as much from stampeders as horrific weather conditions. She could do little to help them other than feed, water, and tend to their wounds. Few returned from the deadly trail, which was already known as Dead Horse Trail.

Abigail had celebrated her quick hire as a stable boy. At first the pack train boss thought she was a boy, and then a *Molly*—an effeminate man—or so he called her. She didn't bother to correct him. No point to it. She'd been hired, and that's all that counted. A dollar a day felt like good money; enough to start putting away for her own ton of goods to cross the summit to the Klondike. The stable provided shelter and she cooked her own camp food on a put-together, sheet-iron stove. On most days, if she combed the beaches, Abigail could find something that had been thrown away, and she'd used it to build her own cache.

Not everyone who landed in Skagway stayed. Their goods were sold or stolen. Though tempted sometimes, Abigail would never steal, especially from a fellow miner. If there had been any handouts, Abigail would have been there. She'd heard tales of angels in the Klondike, cooking and giving out food to starving and sick miners. No angels were to be found in Skagway, at least in Abigail's experience. Plenty of folks got sick from the cold. Bitter chill and scarce food took their toll on the less hearty. So did loneliness and isolation. White liners—heavy drinkers—didn't do well either. Their alcohol problems would dog them all the way over the passes, if they didn't die on the trail from exhaustion and exposure first.

Like so many of these animals will. It killed Abigail to think of these already weary and worn beasts of burden dying on White Pass. The animals had been gathered from near and far, for the purpose of packing over the summit. But greedy gold-seekers would be their death, she knew. Most folks coming to mine didn't know about gold mining or caring for livestock. The inhumane treatment ahead for the animals curdled her stomach. If they dropped on the trail, their owners wouldn't even shoot them out of mercy, but walk over them to come back down to Skagway and buy another.

Horses and mules left dying on the trail were stepped over and pounded to death by the hoofprints of reprehensible stampeders leading still more animals to their deaths. Some horses, Abigail had heard, had leapt to their deaths from steep cliffs rather than suffer another exhausting, humiliating, burdensome, unending moment of agony and misery. If it would make a difference for the animals, she'd let them all go, here and now. But they'd only be rounded up and brought back. There was no escape. There was no Christmas miracle here.

Tears welled inside her and flooded her heart; a river of sadness with no end in sight. She'd tried to make it up to the little boy in Ketchikan whose dog had been stolen, but she couldn't stay here another night only to wake up in the morning and have another animal missing from the line. Dogs fared better than horses in most cases, but inexperienced owners unfamiliar with specific breeds ran them down, too. Overpacked, overburdened animals all suffered in greedy, untried greenhorn hands.

Abigail looked at her own hands, still callused and red from hard work and the cold. At least they were honest hands that healed rather than harmed. She couldn't save the animals from an unfortunate end, but she could save their Christmas, by gum! Abigail shot up out of her corner stall and headed for the feed sacks. She'd leave a note and the money for the cost of feed and determined to serve every animal in the livery Christmas dinner! The animals whinnied, brayed, and neighed at her stirring, a chorus of caroling to her. Unwittingly, she began to hum the Christmas carol, "Away in a Manger." They were, after all, in a stable at Christmas.

Abigail knew she had to get out of Skagway fast. Yes, she'd left money for the feed, but the pack train bosses wouldn't be happy and wouldn't think she'd left enough to make up for the harm she'd caused them all. Humph. They thought she was a Molly anyway and wouldn't be looking for a woman. That's it. She'd change into female garb so she wouldn't be recognized and then get her hide out of there. By now thousands were holed up in Skagway until the Yukon River thawed come spring. She couldn't take the chance of being caught and headed for an outfitter store. Much as she hated to part with any of her hard-earned coin, she had no choice but to buy female Klondike clothes.

Maybe Maud and her troupe were still in town. Abigail didn't know. If they were, she could borrow from one of the women, but they didn't have serviceable clothes for the Klondike. Boomtown clothes, *yes*. Klondike clothes, *no*. Maud, Simone, Francesca, and Lilly had been surprised their friend, Belle Bingham, was really Abigail Grayce, but they didn't fault her for using an assumed name. Apparently they'd all done as much. The women had taken a job at the Royal Theater, but that was a short run. Abigail had lost track of them after that and never told them where she'd found work. She'd only told them she wasn't any kind of actress and had another purpose. Probably they'd all guessed it was to find gold.

For the second time in her recent history, Abigail had to gussy up in female attire. At least this would be Klondike attire and not the type of corseted monstrosity required in Denver. Here she could wear warm flannels, a heavy dress with a short skirt, a suit of heavy Mackinaw, bloomers, arctic gloves and hood, arctic boots, gum boots, German socks, and on and on.

She didn't have the money to go on and on, but she had enough for a basic women's outfit. Getting out of Skagway fast was her biggest problem, second only to arriving in Dyea.

Elias Colt would be in Dyea, or so his note said. This fact unnerved her more than being caught by the pack train bosses. Still, she had to get to Dyea to head up the Chilkoot. Up Chilkoot Pass, miners carried their own gear and didn't force animals to bear their burden. Some miners used dogs to help them up the Chilkoot, but not all of them did. Sleds could only go so far up the trail. Abigail would never head up White Pass. It might be shorter than the Chilkoot, but distance couldn't make up for the heartache and misery that trail caused. She had no choice but to head to Dyea, even if it meant she might run into Elias Colt.

CHAPTER THIRTEEN

Abigail rushed around the busy corner on Broadway Street, looking for an outfitting store where she could disappear inside and change her appearance before being recognized by any of the pack train bosses in Skagway. Uneasy from head to toe, anxiety plagued her; that and pelting snow. Somebody had spotted her! The hair at the back of her neck prickled in warning. Forced to a shivering stop, Abigail dreaded turning around to see which pack train boss was pointing a shooting iron at her. She needed to talk herself out of this, but would she get the chance? Boomtowns were rough places. Few people got mercy. Stealing feed sacks was enough reason to take a bullet if the right man had you in his sights. Some didn't wait to talk but shot first.

Dazed and confused the moment she turned around, she didn't see anybody chasing her; not a pack train boss or anybody else. What just happened? She blinked hard for clarity. Where were all the stampeders, the crowds always milling up and down the street? Had she taken a bullet to the head? *Am I dead?* Mechanically, she removed one of her mittens and ran a hand over her face and skull, searching for the killing wound. She found nothing.

Instead of snow, the sun beat down. Abigail had to shade her eyes from the heated glare. She loosened the collar of her jacket and shirt to breathe easier, everything suddenly having become tight and uncomfortable. Eagles squawked overhead. Other than the indigenous birds calling in the warm breeze, she didn't hear anything else. Abigail put her hands to her ears, tapping them again and again to hear anything that might give a clue to what was happening. But when she tried to take a step, she couldn't, so she held to the spot.

Surrounded by light and silence and all alone, Abigail took purposeful deep breaths to think how to get out of this confounding predicament. She set careful focus and stared hard at an imagined horizon for any kind of direction or a way out. She'd grown up on the frontier in the roughest of mining towns and had got herself out of sticky situations before. Hadn't she pulled herself out of faulty mining shafts? Hadn't she escaped her bullying and abusive family? Hadn't she educated herself to become literate against all odds? She'd always found a way out.

There, in the distance, a dark speck moved toward her, growing larger as it did. Abigail began walking toward the blurred image, barely aware she could take steps now. It was a figure, *a person*, who approached! Abigail stood still and blinked hard to better make out the female figure that was only steps away by this time. Overwhelmed with curiosity rather than fear, Abigail had never been more attentive. Blood pumped at her temple to the point of headache. Her senses strained for answers.

An eerie recognition struck. The approaching figure seemed familiar. The odd boy's clothes didn't, but the way the female walked and carried her pack did. Abigail could almost feel the weight of the heavy gear on her own back. The female looked to be her size and weight, and close to her own age. Nerves charged through Abigail, every one tense, on edge. Only feet away now, the female removed her hat and then repositioned it over her long black braid. *Like mine*, Abigail could see. *Like me*, she thought, the moment she saw the young woman's face. *Just like me.*

The out-of-place figure stood right in front of Abigail now but looked up at something and not at Abigail. Too stunned to speak, Abigail tried to raise her hand in acknowledgment to the figure, but she couldn't move her arms. *She doesn't see me*, Abigail realized. New shudders ran down her spine. Oddly, she wanted to reach out to the young woman, as if she were a long lost friend or a sister, she felt so connected. Becoming more upset as moments passed and the girl kept staring up at something and not looking at Abigail, Abigail's melancholy deepened. If only she could have a look, a smile, any kind of sign of recognition from the girl, that would mean everything in this unlikely moment. Abigail had no idea why, but it was how she felt.

The girl kept looking up.

Abigail followed her line of vision.

White lace curtains billowed out from a frame window that seemed suspended in the air. There was no house, no building; only the window and billowing curtains. A female hand reached for the curtains to draw them inside. Then the window slammed shut. Startled by the sound, Abigail looked again at the girl. She was gone! Abigail turned in every direction to catch sight of the lost girl, but she'd *vanished*.

"Watch where yer going, kid," a man complained as he bumped past her.

"Steamer's coming up the canal!" another shouted.

Noise filled in around Abigail, tipping and turning her already reeling senses. Half-frozen, she quickly fastened the collar of her shirt and pulled her jacket close at her neck. The sunshine had disappeared with the mysterious figure. Snow bit at Abigail's cheeks and bare hands. Her mittens? She had them shoved in a pocket, thank the Lord. Jostled by all the passersby, Abigail took shelter in the first doorway she could find. Things looked normal again. This was Skagway, and she needed to get out of town and

153

not get caught by the pack train bosses. She was back to normal again, or so she hoped.

What just happened? She didn't believe in ghosts, but she believed in *God*. Was this God reaching out to her? Was the girl her . . . *guardian angel* . . . trying to tell her something? Was she trying to show her something in the window with the billowing curtains? Abigail gulped. Was the girl trying to show her something in the window of the Red Onion Saloon? Abigail reluctantly stepped away from the doorway to read the signage overhead. It was the same saloon. She remembered now she'd been on her way to the outfitter next door when she became caught up in this . . . this what?

I'm not a lady on the line. I don't work in brothels. I don't know anybody who lives on the second-story of the Red Onion Saloon. I'm not going loco. I know someone watches from the window. She's watching me, and she's watching the girl who appeared out of nowhere. She doesn't want us to come close to her. I can sense that. She wants something else, but what? Abigail's head pounded in confusion and pure misery. The fact she was conjuring guardian angels *and* ghosts upset her. She couldn't afford to linger in saloon doorways when she had to get out of town fast.

Unwittingly, she reached deep in her pocket for Elias Colt's note and her heart-shaped nugget enclosed inside it. A third connection tugged at her—*the girl who'd appeared out of nowhere.* Abigail had only the image to hold close. She didn't know what any of this meant, but she knew it meant something. As carefully as she could, she replaced the treasured bundle in her pocket and then raced inside the outfitter's next door. She had much to do and little time to get it done. The idea of leaving her stored cache behind spurred her on. She had to fetch what she could.

If Abigail worked things just right, she could get a change of clothes and get to her cache before being found out. It wasn't much, but it was all she had to build on. The pack bosses never learned her hiding place, and she prayed she wouldn't be discovered. They'd be out searching for a Molly and not a female moving a few things here and there. They shouldn't notice her among the usual commotion in Skagway. A small boat could transport her to Dyea. She had enough money to hire somebody to take her, she hoped. So much went on at the docks, with people ready to make a dollar any way they could. She wouldn't leave anything behind except the ghostly image in the second-story window of the Red Onion Saloon.

In time that memory would die.

"Abby Gray is it?" the park ranger greeted when she arrived at the Klondike Gold Rush National Park Station. "We've been expecting you. You're just in time to leave with the next group headed to one of our musher's camps. They're out front now, loading up. Come on with me, young lady."

Surprised to be leaving, having just arrived, Abby followed the ranger back out front to the vans being loaded with passengers and supplies. As much as she looked forward to working with huskies and mushers, she was disappointed to leave here, this spot, this street . . . *Broadway.* Odd, she thought, to think of staying behind when she'd no plan in Alaska, really, other than working with the rangers in Skagway and Dyea on the programs they'd scheduled for her. She'd momentarily forgotten her plan to search for clues to her recent unexplained experiences.

"Hey there, Abby, I'm Mike Turner. Good to meet you. We don't stand on formality here. Call me Mike. I'm your ranger for this mushing experience and will be happy for your help. You can see we've got kids and seniors in this group, which means extra care with the dogs and sleds at our camp."

Abby liked the veteran ranger's friendly manner and relaxed a bit, giving him a smile.

"I see you've just arrived, but no worries, we'll be at our camp in an hour's time, and you can settle in there. Tents are already set up, and the dog yard is well-established. We'll do all the introductions with guests after we get there. Sound all right, Abby?" the ranger asked.

"Yes, thanks," Abby replied, doing her best to pay attention to his words and not her disappointment about leaving town so quickly.

"Hop in the first van with me. Tommy's driving the one behind. He's been on this mushing trail a long time. You're in for a treat. He's a Tlingit and can share much of his heritage with you. The Native Americans here *are* the history of the Klondike Gold Rush. They carved out the trail we all follow today."

Abby looked at Tommy, already sitting behind the wheel, his passengers all loaded up and ready to go. He raised his hand in hello to her. She smiled at him, at once admiring his spiritual connection to this place—the gateway to the Klondike Gold Rush. It would be her privilege to have any conversation with him, despite her not enjoying any lengthy discussions with anybody. But Tommy would be different. The Tlingit people held a special place in gold-rush history, an honorable, sacred place.

"All set?" Mike looked in his rearview mirror at the guests loaded in his van. Two kids in matching ball caps had their noses pressed to the windows, while the adults settled their gear at their feet and grabbed their water bottles. Their excursion to the musher's camp would be two overnights; then they'd board the next Alaska Marine Ferry departing Skagway on which they were scheduled.

Abby sat in the front passenger seat and looked ahead instead of at the passengers. She'd meet them at camp. She felt nervous already about being around so many new people. No one in the group had appeared suspect, but still she couldn't know if *he* were on board.

"All set," she suddenly answered Mike, forcing her thoughts off the impossibly handsome ghost who had come into her life. The apparition had to be a ghost, appearing out of thin air, first in Colorado, then on the plane that landed in Seattle, and next on the *Columbia*. There had to be a rational explanation of her visions. But she didn't believe in ghosts. The same aches plagued her; the same doubts about her mental state; the same worries that she'd conjured someone because she was lonely.

I am no beauty. The thought jarred her. *I don't need to conjure some ghost for a boyfriend!* I don't want a boyfriend. I'm not lonely. I don't need anyone; not my father, not my mother . . . no one. I'm in a van with nothing but people, aren't I? Lonely, humph! Abby caught herself in this wrong-headed thinking and faced forward. She needed to keep those thoughts to herself. This was no time to have a mental meltdown. She was not crazy and had no intention of giving in to her wild imagination.

When the van started down Broadway, Abby chanced a look at the Red Onion Saloon and its second-story window. White lace curtains billowed in the crisp morning breeze. No female hand drew them in, yet Abby suspected the figure was hidden there. Calmer now, Abby studied the curtained window, turning her head to keep the Red Onion in view as long as possible. She wanted to solve this mystery, didn't she? Then her research must start here. The ghostly figure in the second-story window—whether or not in her imagination—held the key to unlock the truth of everything; she was sure of it. Theory or fact, Abby determined to find out. In two weeks' time, after her assignment at the musher's camp, she'd return to Skagway and head for the Red Onion Saloon. It was time to get down to the science of the mystery, and put things in sensible, logical order.

Do the research. Formulate a plan. Implement said plan. Evaluate said plan. Make the changes necessary to achieve results. Abby breathed easier, after reminding herself of the order of things placed in a scientific framework.

She took back control of the situation, or so she thought.

Eli Cole came outside of the Red Onion Saloon and watched Abby Gray's van pull out of sight.

"Darlin', like I said, I'm gonna stay with you as long as I can." He needed a cigarette and a shot of whiskey. One or the other had to help. He pulled out his pocket watch to check the time. The hour was late. Precious moments had dangerously slipped away. This life-and-death game had almost played out. Before he stepped back inside the saloon, he looked up at the second-story window, giving a nod to the female watching him. He understood what her appearance in the window meant, and he knew her time was marked, too.

The female figure pulled the curtains to the window the moment Eli disappeared indoors.

"I saw three ships come sailing in, on Christmas Day, on Christmas Day; I saw three ships come sailing in on Christmas Day in the morning." Abigail sang the carol quietly to herself, so as not to be heard by the boatman she'd paid to transport her the ten miles to Dyea. The skies dimmed to frontier dusk, with light snow reflecting down as if it were gold dust. It looked magical. It is a magical time, she realized. *It's Christmas.*

The tiny steamer carried other passengers and cargo, but no one looked her way. Two of the three passengers were women and made Abigail think of Maud and her group of traveling companions. She missed them all. Knowing them was the closest she'd ever come to having friends. Other than a brief smile, neither of the women on the steamer to Dyea gave her any attention but giggled and talked with each other. They could be entertainers. They could be prostitutes. When Abigail greeted them with, "Merry Christmas," they both gave her a blank look. Abigail wanted to cry, but she didn't.

The third passenger was a greenhorn stampeder, Abigail could tell. He dressed in Klondike clothes but wore a look of bewilderment on his mustached face. The way he sat atop his goods also gave him away. She felt his fear—the fear he might lose everything he had before he even started up the Chilkoot to the gold fields. Her heart went out to the young greenhorn. In truth, she didn't want to lose the little she'd stockpiled so far, for her journey up the Golden Stairs. He didn't look much older than she was; maybe twenty, she guessed. When she greeted him with, "Merry Christmas," he said the same back to her, despite his obvious distraction and nerves. She hoped he'd find gold, pans of it, in the days and months ahead. She also hoped he'd survive the uncertain journey to the Klondike gold fields.

For that matter, she hoped she'd survive, too.

"And what was in those ships all three, on Christmas Day, on Christmas Day; and what was in those ships all three, on Christmas Day in the morning," she sang softly, embracing what Christmas spirit she could. It gave her strength, thinking of God in heaven watching over her and everyone else headed to the Klondike. "The Virgin Mary and Christ were there, on Christmas Day, on Christmas Day; the Virgin Mary and Christ were there, on Christmas Day in the morning." Self-conscious, she turned to look at the passengers who might have overhead her singing. The women paid no attention. The greenhorn smiled and nodded his head at her. She smiled back and turned around to finish the English carol.

"Then let us all rejoice Amen, on Christmas Day, on

Christmas Day; then let us all rejoice Amen, on Christmas Day in the morning."

Even Abigail wasn't prepared for the chaos on the beaches of Dyea. No sooner had their steamer put in close than men came out of nowhere to wade through the black water and start pulling goods off the boat. She didn't have money to pay the men. Abigail got out her gun and hoped she wouldn't have to use it.

"Don't touch me or my gear!" She had to yell to be heard. On the frontier, she'd learned to use a pistol early and knew she'd need to keep it close for this gold rush. Mining camps had taught her as much. You had to look out for yourself, since the law always showed up too late.

The men looked stunned and backed off. None were Native Americans, she could tell. The Tlingits wouldn't charge at a boat like that. They collected fees for services, but she didn't imagine this kind of assault, which was how this felt.

"I ain't helping you lady," the boatman called over to her. "You'd best put that gun away and let these men ferry yer stuff. Otherwise, I gotta dump it in the water. I cain't get in any closer to the wharf."

Abigail took quick stock of her gear. She wasn't worried about her crate of camp gear—her Yukon stove, shovel, gold pan, bread pan, camp kettle, and canvas sleeping bag—but her provisions. The grub sacks of flour, baking powder, dried apples, and potatoes would be ruined in the water. The tins of beans and butter wouldn't. Her cache wasn't all she'd need to climb the Golden Stairs, but it made for a good start.

The greenhorn's goods had already been taken ashore by the beach thieves; that's what Abigail called them at this point. The two women had disappeared. Abigail guessed they'd been carried ashore. They didn't have many possessions, she remembered from the outset. Abigail didn't trust any of this. She didn't trust strangers putting their hands on her gear or her ability to deal with her equipment without help. If she had the money in her pocket to pay off the beach thieves, she would, as she saw no other way out of this pickle.

The boat rocked back and forth in the dark, choppy water. Abigail had trouble standing and keeping her gun pointed at the same time.

"Put that damn gun away, Abigail Grayce."

Caught totally off-guard, Abigail worried she'd conjured a ghost; thinking of Elias Colt but not wanting to. The dim light provided little help in picking out a face in the crowd or picking out where the voice came from. The noisy beach made it impossible to hear, yet she heard what she thought was Elias's quiet, even voice in the thick of it all.

"I gotta dump yer gear, lady," the boat captain warned one more time. "Tide's bad. Hop over the side and I'll dump yer things close."

Hop over the side? Incensed, Abigail pointed her gun at the captain.

"You dump my gear, you're going in next," she threatened.

"Abigail, put that damn gun away," Elias said again, now standing in waist-deep current instead of onshore.

CHAPTER FOURTEEN

Two men waded up behind Elias, who stood next to the boat that had just come in.

"Which is your gear, Abigail?"

Suddenly mute, she pointed to the crates and sacks belonging to her.

"Take these," Elias told the men he'd hired to carry her things ashore. Nighttime snow picked up, creating further problems for everyone in the water and on the beach. Arriving in Dyea wasn't easy on the best of days, much less on this bitter Christmas night.

The men made quick work of their job and had Abigail's gear in hand and onshore before Abigail had a chance to catch her breath.

"You gonna put that gun away or shoot me and the captain here," Elias quipped.

Elias! Abigail lowered her pistol but kept it in hand. Running into Elias Colt the moment she'd arrived in Dyea, after her conjured run-ins with ghosts in Skagway, frayed her nerves beyond the limit. All she wanted to do was climb the Golden Stairs and not have to deal with any of this!

Elias took matters and Abigail in hand, throwing her over his shoulder to get her safely onshore.

"Thanks, mister!" the captain yelled out.

Abigail didn't protest. She couldn't, so caught up was she in the frozen, frenzied atmosphere. The blur of people and brush of Elias Colt next to her assaulted her senses and turned them inside out. Elias had command of her in that moment, and she couldn't break away. She didn't want to break away, and that frightened her as much as conjuring ghosts. It struck her that she'd heard his voice from the beach over the din. It had been Elias telling her to put her gun away. He'd appeared out of nowhere, it seemed. *Like the lost girl.*

Already numb with cold, Abigail tensed even more at the odd circumstance of coming up against Elias Colt right away. Each sway of their bodies in the rough water, with her tossed over his shoulder, jolted her to the quick. On top of everything else, she felt exposed, not just to the weather, but to him. *I am no beauty* rang loud and clear in her head. Elias was as dangerous to her as the treacherous Chilkoot Trail. Both frightened her at that moment. She hadn't survived lawless mining towns by being afraid, and she wouldn't survive this one . . . if she showed any fear.

Unceremoniously deposited on the Dyea beach, Abigail quickly returned to her senses and her dire situation. She couldn't think about Elias Colt; she had to sharpen her thoughts and think about herself. With no money in her pocket, save for her treasured gold nugget, she needed to find shelter and needed to protect her humble cache. One look around her told her others were in the same predicament. Maybe all these people hadn't just arrived, but they didn't have shelter or protection, either. Skagway had been this chaotic, too. Abigail still had her gun in hand and slipped it inside her jacket. She'd need to keep it close and ready.

"Abigail . . . Abigail!" Elias repeated, trying to get her attention. This whole mess confounded him. That's what it was—a mess. He'd just rescued Abigail Grayce from a tight patch, and she wouldn't even look at him. What had he expected if he ever saw her again? Not this, not treating him like a stranger. That's how this felt: like she'd given him the mitten. *Guess rescuing her now makes up for deserting her in Seattle.* That sparkle in her eye for him in Seattle had disappeared. Hell, she wouldn't even look at him in Dyea. The gaming life and no wife, he mentally repeated, attempting to harden his heart against Abigail.

Elias turned to the two men who'd shepherded Abigail's gear to shore and paid them off. The men disappeared into the gathering of stampeders on the beach, probably to get into dry clothes and then look for more customers from whom to make a dime.

"Are you the gals coming to work for me at the Trail?" Elias said to the two women waiting for his attention. These were the same females who'd been on the boat with Abigail, so he guessed they were the ones he'd called over to Skagway about. By this time, two telephone lines had been set up out of Dyea, one up the Chilkoot and one to Skagway. He'd been on the beach to meet their steamer, knowing their approximate time of arrival. Two of his saloon gals were headed back to Seattle, finding Alaska too hard a place to live. Out of all the boats shuttling back and forth between Skagway and Dyea, Abigail had to be on the very one he'd met. *Dammit.* Bad luck for him. He'd expected percentage gals arriving tonight, not Abigail Grayce.

"I'm Charity," one of the young women said, in obvious admiration of her handsome new boss, judging by the way she batted her eyes and warmed up to Elias.

"I'm Sabrina," the other chimed in, her behavior much the same as her companion's.

Abigail looked at Elias at this point, seeing the way the females fawned over him and the way he seemed to respond in kind. They were beauties, she could tell, even in the poor light. He looked at the other two females and not at her. That's what she'd wanted, wasn't it: for him to ignore her and go about his business and leave her alone?

Abigail took a step away from the three and searched the area around them for her gear. She'd no time to lose to find shelter and a safe spot for the night. Maybe there would be a space free along the side of the warehouse across the beach. With a building at her back, she could better protect herself. There'd be no sleep tonight; she couldn't afford to take the chance. She plopped herself down on her crate of goods and would wait for Elias Colt and his *ladies* to leave before she'd transport her gear across the beach. With snow pelting down, and despite shivering head to toe, she'd wait for Elias to disappear from her life. It was the only defense she had against him—against the way he made her feel all jumbled up inside, and right now hurting.

"Hey, Frank!" Elias yelled to a musher and dog team nearby.

Perfect, Abigail thought. He's going to have his ladies ride in a sled to the Trail, and not make them walk like the rest of the world. Huskies love to pull sleds, but not when they were overburdened. Abigail saw those two women as overburden.

"Get up, Abigail," Elias ordered her, at the same time taking hold of her arm to make sure she did. "Frank, help me load this gear onto your sled and take it to my place, will ya?"

"Sure thing, Elias," the musher said, then immediately tossed the designated sacks of provisions onto the bed of his sled. Elias let go of Abigail and lifted the hefty crate onto the sled behind her provisions. The harnessed huskies danced in place, ready to get to work.

"*Your* place," Abigail said. "Put my goods right back on this beach or I'll—"

"Or what, pull that gun of yours on me?" Elias darted.

Abigail stared up at Elias, and his menacing expression. He was dangerous all right.

"Look, Abigail, this is a bad night for all of us. You got no choice, and I don't, either. Tomorrow you can go off on your own, but tonight you're staying at my place."

In truth, she thought she'd suffer frostbite outside with no shelter or enough canvas and wool for protection against the harsh elements. It made sense to take an opportunity at decent shelter. Life was about survival, not feelings. Besides, what goods she had could be ruined or stolen if she took her eyes off them.

"Hike!" The musher gave his order to go, and off they went, quickly disappearing through the crowd of people and piled goods.

"Let's go, ladies," Elias said to Charity and Sabrina, his new percentage gals. He knew Abigail would follow. She'd little choice.

The women bookended Elias; each grabbing one of his arms and feigning the need for help in the ice and sandy snow. Both women turned around at the same time and shot Abigail angry looks.

Abigail knew exactly what the looks meant: jealousy. She wanted to laugh out loud at such a ridiculous emotion shot at her. She was no one to be jealous of, no beauty. Elias had handpicked them to work for him, likely well aware of their good looks. Matching his, she couldn't help but think. Only then did Abigail remember the note in her pocket that held her heart-shaped gold nugget. Elias had talked about jobs when he'd come backstage in Seattle; about her and Maud and Company maybe working for him at his place in Dyea. Well, he didn't make the same offer now, she realized. That this fact bothered her was all the more reason for her to get away from Elias Colt first thing tomorrow.

"There're some suspicious characters come inside tonight, Elias," Nate Farley told his boss as soon as Elias stepped back inside the Trail.

"Which ones, Nate?" The saloon and restaurant were

crowded over with customers. The piano player struck a lively tune.

"One is yonder at the bar in a derby, but not drinkin', and the other is sittin' by the blackjack table in a telescope hat, but not playin'. They've been here nigh onto an hour, just watching things."

Elias eyed the men. Electric lights suspended from the tin ceiling provided a good view of the situation. The men could be part of Soapy Smith's gang, he suspected, the way they appeared to be sizing up his place. So the con man was back in Skagway. Elias's instincts told him so.

"Nate, I've got the new gals outside and need to show them their rooms here. We'll come in through the back. Hold things down for a few more minutes, will ya?"

"Yep, Elias," Nate agreed and took a position behind the bar instead of in the restaurant. Mrs. Farley handled the customers there. Another of Elias's barkeeps served drinks at the bar, while his remaining percentage gal moved through the sea of stampeders, taking drink orders. The Trail bustled with activity on this Christmas night where few people were in church, but inside saloons and eateries in celebration of another day survived in the Alaska wild. The Methodist-Episcopalian Church wouldn't have much business tonight, but the three undertakers in town might do a brisk trade.

Elias signaled to Nate, and then went back outside to Charity, Sabrina . . . and Abigail, who waited for him. Abigail's goods had already been taken around back. He was surprised she wasn't sitting on top of her cache instead of waiting out front. That seemed her job now: to guard her goods and get over the Chilkoot. He remembered his offer to give her a job as a variety entertainer in his place when they were back in Seattle. Suppose that wouldn't work at this point. She didn't appear in any kind of entertaining mood.

Evidently she'd determined to gold mine in the Yukon; that was clear, since she fussed over her goods like they were sacks of gold dust instead of flour and baking powder. She didn't seem like any kind of cook to him, or a percentage gal, or an entertainer, for that matter. Abigail had turned out to be a stampeder like all the rest; yet she wasn't like all the rest. That's what attracted him to her: that she was different. She didn't appear attracted to him. *Given me the mitten, she has. Just as well,* he thought. Abigail had already proved too much of a distraction in Dyea. He needed to keep his heart hardened against her and his eye on his business.

"Let's go, ladies," Elias said the moment he stepped outside, then headed around back without so much as a look for any of the three women.

Charity and Sabrina scuttled behind him, but Abigail stayed put. What had she expected? For him to look at her the same way he had in Seattle? Did she think he'd ask her to work for him again? Had she waited out front to hear him call her "darlin'?" She wanted to cry, but she didn't. She couldn't let Elias Colt see tears or any sign of any feelings she might have for him. Feelings didn't belong in the Alaska Yukon, and they didn't belong in her head and heart. Look at the trouble they'd caused her already, keeping her concentration on Elias Colt and not on her goods where it should be.

Abigail looked up at the Christmas night sky. Snowflakes dusted her skin, the heavy snow over. Oddly, she thought of her family back in Creede. She didn't miss them or wish them here with her, but they were faces she knew. At this moment, she longed for a familiar face, anything to replace the hollowness inside her.

"You coming, Abigail Grayce?" Elias had rounded the corner to find her.

"Yes," she said quietly and followed him this time. Her spirits fell completely. If only he'd called her "darlin'," she might not feel so sad.

Abigail had Elias's cabin to herself. He'd gone to work in his saloon and told her he'd be back in the morning and not before. She'd be gone first thing and wouldn't have to see him again. Getting her gear away would take time, since she'd need to move her things by herself, a little at a time. That's how it would be on the Chilkoot, she knew: having to move her cache bit by bit up the trail. Guarding her things would be a problem that wouldn't go away until she reached the Klondike. This was going to be a long night, and the journey up the Golden Stairs to the gold fields beyond would also be long.

She couldn't afford to go to sleep and miss getting out of there before Elias showed up. The kerosene lamp on the table near the iron frame bed lit the cabin in a soft glow. A potbelly stove warmed the space. For Elias to have such luxury in this remote boomtown surprised her. For him to have his own cabin out back of his saloon surprised her. The money from his business had to be good. He'd earned it. She couldn't begrudge him that. No one hands anything out in mining boomtowns. You have to do your own digging for gold, any which way you could.

Abigail couldn't take her eyes off the quilt and Elias's iron frame bed. What would be the harm in lying on it a few stolen minutes? She wouldn't see a softer spot to lie in all the months ahead. Elias wouldn't come back until morning. Suddenly overcome with shivers, Abigail needed to get warm. Her wet head cover had to go. Then she peeled off her frozen jacket, damp wool skirt, blouse and bloomers, and stripped down to her flannel undergarments. Her teeth chattered, and her bones ached with cold. Her damp braid irritated her skin. She undid the braid to allow her hair to dry. Weary of ghostly apparitions, male and female, she longed for comfort. She'd steal a few moments under Elias's quilt with no one the wiser.

Abigail crawled in bed and snuggled down deep in the feathered mattress. In no time she'd fallen asleep.

Heart-shaped nuggets rained down from the heavens, gently bathing Abigail in golden sunshine. She breathed in their treasured fragrance, her nose filled with purity and sweetness. Wild yellow and white daisies coated the snowy scape and warmed the icy steps ahead. Each careful step strengthened her for the next one up, then the next. It was as if she floated and had no more need for gum boots and German socks. She didn't wear canvas Mackinaw clothes, but a soft cotton gown she'd admired once in a catalog. The nuggets continued to softly rain down, but Abigail had no desire to reach out and catch them. She already held the only heart-shaped nugget she needed, despite the tattered parchment around it. Both were fixed in time in her hand and in her heart.

All of a sudden something—someone—tried to take her nugget and note from her, roaring at her, with shooting irons firing, melting away every icy step she'd made, and sending her tumbling into long-forgotten mine shafts with no hope of rescue!

Abigail woke up gasping for air and tried to sit up. Something, someone held her down, and she had to get away. She had to escape!

"Don't hit me again! The both of you, leave me be!" she shouted, believing her menacing brothers were at it again, trying to bully and beat her. "I'll put you in a grave first. I swear I will!"

"Easy, darlin', easy," Elias crooned, doing his best to hold onto Abigail and help calm her. He'd come back to check on her and was glad he had, seeing her so upset. It hit him, what he'd seen in her eyes back in Seattle: the pain she'd endured in her life, the sons of bitches out there who'd hurt her. He'd readily send 'em to the undertaker.

Abigail thrashed back and forth, hitting at her brothers.

"How did you find me?" she managed through her tears.

Elias held onto her, letting her cry, and waited for her body to relax. She pounded softly at his back.

"How did you find me?" she whimpered against him.

"Easy, darlin', easy," he said again, his chin resting at her head.

At first, it didn't register to Abigail who held her, but she gradually realized it wasn't her brutalizing brothers. She relaxed against the phantom that had come to her rescue and let his warmth flow into her tense limbs. The moment seemed strangely familiar, but it couldn't be. No man would be calling to her. *I am no beauty.*

"Easy, darlin'."

Abigail pushed away just enough to look into Elias Colt's unmistakable brown eyes.

CHAPTER FIFTEEN

He wanted something from her, but what? Abby could tell the handsome stranger with questioning brown eyes asked her for something. Every time she tried to approach and find out what he wanted, he'd vanish. His searching look had frightened her. That he wouldn't stay and talk to her frightened her. She ran after him, calling out to him, but he wouldn't reappear. She didn't know where he went or how to reach him, but she had to find him. Time was running out.

"Abigail . . . Abigail," she heard him call. The distant rasps cut into her the same as ice shards might prick and hurt. Cold fear charged through her veins, enough to numb all feeling and thought. "Abigail—"

Abby woke with a start and sat upright in her tent. Disoriented and agitated to the point of panic, she ran her hands up and down her arms to stop the phantom aches settling in. She jiggled her legs to throw off the sting there. Her entire body felt the bite of cold thawing to warm, prickling and tingling as her blood circulated again. She'd experienced this hypothermia before in the Colorado winter when she'd been exposed to freezing temperatures without enough protection. That's how this felt.

Her confusion began to clear, and she realized she wasn't in Colorado in winter, but in Alaska in summer. Her tent flap was open. She peered out into the twilight sky, though it had to be the middle of the night. A bad dream was all she'd had. No one

172

had called out for her. At this moment she heard nothing but her own heartbeat, her own breathing, her own fear. The musher's camp stayed quiet; no dogs or people stirred. No reason for her to be fearful, yet she was. The handsome stranger had never visited her in dreams. That she'd conjured him in dreams *and* out of thin air cut at her. Whatever was going on was serious and real, she realized at this point. Otherwise, logic would have chased away this mystery by now.

It unnerved Abby that she sought out the stranger. Before, she'd never sought any male to come into her life. How quickly she'd latched onto his face, his figure, his ghostly presence in her academic, ordered life. Someone like him would never seek out someone like her. None of this made sense but for one thing: she'd returned to Dyea and Skagway for a reason. She'd been drawn here by forces beyond her control or comprehension, and she knew she needed to be here. Gold mining had drawn her here. The Klondike Gold Rush had drawn her here. Something else had reached out to her and kept her here. What that was, she needed to find out. It had to have something to do with the mysterious, handsome westerner. She had no other explanation for his sudden appearance in her life.

At first chance, she'd return to Skagway and the Red Onion Saloon. The two-story historic site must hold answers to this mystery. Meanwhile, she'd work with the sled dogs, the summer sleds, and the tourists, helping them enjoy their Alaska experience. In the morning she'd help feed the dogs and get them properly harnessed for the day. Their husky spirits would brighten her mood and ease her worries.

She should try to sleep until morning, but she didn't want to dream about the handsome stranger. No, she didn't want to be unnerved again, so she sat upright on her unzipped sleeping bag and determined to keep her eyes open. Out of nowhere, she thought of the poem by John Keats, "When I Have Fears." The poem made her feel as if time were running out, *the same as I'd felt in my dream.* Her mouth went dry, and she snatched her water bottle up to chase away the eerie sensation.

"E-l-i-a-s," Abigail whispered in disbelief at who held her. The nearby kerosene lamp still burned, carrying ghostly shadows across the cabin space. No brothers hid there. No drunken father or crazed mother. This was no nightmare . . . *but a dream.* Elias Colt held her. Elias Colt comforted her. Elias Colt looked at her and no one else; not the percentage ladies in his saloon or other women fawning over him, but at *her.* She felt beautiful in this dreamy moment. The unexpected sensation caressed her in ways she'd never imagined a woman could be touched. It was, at the same time, the safest and most dangerous moment in her life. Innocent tears started to fall at the impossibility of it all.

Elias stroked her cheek, and she let him. Flushed in dreams, she warmed to his touch. When she felt his gentle kiss on her forehead, she leaned into him more. The new experience of a simple kiss tore at her, and more tears fell. She'd never been kissed like that, or in any other way she could remember. She wanted more; the yearning so deep inside her she couldn't stop the tide of emotion she felt for Elias. Everything about him felt good, smelled good, and tasted good. His touch awakened the woman inside her she'd thought dead. His touch brought her to life—a life she'd never known existed. Abigail prayed she'd never wake from this dream, willing to stay in Elias's loving arms forever.

Blurred in dreamtime, she later fell into satisfied, exhausted sleep.

Abigail stretched along the feathery softness, relishing in the feel of an actual bed and not the hard ground. She didn't open her eyes and wanted to prolong the moment. Warm covers caressed her body in pleasurable ways, and she nestled farther into the feather bed. Gentle pressure pulsed in places, lulling her back in dreams. She yearned to go back to sleep, but she had to get up and get out of Elias Colt's cabin before morning.

"Mornin', darlin'," Elias said in a husky whisper, then pressed a kiss to her forehead. He didn't roll away from her but stayed lying next to her.

Abigail vaulted from the iron frame bed as if in a nightmare. Confusion reeled through her sleepy senses. Her long hair brushed at her back and tickled at her chest. Only when she began fighting to contain her unruly hair into a braid did she realize . . . *she had no clothes on!*

"Come back to bed, darlin'," Elias quietly commanded and held the quilt up for her.

Caught off-guard, Abigail wanted her pistol in hand to help defend against this . . . this assault.

"I'm no prostitute, Elias Colt! You can't take me to bed for any price!"

Elias said nothing, but stared at Abigail in open-faced bewilderment.

Abigail grabbed her jacket from the nearby chair and pulled it on. She kept her eyes on Elias, as if she did have her gun in her hand and him in her crosshairs.

"I'm getting my goods and myself as far away from you as I can. Dyea is a big place. You stay out of my way, and I'll stay out of yours," she said. "I'm no prostitute. I'm no entertainer, either. I have another purpose, *and it has nothing to do with you.*"

"Darlin'—"

"Don't call me that! I'm nobody to you. I know that, and you know that," she said pointedly.

"Abigail, that's not fair." Elias gave her a quiet reply, then angrily threw the covers off and got out of bed.

"Don't call me that, either!" she railed at him and quickly gave him her back. She refused to look at his impossibly perfect body another second.

"I'm going to work. Next time I come back, you'd best be gone," he said in a strained rasp.

His words hurt. This whole predicament hurt. She kept her back to Elias, listening while he got dressed and banged the cabin door shut behind him.

In no time, Abigail had her clothes on and her hands around the fifty-pound sack of flour she needed to cart out of Elias's cabin. The sacks of evaporated fruit and baking powder weighed about the same. The rest of her store of goods filled a heavy crate and was beyond her power to move on her own. After such a night, she had no energy for any of this. Sitting atop her goods and having a good cry would be of no help at all, but it was what she felt like doing. If Elias returned and saw her, she didn't think he'd be in a reasonable mood and would want her gone. That's what he'd said . . . *gone*.

She let go of her heavy sack and pushed open the cabin door, surprised by how much effort it took. Freezing winds met her when she had the door open. She didn't feel cold, but dejected. It must have snowed again. Her heart sank when she realized how much more difficult this would make her task. Dragging her goods through slush and snow wouldn't be easy. Turning toward her cache, she grabbed the flour sack again and pulled it out the front door. It wouldn't do for the sacks to get wet and ruined.

She yanked the flour sack back inside and knew she had to come up with a plan, and fast. Quickly, she undid her canvas bed roll and laid it out flat before heaving the flour sack on top. Now she could better pull the sack to wherever she wanted and keep it dry. She'd stage this; each sack atop the canvas; each sack pulled outside to the alleyway, followed by her crate of belongings. That was her plan—to get all her store of goods in one place before she moved them in stages again. She'd need to do this up the Chilkoot and the Golden Stairs, so she might as well start here.

Abigail had got her sacks of provisions amassed at the end of the alleyway and rested on the strip of canvas, when it hit her again that someone could steal from her when her back was turned. The door to Elias's cabin stood yards away. Could she trust people if she left her things unguarded? She didn't have a choice and hurried to the cabin door, despite the deep snow. She took time to catch her breath. Before she went inside for her crate, she turned for a quick look at her piled-up provisions.

Two men stood by them! They looked at her goods, then at her. She wondered how long they might have been watching her. Neither tried to take her things, but stared at her with questioning expressions on their faces. They must be Tlingit, she thought, the way they appeared. She didn't speak their language and might have to let her gun do the talking. With no money to pay them or anyone else to help her, she'd have to stand her ground and see this first challenge through. She'd no intention of shooting them, but she needed to scare them away. The Tlingit, she knew from talk in Skagway, charged money to transport goods for stampeders, and she could only imagine the price.

Not taking her gaze from theirs, she walked toward the men and reached inside her jacket for her pistol. The Tlingit men appeared to know what she was about to do and both put their hands up in waves of no.

"I'm not going to shoot you, but *get away* from my things," she ordered in as gruff a voice as she could muster. She left her gun in her pocket and used both her hands to gesture to them to leave.

But the men didn't. Instead, they bent down to pick up her goods. Now she put her hands on both their arms to push them away.

One of the Tlingits stood straight and seemed exasperated with her.

"Consarn it!" she exclaimed. "You're upset with *me*? Why? Because I won't let you have my things?"

The man shook his head back and forth in a no gesture and patted the air to calm her down.

Transfixed by this entire lack of conversation, Abigail did relax enough to be curious about their next move. She had her gun ready if she needed it.

The other Tlingit gestured he would pick up the sacks and carry them for her.

At this, she shook her head vehemently, right away putting out her empty hands to show them she had no gold dust hidden anywhere.

One put his hand up and shook it slightly as if to say there was no need for payment.

"Shee ax eet wudishee i. Tleik Tee aade awsitee daanaa," the Tlingit said. *"Tleik Tleik,"* he repeated and kept shaking his head in a no. *"Tleik . . . no . . . goon,"* he added and pointed to her empty pocket.

Goon? Was that gold? Was that what he meant? Could these native Tlingit actually be offering her help for no gold? Impossible, yet that's what Abigail thought. She warmed to the idea because she didn't have any others at the moment. Since she was dressed in female clothes, maybe they just wanted to help someone they understood to be a greenhorn woman who was all alone and apparently didn't have any money to pay them. She'd find out soon enough if they meant to rob her and not help her.

Abigail gave them both a firm nod yes, then pointed to the

open door of Elias's cabin and motioned for them to follow.

They did so without question.

She pointed to the big crate, then put her hand on its edge and tried to move it toward her.

One Tlingit nudged her out of the way while the other lifted the crate onto a shoulder. Abigail could hardly believe his strength. He went out the door as if carrying a bale of hay instead of such heavy weight. The same man stopped at the piled-up sacks and evidently wanted to know where to take her crate. Abigail took a last look around Elias's cabin for anything she might have left behind, and then pulled the door closed behind her. She scurried in front of the Tlingit men and led the way.

With no other option at the moment, she prayed there'd be space free along one of the warehouse's outside walls. Beyond that, she had no plan. That she'd had such good fortune in the Tlingit helping her the day after Christmas was her present, she decided—the best she'd ever received during this festive season. She'd already determined the Tlingit had no wish to rob her and forgot all about ever thinking of pulling a gun on either of these guardian spirits.

Elias didn't know what to expect when he got back to his cabin, but he didn't think Abigail would be gone. Yet in an hour's time, she'd cleared out. He'd had a chance to cool off and thought she had, too. They had made love and their lovemaking had left its mark. She had him all stirred up. He wanted her, all right. The moment he'd seen her in his bed, he meant to check on her, not make love to her. He'd made the mistake of stroking her cheek, then kissing her. She'd kissed him back. Her whole body invited him to her bed. Dammit! He'd been afraid of this all along—that he'd fallen for her.

She hadn't fallen for him, or else she'd still be here. First time a gal ever walked out on him. He knew Abigail was different but still, he didn't expect her to leave so fast. His cabin felt empty. He felt empty.

Dammit!

Elias took a final look around, stalling for time, not wanting to leave Abigail and his night with her behind. He didn't have a choice. She'd left him.

CHAPTER SIXTEEN

Abby hopped out of the van and helped the tourists offload at the ranger station on Broadway Street in Skagway. Two weeks had gone by without another incident like the one she'd experienced her first night at musher's camp. The huskies comforted her every day she spent with them. Their spirits, like Tommy's, kept her steady in this wild gold-rush country. This remained the land of the Tlingit and the husky, and she was privileged to walk in step behind them. Her next assignment waited for her at the ranger station, but she'd stow her gear inside the door and head to the Red Onion first.

The town looked empty. It matched her mood. No cruise ships had arrived yet, Abby supposed. It struck her how few residents lived in Skagway, and she could recognize the importance of tourism to the area. Gold-rush days had ended long ago, yet Skagway hadn't completely died out, as Dyea had. The three cemeteries in Dyea crossed her line of vision, all vivid, all real to her. Dyea was a ghost town, but had all the boom towners and stampeders truly died out? This idea haunted Abby. She picked up her pace to the Red Onion and determined to find out for herself soon enough.

Downhearted from the start, Abby stood on the planked walkway outside the infamous saloon and studied the upper windows. No curtains billowed. No windows opened in greeting. No ghosts. *Of course, no ghosts!* That's not what got to her.

181

The fact that the handsome westerner in her dream didn't come outside in welcome did. What did she expect? For all the ghosts inside to open the doors of the Red Onion and invite her in and answer all the questions she'd held inside her for two weeks? It unnerved her that she so willingly believed in phantoms and pseudoscience, when she'd no evidence of same other than her turned-upside-down emotions.

For long moments Abby stared at the white clapboard, two-story building, peering through the windows that spanned the entire front of the saloon. Even the front double doors were largely glass. She couldn't see much through the panes, the light inside being dim. The place looked dead inside. She shuddered at the thought, just as if someone were walking over her grave. Abby always thought this myth was nonsense, but she had goose bumps nonetheless. She did her best to ignore them and pushed through the front doors.

"We're not open just yet," a friendly costumed "saloon gal" greeted Abby the moment she stood inside the restaurant and bar.

"Oh," Abby said, embarrassed by her mistake. The temperature turned icy, and Abby's shivers picked up.

"Are you all right, miss?" The attentive young woman sounded concerned.

"Sure. Just tired," Abby said, trying to cover her sudden fear. "When do you open?"

"We open at ten, in a half-hour."

"Thank you," Abby said, then spun on her heels to get out of there.

"Oh, miss," the costumed gal said to Abby's back. "Tour times are posted out front if you're interested in our brothel museum."

Abby heard her but didn't stop to give a response. She needed to get warm and find answers to what was going on. The instant she'd cleared the saloon, the warm day soothed her. Steadier now, she read the sign out front regarding hours and age requirements. Tours ran every hour, depending on the day. At nineteen, she couldn't go into the brothel museum without a parent or guardian. The youngest age allowed to take the tour was fourteen. To order alcohol, she needed to be twenty-one, naturally; but she couldn't go upstairs to that second-story window by herself. A quick check of prices informed she also needed ten dollars for the brothel museum tour. She'd find the money to pay for entry, but she also had to find an adult to accompany her.

Abby made a dash for the ranger station, unsure what time her transport left for Dyea. She couldn't wait weeks and weeks to get back here and get inside the Red Onion Saloon. Where her trail went cold was exactly where this mystery heated up.

"We're leaving for our Chilkoot base camp in Dyea around three. Should have our climbers grouped here by that time, Abby," the ranger, Sam Ballard, told her. "Two are on the ferry coming in at one, and the others spent last night in Skagway. Mike tells me you did a great job at musher's camp, and he'd be glad for your help every summer season."

Embarrassed by the praise, Abby stared at her booted feet and not at the new ranger. It was difficult for her to accept a compliment about her intellect, her looks, or her gold-mining prowess. Abby forced her head up and gave Sam the best smile she could muster.

"I know you've done some hiking in Dyea, but did you ever tackle the entire Chilkoot to Canada?"

"No, I haven't," she answered, warming to the subject of the famous gold-rush trail.

"Are you ready to be a stampeder and climb the Golden Stairs?" Sam gave her a quick wink.

Abby's smile broadened and she nodded yes.

"Well, good," he said. "I think you'll have a good group gathered and a good climb to all the camps over the summit to Lake Bennett. Be back here by two, to help load up. Meanwhile, see a bit of Skagway and take in the history."

"I will, and I will," she told him. "Thank you, Sam."

"I should be thanking you," the veteran ranger quipped. "It is young people like you who will take all you learn here and share it with the outside, so no one will forget our gold-rush history. It's I who should thank you, Abby Gray."

"I will never forget," she said, touched by his respect for the history here. She felt akin to Sam Ballard, at his careful choice of words. *So no one will forget.*

"Right then," he said. "See you at two, Abby."

"Yes," she replied, then turned to head out the door and to the Red Onion Saloon.

A cruise ship had docked at the Skagway wharf. Hundreds of tourists milled in the streets. Abby joined in the crowd along Broadway, and thought to join in with those headed to the Red Onion for a tour of the brothel museum. She'd try to blend in and go unnoticed. The push of tourists would be cover enough, she hoped.

The costumed "madam" started the eleven o'clock tour on time. Abby was so intent on mixing in with the group and paying for her ticket, she didn't catch the madam's *nom de plume*. Abby paid ten dollars for her ticket for a twenty-minute tour and fell in line behind an elderly couple to give the impression she was with them. The costumed tour guide hadn't noticed, and Abby was relieved not to be caught. She listened intently while the "madam" began her talk about how, in times past, prostitutes earned five dollars for fifteen minutes with a customer. Abby didn't feel as cold as she'd expected to feel the moment she entered the Red Onion, thankful no pretend spirits tried to chase her away. She needed to pay attention and keep her wits for this tour. She needed to find answers to the mystery plaguing her since spring break.

"Come follow me up the 'Stairway to Heaven,' " the madam said, raising her eyebrow as if to underscore her intended meaning. "Climb the same steps and walk the same floors the miners did in Klondike gold-rush days. Follow me down the hallway of doors leading to the cribs where prostitutes entertained their customers."

Abby strained to hear what the madam said over the chatter of tourists, at the same time scrutinizing every detail of the infamous brothel. *Gasp!* She experienced a sudden chill as if she stood in a cold spot similar to those described by paranormal investigators. *Ghosts.* The crib in the corner might house a ghost. Abby needed to reach the corner crib and find out. That's why she was here.

The costumed tour guide spoke loudly enough about prostitutes who'd worked the brothel, for Abby to hear a good number of their names. "Birdie Ash, Big Desire, Babe Davenport, Pea Hull Annie, Kitty Faith, Klondike Kate," and someone whose name was *"Lydia"* had occupied these cribs. Maybe they were prostitutes, or maybe other madams; Abby couldn't be sure at this point. There were ten cribs along the large hallway, and each plank-walled crib measured ten by ten feet. Each crib had three doors, with one to the hallway and one to each adjoining crib.

The tour group moved way too slowly for Abby, who wanted to get to the corner crib—the one where Abby believed she'd seen the billowing curtains out the second-story window. Abby peered inside each crib and could see remnants of wallpaper left on stretched linen that had been tacked up to cover the planked walls. The women working here had tried to decorate their tiny cribs, Abby could see. Each room had iron beds covered with patchwork quilts, a stand with a wash pitcher and basin set on top, and a lamp placed alongside. Most cribs contained beveled mirrors and risqué paintings.

Abby overheard the doll story, where each prostitute had a doll carved to her likeness behind the bar downstairs. When a prostitute sent her five dollars down the copper tube running from a hole in her crib floor to the bar downstairs, the barkeep would sit her doll upright again. This indicated she was available. Gold was the preferred payment, and the barkeep safeguarded a prostitute's earnings for her. A prostitute would hide any tips and nuggets given her in crawl spaces between floors or in loose boards.

"A silver dress was found in a crawl space and is on display here," the madam added.

This interested Abby: the idea of a silver dress discovered in the crawl space. Which of the ladies on the line at the Red Onion Saloon and Brothel had worn this dress and kept it hidden? Maybe the prostitute was afraid it would be stolen? Maybe the prostitute had stolen the dress from somebody else?

"And this is the corner crib where Lydia, the madam, kept company," the tour guide announced.

Abby leaned through the crowd for a better look inside Lydia's corner crib. This crib interested her the most; a *ghost* lived here. A sharp, cold breeze suddenly knifed through Abby, enough to put her off her footing. The man in front turned around and stopped her fall.

"Thank you," she said, embarrassed by her actions.

"Lydia was one of the madams here—"

Abby strained to listen to the tour guide, but everything went silent. She shook her head to clear whatever blocked her from hearing. Silence still. The next thing she knew, cold water had been splashed on her! Before she could react to this, sounds picked up again, but none of the voices or sounds seemed familiar. Abby listened carefully, even closing her eyes to better concentrate. Chatter came from all the crib rooms. She could hear conversations through the thin walls. Bawdy laughter echoed along the hallway, with doors opening and closing behind the clink of gold nuggets sent downstairs to the barkeep. A perfumed fragrance permeated the air, momentarily interrupted by a whiff of lit tobacco. Abby opened her eyes. Light in the hallway had dimmed to nighttime sconces and tunneled passions.

"Abigail . . . Abigail . . ."

Abby stayed frozen. She recognized the voice calling her name. *He* was here!

"Miss, are you all right?" asked the same man who'd prevented her fall moments before.

"Yes," she answered numbly. "Thanks. I should pay better attention to where I'm going." *And just where is that?* Abby asked herself, at the same time trying to pull herself together.

"This was Lydia's corner crib, and no one knows if she died here, but we do know she's our most famous ghost," the tour guide said, keeping up her talk.

Abby craned to hear every word, only now realizing her arm actually *was* wet with water spilled on her. The sensation had been real!

"These days Lydia is known to dash down the hallway, and her footsteps are often heard. She's also known to water plants, and we know that since the plants have all been watered when we next attend to them. Her perfume is obvious, and she sometimes gives the impression of not liking all the men who come through here. So you gents in the group, best look out. She might give you a poke and send you on your way," the tour guide teased.

"Does anyone ever stay in these cribs?" Abby blurted, paying little attention to the titter of laughter around her at her question.

"No, dearie," the guide said, keeping in Klondike gold-rush mode. "We don't rent these out as a B&B or hotel accommodation. This is a brothel museum, and we cherish every artifact and bawdy memory. No one stays in these cribs except any ghosts who might choose to," the guide added humorously.

Abby heard the laughter among the group, but she didn't scoff at the tour guide's remarks. She knew the tour guide and the group around her hadn't experienced what she just had, and didn't believe ghosts really walked this hallway or spent the night in any of the cribs. Abby believed differently. How else could icy water have been spilled on her, on top of the sensation that something or someone had passed through her to get by, on top of the smell of telltale perfume, and how else could she have heard, "Abigail . . . Abigail . . ."

Abby kept calm on the outside, but inside she twisted in knots. She'd found the evidence she needed at the Red Onion Saloon. *She* was the evidence! That these experiences and sensations happened to her—a person of science and hard facts—baffled her, yet proved pseudoscience had toed its way into her ordered life. Disorder ruled, and would, until she played the mystery out. As it was too late for her to go anywhere but forward, she felt oddly akin to the ghosts from the past, especially the handsome westerner.

Now she understood he didn't exist in her reality today, but from a time gone by. This was what she'd come to believe. What had she expected anyway? That someone who looked like him would have any affection for someone like her, today or yesterday? This whole experience represented nothing more than her dreams of gold-rush days and her yearning to have been a part of such a romantic, adventuresome time. That's all any of this seemed—*a blur, a slip in time.* For unknown reasons, she'd laid herself open to this ghostly venture, and she'd no choice but to see it through.

Downhearted and depressed at the cold reality of her situation, she felt like nothing more than a paranormal activist, going about with her EVP devices and cameras, picking up white orbs and electronic static. A fat lot of good her scientific thinking had done her, since she'd fallen into the same ghostly trap every other TV-watcher had. Worse, she'd fallen for a handsome ghost when she'd rather not have. The truth stared her in the face, and it hurt. She believed now the handsome westerner from the past didn't want her . . . but something *from* her. Evidently he could get through to her enough to pique her curiosity and solicit her help.

Abby's spirits plummeted farther. Had she really come back to Alaska to chase after a ghost? Yes, she had. She'd come here to ghost mine, as Ebony had predicted. The sad truth gnawed at her. Deep in her subconscious, she did want a boyfriend, and evidently had to go chasing ghosts in another time, trying to find one! She didn't have the energy to pity herself. Drained of everything but knowing she had to return to the ranger station for her next assignment by two o'clock, Abby didn't want to think about the Chilkoot Trail ahead and didn't want any part of gold-rush dreams.

They wouldn't come true after all.

Eli watched Abby leave the Red Onion Saloon. He knew she was upset, and he knew she wouldn't be back to the brothel. He willed her to stay strong and see this through. A quick check of his pocket watch showed the late hour. Rattled head to toe, he wanted to throw the timepiece to the ground and crush it beneath his boot, but he didn't. Nothing he could do would hold back time. The pocket watch had been set and it never lied.

Chapter Seventeen

Abigail warmed to Elias's touch and to the love she read in his mischievous brown eyes. Every part of her wanted every part of him. She heated to his tautly muscled body until she could bear the fevered pitch no more . . . then completely gave herself to him. The moisture between their bodies sealed them together for all time; their love a bond never broken. She'd come home to Elias Colt, safe and secure at long last. I am a beauty.

Startled awake by a jolt at her knees, Abigail tried to come out of dreams and not fall off her piled-up sacks of provisions. The reality of her situation unnerved her. She must have dozed off, a dangerous thing to do on Dyea's beaches. So fixed was she on her predicament, she'd failed to notice the two Tlingit men standing in front of her: the same men who'd helped her move her belongings to the wharf. At first sight, they blended in with the crowd around her, and she didn't react. When one of the Tlingit pushed something against her knees again, she shot to attention.

She recognized the men and didn't try to pull her pistol on them.

"*I du tlaa,*" one said.

"*I du tlaa,*" the other repeated then pointed to her. "*I du tlaa.*"

Abigail had no idea what they said, but saw right away they'd propped a bundled tent against her. Curious about their action, she pointed to the tent and repeated what she thought they'd said.

"*I du tl . . . aa?*"

"*Tleik,*" one of the men said, shaking his head in a clear no. He pointed to her and not the tent in front of her.

"*I . . . i du tlaa.*"

"I'm *du tlaa?* Me?" she understood the Tlingit to mean.

The Tlingit nodded the affirmative.

She pointed to the tent again and then touched her hand to her chest, asking if the tent were for her.

The Tlingit nodded yes.

Abigail didn't know what to say, what to think. Their generosity overwhelmed her, and she had no idea why they'd gifted her with something so valuable. A tent meant shelter from the wind and the cold. A tent meant her provisions wouldn't get ruined in rain or snow. A tent breathed life into her journey up the Golden Stairs! When she looked up to thank the two men, they'd disappeared. It was still the Christmas season, Abigail thought as she looked to heaven, grateful for this gift outright from the Tlingit *guardian spirits* who'd brought it to her.

The day had broken in Dyea, but she hadn't, yet. Dreams of Elias Colt just plain hurt her in the light of day. It hurt that he didn't love her. Their lovemaking had left its mark at her female center. The passion of their intense night together left her whole body edgy and agitated, where before she'd remembered only pleasure at Elias's touch. She'd never know it again. He'd told her to get out. "Next time I come back, you'd best be gone," he'd said.

Abigail didn't think she'd ever be warm enough from this day on, without Elias's arms around her. She braced against the cold. Too much had happened too fast. Time wasn't on her side with the day leaving her behind. The press of more miners arriving on the beach and their goods piling around her didn't help her mood. Any space left for her tent would be taken soon. With the Yukon River frozen, more miners would crowd into Dyea in the coming weeks. Abigail hopped off her cache and peered through the chaos for direction. She'd make her own way, as she always had.

It had taken Abigail the entire rest of the day to transport her tent and what goods she had the short distance to her encampment by the Taiya River. It was now near dusk. Other set up tents dotted the area alongside the river and inland. Luck had stayed with her, not only in keeping her provisions from harm, but in finding the campsite in the first place. She'd decided to break down her things so she could carry them herself. This had taken precious time, but she'd no choice. She didn't think the Tlingit would appear again to help her, guardian spirits or not.

With not one item stolen while she transported her smaller loads back and forth all day, Abigail still couldn't believe her good luck. Maybe stampeders, cheechako or sourdough, already lived by a trail code the moment they hit Dyea's beaches. Everyone couldn't afford to hire packers or buy horses or mush a dog team to get their ton of goods up the Golden Stairs. That took gold many didn't have. She'd heard packers charged as much as a dollar a pound to transport goods, a fortune to her at this point. A roped tram operated near the summit, with a horse circling and turning the wheel from a lower elevation to power the setup. Abigail could only imagine what that charge would be.

Her heart-shaped gold nugget burned a hole in her pocket, but she never thought of parting with her treasure. Elias's note, either. She'd keep them both. They mattered to her when not much else in life did on this cold evening. She'd fallen in love with Elias and there was nothing she could do about it but keep on going up the Golden Stairs. She had to, for her life to count for something. If she died on the Golden Stairs, she'd die content, Abigail told herself. Odd that this notion came to her. She'd no intention of dying on the journey ahead, despite the dangers to be faced. She started to shiver.

Who wouldn't on such a cold night?

She needed to get a campfire going, and would as soon as she finished hammering down the wood braces of her canvas tent. Luckily she had an ax. It came in handy to tamp down the braces; then she'd use it to cut wood and build her fire. The forest would provide what she needed. She wasn't above the tree line yet. This seemed a good place, by the river and out of the way of the rushing stampeders. In fact, she'd hardly noticed those around her, she'd been so intent on her tasks. Other than an occasional curse or grumble, she didn't pay much attention.

With her tent setup and her belongings stored inside, she closed the flaps and stood outside. It was then she realized she wasn't alone, far from it. Neighboring tents banked all sides except for her river exposure. She didn't want company, not tonight. She wanted to get warm and go to sleep. Elias's parting words cut deep. Others were trying to cook something to eat over their campfires. No one even looked her way. The unfriendly atmosphere didn't surprise her. People had one thing on their minds: getting to the gold fields. None of them, including her, knew what lay ahead. That might be on a few minds, too. They all wanted to survive the Alaska wild.

A woman screamed.

Abigail put her hand on her pistol and kept the gun hidden in her pocket. She listened hard and scanned the tented area. The foggy twilight sky gave off little light. The woman screamed a second time. Abigail tried to pinpoint where the shrieks came from. No one milling about appeared curious. No one came running out of a tent. She heard no shouts or gunfire or anything else. When the screams turned to wails, Abigail headed in the direction of the disturbing sobs.

She didn't have to go far. Stacked crates and supplies were piled up on either side of the tent's entryway. The flaps remained closed. No campfire burned outside. The woman's sobs came from inside.

"Ma'am," Abigail called through the flaps. "Ma'am, can I help you?"

Silence from inside the tent.

"Ma'am," Abigail repeated, this time louder.

A woman's ungloved hand appeared through the flaps then slowly pushed one side open. The white bloused arm seemed familiar to Abigail, and she thought of the figure that appeared in the second-story window of the Red Onion Saloon, as if she'd been in the moment before.

"Ye . . . yes," a faint voice sniffled from inside the tent.

Abigail took this as her invitation and bent enough to pass partially through the flaps. The distraught woman knelt by a man laid out on the canvas ground. The lantern light's glimmer revealed the sad scene. He looked dead. Goods were piled around them in the small space, providing little room for Abigail to do anything but stay crouched at the tent's entrance.

"What happened, ma'am?"

"He's . . . gone. My Jonah . . . is gone," the distraught woman sobbed and clasped her husband's dead hands in hers. Then she stroked his face and placed a gentle kiss there. "I don't know why God took him. Why did He?" She seemed to put the question to Abigail.

Tears streaked down the young woman's face. This dreadful moment was difficult to believe. A young couple coming here for gold, and their dreams ended like this! Abigail grieved inside. She understood mining accidents, disease, bullet holes, and savage winters that killed, but she didn't want to believe a young man could be taken by God in his prime.

"Had he been sick?" Abigail asked in a quiet voice.

"No. Jonah is strong as an ox and stubborn as a mule." *Sniffle. Sniffle.* "I declare, he can take on any frontiersman and come out the winner," she said and brightened. "Our community in Kansas believed in him so much they sent us here to the Klondike to find gold. *Jonah can do it,* they'd said. I wanted to stay and work the fields, but Jonah wanted more than a farmer's life. We packed up and got here to Dyea. I've never seen my Jonah so happy," the widow said and placed another kiss on her husband's stone-cold face. The sensation appeared to bring her back to the moment, and the realization her man was dead. She laid her head on his chest and encircled him in her grieving arms.

The young woman was cold and alone now. Abigail was cold and alone, too. She felt a kinship beyond the tragedy of sudden loss. Strangely, Abigail envied the woman—that she had someone to grieve over, when Abigail had never experienced the loss of someone she loved. The only one who came close was Elias Colt. She gulped hard and struggled to chase his unforgettable face from memory. The widow's sobs picked up. Abigail's heart wrenched for her, at her lost love.

"Would you like me to find the undertaker?" Abigail hated to ask but knew it was necessary.

"No!"

"Ma'am—"

"It's Martha. My name is Martha," the young woman said, her voice calmer now.

"I'm Abigail."

Martha nodded to Abigail, then laid her head back on her husband's chest. "In the morning . . . would you fetch the undertaker in the morning? Until then, would you stay with me? I don't want to be alone. I've never been alone before, Abigail. Will you stay with me?"

"Yes," Abigail replied without giving a thought to her own tent, her stored goods, or her own comfort. She didn't want to be alone on this cold, desolate night, either. She took up the blanket nearby and draped it around Martha's shoulders, to help Martha hold close, warm memories of her beloved Jonah for the last time.

Abigail steered clear of the Trail and Elias Colt in her morning rush to find an undertaker. There were three undertakers in town, she discovered, with only the last open for business. He wanted money up front; money she didn't have.

"How about I give you my fifty pounds of flour in trade?"

The wily undertaker scratched his graying beard.

"You got a deal, missy," he said. "Show me where the poor soul met his Maker."

Abigail bristled at "missy," until she realized she did wear female clothes and not her brother's mining hand-me-downs anymore. She must look like a "missy," a girl, and not a sourdough. When she had the chance, she'd try to dress more befitting a gold miner.

"C'mon, missy, the day ain't waitin' on either one of us," he said, and opened the door for her.

Abigail hurried outside. No one opened doors for her. How odd that the first man who did so was an undertaker. It surprised her, that's all.

"He's down by the river on the last tented street," she informed him and stepped into the throng of miners already busy with their day.

"Slow down there, missy!" the undertaker called. "You tryin' to put me in an early grave with your hurryin'?"

Abigail heard him and slowed down for the man to catch up. Jonah was dead. There wasn't any rush to lay him in the ground.

An eerie sense of time slipping through her icy fingers overwhelmed her and made her want to hurry. The Yukon River wouldn't break up until spring, and that was a ways off. She had time to find work and supply her ton of goods, then get them up the treacherous Chilkoot to the Klondike. Why *did* she hurry, with so much time until the spring thaw? It nagged at her, that she didn't have a good answer. Abigail walked swiftly toward Martha and Jonah's tent, seeing that the undertaker kept up with her.

"No, Martha, I couldn't," Abigail replied when the widow offered her half of her and her dead husband's goods. Abigail couldn't have imagined this sort of kindness before now. Martha had fallen on grave misfortune, and Abigail didn't want to take anything from her. Her husband had been taken from her. How could Abigail take any part of Martha's fortune in goods and leave her without means? It would be stealing. Abigail wanted no part of it.

"Dear Abigail," the young widow said and caught Abigail's roughened hands in her own.

Snow dusted the bitter air, sprinkling as gold dust might if allowed to escape its poke. Abigail wanted to get back to her tent and her things where she belonged. The sooner she did, the sooner she could work for her own cache. She'd been away for such a long time, someone might have tampered with her gear, and she needed to check.

"I'm going back to Kansas. Jonah would have wanted me to," Martha said softly. "You are the only one here who helped me and Jonah, the only one. I'll never forget your kindness to me. I saw that you paid the undertaker with the promise of your fifty pounds of flour. I know what that costs. I need to pay you back in kind, Abigail."

Abigail pulled her hands from Martha's.

"No need," Abigail muttered self-consciously. She didn't look the widow in the eye but stared down at her own sodden boots.

"I need to do this, Abigail, for my sake and yours. You're going to the gold fields, and I'm not. What am I supposed to do with all of this?" Martha asked as she gestured to the crates and piled goods stacked close by. "I can't get back home without your help. I want to sell the goods you don't need, and get the money to go home. Will you help me do it?" Martha pled.

People scurried past the two women, sometimes bumping them with the end of a number-two shovel or the edge of a cumbersome crate. People yelled in argument or giving orders. Dogs barked. Horses neighed. Men cursed. Hammers banged. Steam engines bellowed. Campfires burned. Women kept to their tasks in silence, intent on their day.

"Only if you let me pay you back," Abigail finally answered. She fumbled in her jacket and skirt pockets for pencil and paper to write down Martha's address in Kansas. All she had was Elias's note. She gingerly pulled it from her deepest of pockets. Spreading the paper out full, she turned it over to the blank side. "Do you have a pencil?" Light snow fell. Abigail worried about the snow. She didn't want the note to get wet.

"Here," Martha said and pulled a marker pencil from her jacket pocket.

Abigail bent down, went inside Martha's tent, and spread Elias's note on a smooth crate surface. Martha followed her inside and did Abigail's bidding, quickly writing down her full name and where she could be reached in Kansas. Abigail took up the note and carefully replaced it in her pocket with her treasured gold nugget; not wanting the two separated.

The two women forged a plan to sell Martha's goods in Dyea. Abigail would take what she needed to finish supplying her goods for a year; that and no more. Choked up by this unexpected fortune, Abigail realized she didn't have to stay in

Dyea and work after all. She didn't have to chance spending the rest of the winter in the same town as Elias before beginning her journey up the Golden Stairs.

CHAPTER EIGHTEEN

"Which one of these ladies is your left-handed wife?"

Elias looked up from behind the bar at the man standing in front of him. Medium height, medium build, wool suit and vest, white-collar shirt, flat brim, medium-crown hat, black hair and beard, about thirty-five years old, lit cigar in hand, easy smile, con-man eyes, and razor-sharp attitude.

"Who wants to know?" Elias asked, already suspicious that his new customer was Soapy Smith.

"Name's Jefferson Randolph Smith."

Elias wasn't happy to be right. "Well, Jefferson Randolph Smith, you want a drink or the door?" Elias asked in a flat voice. Most men went by first names only in saloons, but this customer wasn't like most. Elias usually left his customers alone and didn't ask questions. Curiosity could get a body killed, no matter on which side of the bar he stood. Elias set his jaw.

Soapy Smith puffed on his cigar a few times, then crinkled the corners of his mouth into a smile.

"That's not very friendly, barkeep. I was under the impression you ran a friendly place," Soapy intoned evenly. "These ladies of yours appear friendly. Which one is yours?"

"This is no hook-shop. No mistress for any price in my place. The drink or the door, Soapy; which will it be?"

"Give me a shot of your tarantula juice, Elias Colt."

"Don't serve that here."

"My mistake," Soapy corrected with an easy smile. "Give me

a shot of your *fine whiskey.*"

Elias poured a glass for the notorious con man, setting the shot square on the bar in front of him. He knew Soapy had to be heeled and carried a gun. Elias noticed the two men standing behind Soapy were the same ones who'd been here before, checking out his place. Elias had his six-shooter holstered and a loaded Winchester resting on the shelf below. He wasn't nervous about this situation. He was mad.

Soapy finished his shot and gestured for one more.

"That'll be four bits," Elias said.

Soapy laughed to himself, then took the right coins from his vest pocket and set them on the bar with the same care a gambler might use to place his bet.

"Let's have us a friendly conversation, Elias Colt. Pour yourself a drink and we'll talk business."

"I know about your kind of business. It's not how I run things." Elias held his temper. He didn't cotton to cheaters, big-time or small-time. Soapy was big-time, but he'd bleed the same as a small-time cheater. It wouldn't do any good to go for the deputy marshal. Elias figured the law had already been bought off.

"Well that's real disappointing, Elias Colt," Soapy told him, then downed his second pour. He made no pretense of smiling. "Reckon you've heard of me," he said and scratched his bearded chin. His men moved in to stand on either side of him.

Elias glanced around the crowded room, looking for any more of Soapy's gang, but it was hard to tell on this busy night. Elias caught Nate Farley's eye and sent a nod to alert him. Nate left the restaurant side and slipped to the saloon side. Elias had two dealers who doubled as guards. Nate tapped them both on the shoulder, then stood by the front door of the Trail, watching for any more trouble. The dealers kept one eye on their faro play and the other on the action at the bar, ready to pull out their guns and back up their boss.

"You want to stay open, you do business with me," Soapy spelled out to Elias.

"Is that a fact?"

Soapy chuckled.

"I took you for smarter, Elias Colt, a fella like you who's sitting pretty with your place here. The take has to be good. If you want to keep all this gold dust coming in, you do things my way, and nobody gets hurt."

Elias guessed Soapy had already stopped by most of the saloons in Dyea and intimidated them in the same way and with the same threats. From most accounts Elias had heard, Soapy worked under the table with his con operation and didn't come right out and tell people to pay up or pay dearly. Hell, Soapy had taken over Creede and most of Denver with his con. Elias wondered how many folks Soapy had hurt in Colorado, sending them out of the game without a nickel left, or sending them to an early grave. Elias believed Soapy had the law in Dyea and Skagway in his pocket, or else he wouldn't come in like this to the Trail.

"Hurt, you say?" Elias finally shot back.

"Now we're talking business," Soapy said with a wry smile on his bearded face.

"I run an honest place here. I don't like cheaters. You're a cheater, Jefferson Randolph Smith. The only 'business' you'll have with me is at the end of a gun." Elias looked Soapy in the eye and didn't blink.

Soapy stood back from the bar and eyed Elias the same way.

"I'm right sorry to hear that, Elias Colt."

Elias slipped his hand to his holstered gun. His dealers stopped their game play and followed suit. The piano player ended his tune, and the noise in the saloon dulled. Soapy Smith stood at the bar with his men. Word spread quickly around the bulb-lit room. A few men recognized Soapy, and a few had already been taken by him.

Elias didn't like long conversations. No good came from 'em.

"Your move," he called.

Soapy took his eye off Elias and looked around him, then fixed his gaze back on Elias.

"Appears your customers are smarter than you," he said and chuckled.

"Your move," Elias repeated.

"I'll fold this hand," Soapy said, yielding, "but our game ain't over."

Elias relaxed his gun hand, yet kept it positioned over the familiar steel.

Soapy turned around and left. His men followed.

Elias stood behind the bar for long moments before he took his hand from his holstered pistol. A lively piano tune replaced the silence. The saloon girls milled around in the crowd of miners, smiling and asking for drink orders. Table play resumed. The guards went back to dealing, and Nate went back to the restaurant side of the Trail. Everything looked normal. Boomtowns always returned to normal after such goings-on.

Elias exhaled and reset his jaw, relieved no one had been hurt in his place tonight. He'd need to keep a sharper eye out, now that Soapy Smith was back in the area.

Weeks had passed, and Elias had still heard no word about Abigail. Elias was worried about her safety. He hadn't gone out looking for her but thought maybe he should. 'Course he didn't expect her to come by and see him. She'd given him the mitten. It gnawed at him that he'd let her get to him. It gnawed at him more that something might have happened to her and he'd never know. He'd stayed close to the Trail, on the lookout for Soapy Smith or any of his gang.

Word had come from Skagway that Jeff Smith's Parlor opened for business. Despite setting himself up in Skagway, Elias didn't doubt Soapy and his gang patrolled in Dyea, too. He just hadn't seen any sign of 'em near his place since the con man came in over a month ago. That didn't mean the post office, freight companies, supply houses, steamship agents, restaurants, hotels, or other trades and saloons had been left alone. If Soapy hadn't set up some kind of a swindle involving the businesses, he'd likely intimidated them out of half their profits. Too many stampeders still waited in Skagway and Dyea for the Yukon River freeze to break for Soapy to miss out on what he could get from them first.

Elias made the rounds in his place, letting his staff know he'd be gone a couple of hours, and put his guards in charge. He grabbed his cattleman's jacket and flat-brimmed hat, then headed outside into the cold February afternoon to search for Abigail.

Elias checked his pocket watch. *Eight o'clock.* He needed to get back to work, but he'd come up empty in his search. No sign of Abigail anywhere. He'd checked every business on every block, expecting to run into her. As far as he knew, she didn't have her full store of goods, and he believed she had to be somewhere in Dyea earning the money she needed. No saloon gal. No entertainer. No sign, period, of her working in places he expected she might. If she were a man with a number-two shovel in hand, she'd find work easily. She'd dressed in female clothes and not miner's when he'd last seen her. He thought she'd stay in the same clothes to get a job for which a female would be hired. Saloons and theaters and brothels hired females all the time.

Elias didn't like the idea of any man touching Abigail but him. In fact, the thought made him edgy. Her slender body fit *him.* Her sapphire blue eyes shone for *him.* Her shimmering black hair entwined around *him.* Her soft, giving mouth opened for *him.* Her essence filled *him.* She'd given herself to him. He was her first, he knew. He needed to be her last. The fragrance of her body and sweet spirit lingered still. Elias's every muscle tensed, his senses caught up in Abigail's soft hold on him. He was in love with her, and there was nothing he could do about it.

He hadn't checked the rows of tents near the wharf yet!

The late hour didn't deter Elias, so he charged toward the Taiya River and the wharf. Abigail had to be housed in one of the tents, guarding her cache. He'd only make sure she was all right, he told himself, grateful that he'd at last thought where to find her.

In two hours' time, Elias stood back behind his bar, serving up drinks and watching the doors for any signs of trouble. He'd checked every tent and walked every foot of the beaches, looking for Abigail. Disappointment and regret was all he'd come up with. Right now he tried to keep his mind on his job and not on the possibility Abigail might be gone—or worse—dead. The Trail was full of people, but Elias felt alone in his worry. He hated himself for having let her go when she'd needed his help. Two times he'd let her go; first in Seattle, and then from his bed. His insides twisted over not finding her. He'd never hurt so bad, not like this.

"I'd like a whiskey," the cheechako miner ordered, "and one for my friend here."

Elias mutely set a glass in front of each man and poured their drinks. He didn't scrutinize their faces to see if they were suspicious; he just waited for his next order. He felt like hell and wanted this night over with.

"I'm dang glad to be back, Seth," one of the young men said.

"Canyon City's rough enough. Don't think goin' yonder to the Yukon is worth it. No, sir."

"Yep, I agree. These mud pipes of mine wouldn't last in any toad strangler on the trail come spring," the other responded. "It's bad enough with all the snow and mud in the narrows at Pleasant Camp. A big rain comes, and that's all she wrote, far as I'm concerned."

"You still riled over that girl what showed you up, Seth?"

"Me? Naw," the greenhorn miner answered.

His friend laughed.

"Yep. Yer still riled," he joked. "She done went right past you with her gear, load after load. A pretty gal, too."

"She wadn't dressed like any pretty gal," Seth muttered.

Elias listened more closely to their conversation.

"Thought I'd bust my gut when she pulled her pistol on you, thinkin' you took somethin' from her cache."

"I was just tryin' to help, that's all. She didn't need to go and get all mad over a fella tryin' to help her."

"Left you in her dust; that one did. You ain't never gonna get over it," his friend taunted.

"Seth?" Elias pointedly interrupted their conversation, trying not to get his hopes up. "Did you catch the name of the gal on the trail with you?"

"No, sir," the greenhorn answered sheepishly, seemingly embarrassed at being overheard.

"Can you tell me what she looked like?"

"Uh, pretty. Black hair, blue eyes, skinny, dressed like a miner but movin' like a girl," he said.

Abigail. Elias's pulse picked up.

Seth's friend started to laugh again at the phrase, "movin' like a girl," as if admitting a girl had bested him.

"And she pulled a pistol on you?" Elias remembered when Abigail pulled a pistol on him. She'd looked mad enough to shoot him and the boatman, too.

Seth nodded yes.

"So she's all right," Elias said to himself. "How long ago did you see her?"

The two greenhorn miners exchanged puzzled looks about Elias's interest in the girl on the Chilkoot Trail.

Elias noticed and momentarily stepped back. He wanted to ask more questions about Abigail, but didn't want to scare the two off.

"Another round on the house, boys?"

The pair brightened at this surprising offer and shoved their glasses toward Elias. He waited for them to sip their whiskey. They were cheechakos, all right. Neither one probably had a clue what they were in for when they joined the Klondike rush. Probably farm boys or ranch hands who believed what they'd read in the newspapers and expected gold nuggets would be waiting on the ground and in creek beds for 'em not far outside Dyea or Skagway, instead of five-hundred miles up steep trails and over dangerous rapids to reach Yukon gold diggings.

"I was plum surprised to see so many winter stampeders camped out, 'specially in the narrow canyon." Seth finished his drink and talked more to his friend than Elias. "The bridge crossings held 'em up, I reckon, what with the Taiya River either floodin' or freezin' up. It's a gall-dang mess, I know that much."

"Look how long it took us to move our gear to the canyon camps, Seth. The rest is just gonna get rougher," his friend opined.

"How long since you left the canyon?" Elias asked in an easy tone.

"Took us a whole week," Seth readily answered.

"And you still ain't over that pretty gal showin' you up," his friend kidded again. "Left out of the canyon right after that," he said and had another laugh.

Elias stopped listening after that. Abigail had been alive and doing all right a week ago. That meant she'd gathered enough of her cache together beforehand and had carried it seven miles to the first camps on the trail. How she'd managed to do so in winter puzzled him. How she'd managed to supply her ton of goods puzzled him. How she'd managed to do any of this at all had him stumped. Maybe he shouldn't be surprised. She carried her own pistol and her own burdens. Elias leaned against the heavy mirror at his back, his emotions raw.

Abigail took care of herself when he wanted to take care of her. He'd never have the chance now and blamed himself for not trying to find her before. *Holding her, I held everything.* His arms ached without her in them. He shoved away from the mirror and tried to swallow past his own vow, the gaming life but never a wife. He hurt bad and knew this night wouldn't end anytime soon.

CHAPTER NINETEEN

Abby's notebook poked out the side of her backpack, and she tried to shove it back, in a hurry to get to the ranger station and hop on her transport to Dyea. She stopped short. The notebook reminded her she had letters inside to mail to the School of Mines. At this moment, she regretted not bringing her laptop with her to Alaska since she was going back in time when computers didn't exist. She'd promised to submit her articles and postings to the National Academy of Engineering and the *Oredigger* after each internship experience. She'd promised "to identify challenges faced by our world in the past (as opposed to the present)." She'd convinced Mines that gold-rush history would be a valuable freshman internship option in the Grand Challenges Scholar Program. She didn't have her laptop to simply email the school. Snail mail would do, but if she didn't mail her articles, she couldn't make her case. Wasn't this why she'd come to Alaska in the first place?

No, it wasn't, she admitted. *It's not my reason but my excuse.* Even so, she had to find a post office, and quick. An American flag waved in front of a building down the block. Abby guessed it to be the post office and made a dash down the tourist-filled street. Suddenly everything around her irritated her and set her nerves on edge. She never liked to be late or behind in anything, but she seldom allowed things to bother her this much. This unwanted disorder in her life, all at once and all the time, where figures moved in and out of her conscious and subconscious enough to blur fact and fiction and make her doubt herself . . . had to end!

It wouldn't, she knew, until she got through this summer of ghost mining and ghosts, wanted: dead or alive.

"Hey, everybody, gather round." Ranger Jake welcomed the newest hikers to Dyea Campground. "I'd like to introduce Abby Gray, a student from the Colorado School of Mines, who will hike the Chilkoot Trail with us."

Abby raised a self-conscious hand in acknowledgment. She fought the urge to pull her North Face beanie down farther over her ears.

"Abby's looking to be a gold miner, same as the one-hundred-thousand stampeders who took to this trail over a hundred years ago, and one of the thirty thousand who made it all the way to the Yukon. She's going to take our Klondike gold-rush history back to Colorado and her engineering school, which was founded in its own gold-rush country. A lot has changed about gold mining due to modern technology, but the basics stay the same. That's what we're all doing here—getting down to the basics," Jake Newman proudly claimed.

The hiking group of ten—one couple in their fifties, one in their twenties, three college-age buddies, and a family of three—paid careful attention to the ranger's opening talk about their journey ahead. Other hikers with permits, and walk-ins needing permits to hike, had taken up the remaining campsites, of which there were twenty-two in the entire Dyea base. Those independent hikers didn't listen to Jake, but kept busy setting up their own gear. The ranger stationed at Dyea Campground for the summer months would give Abby specific instructions and advisories about the trail later.

"The Chilkoot trailhead is a half mile from here," Jake pointed out. "I want you all to imagine stepping back in time to eighteen ninety-eight when you take your first step on the Chilkoot. The moment you arrived in today's Dyea, you stepped into a living history museum. This entire national park region, in the United States and in Canada, is a living history museum. The Chilkoot will take you back into a history of danger, hardship, and heartbreak, all faced by the stampeders on their journey up the Golden Stairs."

The group stared, transfixed by the ranger's words, as did Abby.

"Mind you, the stampeders didn't have polyester clothing, winterized waterproof boots, modern-day camping equipment, warming tents waiting to give shelter, meals packed in powdered ounces ready to cook, energy bars, and water bottles, Advil for muscle aches, updated weather reports with details of conditions ahead, or guides like me. Those fortunate enough to afford a Tlingit packer could rely on them to help with goods and help them survive the treacheries ahead."

Abby thought of Tommy at the musher's camp. She easily imagined him guiding stampeders to safety. This whole passage began with the native Tlingit—their home, their trail, their pathway over the summit. The Tlingit issued the first permits to climb the Chilkoot. They didn't value gold, but trade to the interior with the Athabascans, Abby understood. The Tlingit paid a heavy price for their generosity. No amount of gold given them today could make up for the losses they suffered.

"We're going to climb the Chilkoot and traverse thirty-three miles to Lake Bennett, in five days, and then we'll take the White Pass and Yukon Railroad back down thirty-eight miles to Skagway instead of going another five-hundred miles down the Yukon River to the gold fields," the ranger said, staying on history. "The railroad reached Bennett from Skagway in eighteen ninety-nine, and Whitehorse the next year, which meant the end of Bennett. Railway lines mark history the same way telegraph and telephone lines do. Follow their path, and you won't get off course."

Jake must be a history teacher, Abby guessed. She'd make sure and ask.

"Stampeders couldn't make this trek in five days. It often took months to haul their gear from Dyea to the summit and the waiting Canadian Mounties. Remember, stampeders hauled what poundage they could carry themselves up the trail to a cache point, then went back for more of their goods. They had to haul the so-called ton of goods established by the Mounties, who knew many people would die of starvation if they did not. Stampeders had to go back and forth, forty times or so, to haul what weight they could in five-mile clips on average. Why were they so careful with their haul of goods? Forty thousand reasons. That's the cost of their goods in today's market.

"Here on the Chilkoot, some stampeders had dogs, horses, and packers to help with gear, but most carried their own. It didn't matter the season. Every day was either rain-soaked, trail-flooded, mosquito-bit, snow-blinded or heart-wrenched. Seventy thousand stampeders turned back and couldn't go on. Unknown numbers died. You're all about to take to the same trail, and I know you'll carry the same respect for the stampeders as I do each step of the way."

A rush of excitement shot through Abby as she listened to Jake's description. She'd imagined herself here before, and climbing the Golden Stairs. How amazing it was that so many women had tackled this challenge so many years ago. If only she could have been one of them. Time stood still in her head and heart, as she envisioned such possibility. She should keep listening to Jake, but she couldn't concentrate on him as she was too busy climbing each golden step in her mind's eye. All of a sudden everything went blank!

Abby blinked a few times to get her concentration back. When that didn't work, she shut her eyes and waited for clarity to return, sure that it would. Long moments passed before she dared opening her eyes. The instant she did, she found herself in swirls of blurring snow. Her ears rang in alarm, and her chest hurt. Abby shuddered in the freezing panic of this ghostly bubble. She'd had similar imaginings before and knew they would pass. It took effort, but she found a deep breath, then shut her eyes against the fiction playing out in her head.

"Abby, let's help everybody get their tents set up for the night," Jake said. He'd ended his talk with the necessary warning about bears and how to keep the campers and their food safe.

Abby opened her eyes and immediately followed Jake to help with tent setup, relieved that everything appeared normal. No storm swirled around Dyea Campground. There was no reason for alarm. Drained emotionally, Abby worried about how her thoughts could so easily spin out of control. *The unexplained* can *be explained. I'm here for answers. I'm not going crazy, but ghost mining. I'll find the facts behind this fiction. I will!*

Eli rounded the corner behind an RV parked at Dyea Campground and stayed out of Abby's sight. She looked so lost. He wanted to take her in his arms and comfort her. If only he could. He wanted to tell her everything would be all right, but he wouldn't lie. Things might not be all right.

The late June day eased into nighttime without the campers at Dyea Campground giving this much notice. They were all too busy getting ready for bed and too excited about their trek in the morning to pay much attention to Alaska's summer skies. It was still fairly light out. Some might notice nightfall when they tried to shut their eyes against its gentle glow. Hikers had to bring their own firewood and water to this first camp, where pit toilets were in place and garbage receptacles had been provided. Several fire rings still burned, with a handful of campers circled around and quietly talking about tomorrow's trek. Polar fleece jackets protected them against the cool evening. The multiple tents erected on planked, ten-by-ten sites, were reminiscent of gold-rush days, when stampeders would set up encampments on Dyea's beaches. That's where any similarity ended, except for following the same trail come morning.

Abby stood by her tent and looked out over this camp setting, watching campfires flicker and listening to the easy conversations. Most of her group had already gone to bed, and she knew she should do likewise. She didn't want to be by herself or go to sleep yet. She didn't trust her dreams. And right now she couldn't trust herself. The handsome westerner wanted something from her. He didn't want her. By this time she realized she wanted him for a boyfriend and more, despite the fact he had to be a ghost. She dealt in facts and had to accept this ghostly reality.

Agitated and confused, Abby slipped inside her tent and sat down hard on her sleeping bag, fighting back tears over her pitiable circumstance. Crying over a ghost! A stranger, at that! She couldn't. She wouldn't, but she did. She cried softly into her hands, then turned and buried her face against her down sleeping bag so no one would overhear her sobs.

I am no beauty. If I were, he might want me.

This thinking brought on more tears. Her father had told her she wasn't a beauty all her life. Her intellect made her question his reasons, but her emotions ruled over this situation. She pulled her North Face cap snug over her ears, not wanting to hear her father's taunts. She'd never cared about how she looked until now—now that she cared for a handsome ghost who stepped out of dreams and into her reality.

Exhausted and out of tears, Abby sat up and wiped her face

with her fleece sleeve. *Sniffle. Sniffle.* She had to buck up and deal with the situation, no matter how many times she wanted to cry. If she could get through this climb and this summer, she'd be all right again. Once back at Mines, there'd be no time for these pseudoscience meltdowns. No more ghost chasing after this, she lectured herself. No more wanting any kind of boyfriend! *I've done just fine by myself, a girl alone.*

"I'm here for reasons I don't understand," Abby whispered. "I'm afraid of tomorrow." The unnerving realization hung in the stiff air and didn't make a move. She couldn't chase away the emptiness inside her, how helpless she felt, and how alone. She'd no compass for direction or scientific principle to guide her out of this blur of confusion. No one could help her get through it.

No one helped the stampeders. They were probably afraid of tomorrow, exactly as she felt tonight, before the next day's climb. Uncertainty followed stampeders every step along the way. Men and women carried their own burdens up the Chilkoot. *So will I,* she vowed, determined to face her fears. It would be foolish to turn back after having come this far.

"Good night," she whispered through her tent flap to no one at all, then crawled inside her sleeping bag intent on getting some rest.

"Good night, darlin'," Eli whispered in a static-coated rasp. He'd stand outside her tent the night through, but she'd leave in the morning without him. It had to be. Voices carried down from the heights of the Chilkoot, and Eli could hear them still. He didn't call back in answer; the distance too great. Everything was up to Abby now.

Abigail couldn't afford to hole up in Pleasant Camp or Canyon City and wait out the rest of winter. The Taiya River froze up here, enough to make crossing it a peril. She should have stayed in Dyea another month for obvious reasons, but she'd refused. Being so close to Elias, yet so far away from him, hurt too much. She'd rather suffer the pains of the Chilkoot in winter than the pain of longing for Elias. Someone like him would never want someone like her. Elias could have any girl he wanted, any proper lady, or any girl working the line. What was she? *I don't work in brothels, but I'm no kind of lady. I'm a girl in boy's clothes wanting to count for something more than callused hands and empty pockets.*

Abigail wanted to count for more to Elias Colt.

She never would.

"Consarn you, get outa the way!"

Abigail didn't budge from her spot in the narrows of the canyon. Hundreds of miners had dragged and carried supplies along this same route and camped, as she did now. The snow and mud slowed all of them down, but the line up the trail kept moving at a snail's pace. She wasn't about to give up her hard-fought place in line. The trail here narrowed, and there was little room for horse or human.

"I said vamoose, you son of a bitch!"

Abigail might consider making a path for a horse or dog sled, but not this sour stampeder.

"Get in line like the rest of us," she told him. She didn't yell.

"Hell, there ain't no line, you cussed excuse for a miner!"

Abigail stood to her full height of five-foot-three and reached inside her heavy jacket for her pistol. If she had to make threats, she would. The dark night didn't help the situation. She couldn't see much in front or behind her, due to the wind and snow. She worried her supplies might get ruined.

"Hear me out, *Miss Nancy*! You git, or you'll be sorry," the lout threatened.

He thought her a Molly. It wasn't the first time someone had mistaken her for a man with girly ways. Moving deliberately,

217

she pulled her pistol out and pointed it at him.

"Get in line like the rest of us," she said a second time.

The angry stampeder looked stunned.

Abigail tried to read him and what he might do next. Wind batted at her face and made her blink. She couldn't afford to blink at the moment. Tense, she held her ground.

"G. Rover Cripes," he grumbled and took a step back.

Abigail watched him turn around and climb over the supplies and people behind her, until he disappeared from sight. Thoughtless man! Thoughtless world! Bitter tears welled in her, despite the freezing temperature. *Few folks on the trail are kind,* she lamented in a heavy exhale. Abigail thought of those who'd shown kindness to her in life and could count them on one hand: the aging miner in Cripple Creek, Mary at the Women's Exchange, Amos from the *Rocky Mountain News,* Maud and her troupe, the Tlingit in Dyea, and the widow Martha. She purposely left Elias off her list when she knew better since he'd shown her kindness, too.

An even sharper, high wind assaulted Abigail and forced her to hunker down with her goods in the unfriendly ravine. She'd struggled for weeks to get her cache to this point, and exhaustion set in fast. Come morning she had to get moving again. No going back. No reason to. Despite the hundreds of thoughtless stampeders on the same trail where speech was silver and silence gold, she had to press forward with what she could carry, load by load, step by step. Determination filled her emptiness and motivated her on.

She imagined the Golden Stairs and her first glass step.

CHAPTER TWENTY

The Yukon River had begun to thaw. Signs of spring motivated stampeders waiting in Dyea and Skagway to leave at once. Hundreds became thousands taking to the trails. Over one thousand a week arrived in the boomtowns to begin their climb. Beaches turned more chaotic, and the trails were jammed. The warmer temperatures melted snow-packed, permafrost trails to mud and slush, with some sections suddenly flooded. Conditions never eased. Animals broke. Men broke. Still, the black line in history up the Chilkoot and the sorrowful line up Dead Horse Trail kept on moving.

It might be a sunny day, a foggy day, or a stormy day along the ascent. The sun brought warmth but also trouble. Melting snow at these heights caused new dangers for stampeders, many of whom were unfamiliar with the hazards of such a slippery slope. A wrong move could bring a quick death. Whether sourdough or cheechako, most miners attempting to reach the Klondike had never experienced this kind of gold rush, with its inherent dangers of impassable rocks, avalanches, sudden snowstorms, sheer exhaustion, and hopelessness.

In fact, most stampeders couldn't call themselves miners—veteran or greenhorn—but were businessmen, cooks, farmers, policemen, teachers, or clerks; men and women from every kind of trade, from all walks of life, and from many countries around the world. This crush of humanity stretched from boomtown beaches, along sometimes flat but often steep trails, up the

Golden Stairs to lofty summits, then into Canada and the Yukon. After a thirteen-mile sojourn up the Chilkoot, over five-hundred watery miles lay ahead before a fellow reached the gold fields.

Thirty thousand made it. Seventy thousand did not.

A few thousand found ample riches, while a few hundred claimed untold wealth.

Most found only heartache.

Stalwart winter stampeders had kept on their icy move up the Chilkoot with spring stampeders crashing in line behind them, camping along the way wherever they could. They lived on the trail, this steady current of humankind. Camps sprang up, first Pleasant Camp and Canyon City, then Sheep Camp and, last of all, the Scales. The first camps quickly turned into tent towns in which a weary stampeder could get a meal and find a bridge to cross the surging Taiya River that blocked the path upward. If the bridges had not washed away, then there would be a toll to pay. From Canyon City, stampeders might send letters back to the post office in Dyea, yearning to communicate with loved ones back home.

Sheep Camp, eleven miles from Dyea, at 1,058 feet, housed tents dedicated to the restaurant, hotel, saloon, and supply trades. Didn't matter. A stampeder could still be wet, cold, sick, melancholy, or flooded out, even at this established tent city. Exhaustion followed every stampeder and plagued every animal working on the trail. Sheep Camp was stuffed with stampeders jumbled together and trying to catch their breath in such a thick atmosphere. Aerial trams transporting goods from the Scales to the summit were based here, at first horse-powered, then powered by steam. A telephone line connected Dyea and the uppermost camp. Tents stretched from Dyea to Sheep Camp, much as if the two towns connected with no open space between them.

The Scales waited ahead for stampeders after Sheep Camp. Goods were weighed there, ensuring stampeders had enough supplies to pass muster with the Canadian Mounties. Despite having tramway offices, six restaurants, two hotels, a saloon, and several warehouses, this was a wretched place, as some people described it. From this point on, the trail was too steep for animals, yet some dogs were still made to toe the line.

The Golden Stairs lay ahead.

After having traversed a wide snowfield from the Scales, stampeders carried their goods up the forty-five degree, ice-carved Golden Stairs to Chilkoot's height of 3,400 feet. It might take a stampeder six hours to make even one trip. Snowslides threatened and gave no hint about when they might collapse. Clear skies could turn stormy on the next rush of wind and cut off visibility. People caught at this altitude and in such weather were vulnerable. Anything might befall a stampeder before he reached the summit—anything from abandoned supplies to abandoned dreams . . . to an early grave.

Such was the risk taken to find riches in the far-off North; the dangerous gamble made the moment the first cry of *"Gold!"* echoed across America in the summer of eighteen ninety-seven.

Stampeders ran out of Dyea like salmon going upstream to spawn, so many had left with the spring thaw. *Then they die, the salmon that is,* Elias thought. He struggled to keep his mind on fish and not the fact that Abigail was somewhere out there, climbing the Chilkoot, and could die. Two months had passed. If something had happened to her, he'd have no way of knowing. Dammit! Elias got out of bed and lit his kerosene lamp. He didn't have electric lights in his cabin, but did in his saloon. Frustrated, he ran his hands over his face, then through his hair.

God knew he'd tried, but he couldn't let go of Abigail; not

yet, not like this. He couldn't shake the feeling he'd let her down. Not a day passed during which he didn't see that look in her sad blue eyes, reaching out to him for something. She hurt; he could tell. Whatever it was he had with Abigail, it had started in Seattle, and it wasn't finished; not to him. He rifled through a drawer for his pack of Old Golds and found a match. A smoke might help him sort this out.

It didn't. He opened his cast-iron stove and tossed the half-burned cigarette in with the embers. Whiskey didn't appeal to him. Drink dulled his guard, and he needed to stay alert with so many of Soapy Smith's gang patrolling in Dyea. They hadn't stirred up trouble in the Trail, but Elias couldn't count on his luck holding out much longer. Jeff Smith's Parlor in Skagway ran the table in both boomtowns. Elias ran his table at the end of his holstered Colt Six-Shooter. Soapy knew he'd use it and had left him alone for a time. The con man would try again. *When my back's turned*, Elias thought.

Soapy didn't grate at him as much as losing Abigail did. He shouldn't have let her go, not from his bed and not up the Chilkoot. If anything happened to her, it was his fault. How the hell could he track her down at this point? What was he supposed to do? Call up to the store, or wherever the telephone line ran from Dyea to Sheep Camp or the Scales, and ask if Abigail Grayce was there? Hardly.

He could take off up the trail. He could do that.

Elias would think about it.

As it was too early for work and too late for sleep, he stoked the fire and got dressed. He strapped on his gun belt and threw on a jacket, needing to get some fresh air and walk out his worries.

Abigail finished with her last forty-pound pack to Sheep Camp, and eased the heavy load off her back onto the slushy ground.

The snowpack, she'd observed to this point, appeared to be melting at a faster rate than she'd expected. Born in the Rocky Mountains, she knew about spring thaw and everything it could bring. Not just mud and slush, but snowslides and flooding. Tension rose inside her at the thought. Caught on this trail, she felt exposed and completely vulnerable to Mother Nature. The Chilkoot Trail didn't welcome any of the stampeders, Abigail included.

All of us will have to fight our way up the Golden Stairs, she believed. The mountains pushed back. An eerie sensation struck her right after she left the narrows of Pleasant Camp and Canyon City. The feeling weighed her down more than her forty-pound pack, each ice-covered, mud-pitted, slush-ridden trip she'd made to move her supplies a little farther every day. More often than not, she felt frozen and couldn't catch much sleep as she tried to keep warm and not lose her fingers and toes. She'd crawl into her sleeping spot and cover herself with every bit of available canvas and wool to keep warm. Socks, blankets, oilcloth . . . anything that might protect her from the cold. Then she'd work her fingers and toes to keep the blood moving, shivering all the while. Sometimes she had a little fire in her stove, but rarely. When she couldn't stand the cold or the loneliness another moment, she'd strike a match and light the candle in her lantern. The glimmer served as her companion on this desolate journey. God help her if she ran out of candles.

Sometimes she thought of turning back, to Elias. She'd chosen the Golden Stairs over him. Yet daydreams of Elias followed her up the Chilkoot—dreams of going back to Elias to ask him to love her—dreams in which he took her in his arms and promised to hold her there forever—dreams he loved her. She'd felt like a beauty in Elias's arms.

It's only a dream, Abigail knew, and she tried to shrug off such fanciful thoughts and get her mind back on the trail. Elias

Colt had every proper lady, every percentage lady, and every lady on the line vying for his attention. Just because he'd taken her to his bed once didn't mean he wanted her forever. Forever belonged in dreams, not here on the Chilkoot.

Sheep Camp bustled around Abigail, pulling her thoughts from Elias and onto the reality of her circumstances. Had all these stampeders passed her on the trail? They must have, since hundreds camped here. Struggling with her own worries up the trail, she hadn't paid attention to others, and for good reason. Men cursed at her, and she practiced ignoring the noise. Few were friendly. Even more stampeders would arrive, what with rivers breaking up and people on the move.

This camp looked like a town, and Abigail hadn't expected it. She had to squint in the afternoon sun. When she peered around her at all the tents set up for business, she spotted a group of Tlingit packers. They traveled this route no matter the season, she knew. They understood the mountains and kept a steady path over them.

One of the men in the group turned, and she recognized him. He'd helped her in Dyea. The Tlingit nodded her way and she responded in kind, heartened to see a friendly face in such an unfriendly place. She watched the Tlingit packer until he disappeared inside a large tent, maybe a warehouse. He'd been hired to pack goods over the summit for some able-to-pay stampeder and stored the goods inside the appointed tent for protection from the weather, she guessed.

Abigail had the same worries about her goods: that they stood in mud and slush. Her supplies could be ruined. She went to work finding more solid ground. The best she could do was to prop pieces of scattered wood under her goods to help keep them dry. The tree line ended at Sheep Camp. She looked up the trail and saw nothing but snowfields and icy ridges, no more trees. Any trees left around Sheep Camp would be cut down, what with so many people working their way here and needing firewood and building materials.

If she'd had the money, Abigail might be tempted to find a restaurant tent and buy supper. Instead, she found her camp stove and picked up a few splinters of wood to get her own cook fire going. Coffee and beans appealed to her; that was a miner's meal. She scooped up handfuls of snow and filled her coffee pot to set on her stove. She didn't feel hungry and hesitated to open her can of beans. Maybe she should wait and save them for when she was really hungry. During most of this trip she hadn't been hungry. No wonder she'd been so cold. Food was fuel. Food also kept weight on her, and she feared she'd lost too much. Reluctantly, she reached for the can of beans and pried it open, then took out a bit of dried fruit from her pack. She needed to eat, hungry or not, if she wanted to make it up the Golden Stairs.

Abby woke up fresh, her spirit for the day renewed, despite her uneasy night. Her hiking group would spend the night tonight at Canyon City Camp, and reach Sheep Camp tomorrow. In five days' time they'd arrive at Lake Bennett and catch the train down to Skagway. In five days' time she would have climbed the Golden Stairs!

"Let's hustle, Abby," Jake called from outside her tent. It was six in the morning and time to get the cook fire going for breakfast. Ten hikers needed to eat a fortifying meal before the day's hike.

"Be right there," Abby answered the ranger and quickly got out of her sleeping bag. Excited to leave Dyea Campground, she couldn't wait to take to the Chilkoot Trail; the start was only a half mile away.

Abby took to the trailhead at the rear of her hiking group, where

Jake had asked her to stay from the outset. He knew she was familiar with Colorado hiking conditions, sudden weather changes, bear danger, and other unexpected pitfalls of high altitude hiking. Her assignment: to keep a close eye on everyone and watch out for their safety. The college buddies heard Jake ask Abby to stay in the back of the line and exchanged surprised looks. No doubt they recognized Abby was their age or younger, and they figured they could just as well bring up the rear as any girl in the same hiking gear. They were probably a little embarrassed. Abby smiled at this. It felt good to smile, and she meant to keep the smile going the day through.

The well-maintained trail led into coastal rain forest with planked bridges over creeks that couldn't be stepped over with ease. Abby adjusted her waterproof hoodie. The straps of her backpack needed a little adjustment, too. She had the weight distributed in the right manner, but something nagged at her. *Like the fairy tale of the Princess and the Pea,* she thought with a chuckle. Before leaving Dyea Campground, she and Jake made sure everyone in their group wore their waterproof slickers as well. It might not be raining, but you could get wet anyway, with large hemlocks and spruce dripping dew all around them.

The trail stayed flat, any elevation negligible. The morning passed quickly for Abby, entranced by the scene unfolding. The path took her past dozens of waterfalls, rushing streams, and beautiful fern-covered ground. Every light step brightened the already sunny day. To at last be on the Chilkoot stirred her spirits and pushed all thought of second-story-window ghosts out of her mind, but not thoughts of the handsome westerner. She caught herself more than once thinking about his ghost, and had to drag her attention back to the ten hikers in front of her. Their safety counted here, not her fanciful dreams of the Chilkoot and its Golden Stairs . . . or her fanciful dreams of finding love.

Sheep Camp couldn't come soon enough.

Chapter Twenty-One

Abigail woke up cold and felt sick to her stomach. Although she was used to the cold, she wasn't used to the ague. She sat up in her tiny tent and pulled the flaps closed. The ties had come loose during the night. It had snowed again. Her aching bones groaned at the thought of finding her shovel and digging her goods out of snow. She'd stayed two days at Sheep Camp, trying to rest and better pack her gear. Strong, warm winds had blown in, but the snows kept up. She wanted to wait for the snow to stop in order to make her first climb to the Scales easier. The Golden Stairs waited for her above the Scales.

Easier? She had to laugh at her choice of words to describe the Chilkoot. Nothing came easy on this gold-rush trail. She couldn't afford to be ailing, although she supposed she'd been lucky not to die so far in some accident or by freezing to death. Dying from disease didn't appeal to her, either. Others had probably fallen on the trail, and Abigail didn't think greedy stampeders would stop to help them. If she died, she'd die alone, she knew. Sick or not, she'd pay more mind to those around her from here on out, and not leave them to die alone. No one and no animal should be stepped over or kicked aside—dead or alive.

Admittedly, she hadn't been exactly friendly to others on this trail. *I've never thought of myself as greedy.* The idea that she might be gnawed at her. Gold in your pocket meant you had independence, safety, and shelter for the rest of your life, at least it did to Abigail. She'd never thought of riches in any way but this. It counted for something to her, to climb the Golden Stairs and at last find the shelter from harm she'd longed for her entire life. She'd do it alone.

Unconsciously, she reached deep inside her jacket pocket and clasped her heart-shaped nugget and Elias's note, squeezing shaky fingers around the treasured bundle. She thought of the nameless miner in Cripple Creek and of Elias, almost wishing them both here with her now. When she caught herself thinking that way, she pushed their memories away and shoved the bundle back inside her pocket. It was time to let them go. She should toss the bundle away, or at least Elias's note, but she hesitated. I will do it tomorrow, not today, she told herself.

Loud chatter picked up outside her tent, and Abigail got up to see what caused the commotion.

"Storm's broken!" Someone shouted.

"Sun's out. Let's go!" Another yelled.

"Hurry, before it snows again!" Still another warned.

The hubbub at Sheep Camp continued over the next hour, with stampeders in a frenzy to collect their gear and head up to the Scales. Abigail watched them for long moments, and then decided to start out herself. Her fever and stomachache wouldn't stop her. Despite being dragged down by days of snowfall and now the ague, the bright sun encouraged her to leave while she had the chance. It might not be smart, but she thought she'd be all right. The Scales wasn't so far ahead that she couldn't make it, even sick and beaten up by the trail. She took down her tent and packed it up, then put on her arctic mittens, heavy wool hat, and snow glasses, before looking to secure the first load she would hoist onto her back.

Dizzy when she stood back up, Abigail waited for the feeling to pass. The ague had got her good. She needed to fight the weakness inside her and get on up the trail. Time was wasting.

It could snow again any time and the trail would be cut off. She shut her eyes to better think about the day ahead and plan her careful steps.

"*Tleik. Tleik.*"

Abigail opened her eyes and recognized the Tlingit standing in front of her—the same one who helped her in Dyea, and the same one she'd seen when she first made it to Sheep Camp. She smiled, glad he'd approached.

"*Tleik,*" he repeated and pointed up the mountain. "*Tleik,*" he said again and shook his head in a no gesture.

Abigail looked up the snowy mountainside and tried to make sense of his meaning. She shot the Tlingit a questioning look.

"*Tleik. Dleit Kaadi,*" he said and affirmed his words with a nod before pointing up toward the Scales again. "*Dleit Kaadi.*"

She gave him a blank look.

The Tlingit pointed at her now, then waved both hands over each other several times to indicate no. He pointed to her again and indicated no.

He doesn't want me to start out, she understood him to mean. Her look of recognition must have been enough for the Tlingit, and he stepped away to go back into the large warehouse tent. She could see he wasn't going to pack today. He must have good reason. Abigail looked around and discovered others also stayed behind and were not packing to head out. Not one Tlingit, she could tell. Not all white packers or all stampeders, either. She ripped off her snow glasses to make sure what she saw.

So, that was it. There was something up ahead, something bad. No, the Golden Stairs lay ahead. If she lingered at Sheep Camp another day, she'd just be sicker and less able to travel, she could tell. The choice was hers, and she made it. She'd go on. She'd survived this far. Every day she took risks, and today wasn't any different.

Abigail repositioned her snow glasses. The snowfields blinded people in the spring sunshine. She took care to shore up the cache she'd leave behind, then settled her heavy pack on her back. The weight brought her spirits down as much as the reality in front of her. She couldn't weigh much more than a hundred pounds at this point. Her burden increased on each hard step she took. She inhaled an encouraging breath and found her place in line up the unforgiving trail.

Abby stopped and read each iron-framed interpretive sign posted along the Chilkoot Trail. She couldn't help but think how helpful such signage would have been to Klondike stampeders in terms of distance and topography. They'd had nothing to go on but their dogged spirit and dreams of gold. She wondered how many might have turned back at this point and she decided probably not many had. The rain forest still seemed welcoming. The subalpine terrain only hinted of what might lie ahead.

Abby's welcome to Canyon City Camp: a rusted-out boiler. It was the first artifact she'd seen from gold-rush days. She needed to make a note for her article back to Mines. The others in her hiking group had already begun to set up camp for the night near an old log cabin. Jake had mentioned the cabin before and said hikers could use it to dry out, cook in, and warm up. There were bear lockers at Canyon City, too. Word hadn't come down the trail that a bear might be in the area, but no one could take the chance. Food could also be suspended over a high bar to keep it safe. Abby didn't see any droppings or sign of bears so far.

"Good first day, I'd say." Jake came up to Abby when she filed into camp. "Any problems on your end?" he asked.

"No. No one in our group stopped for as long or as often as I did," she admitted.

"I thought you were taking a little time there, Abby, but I understand. There's a lot of history to take in here."

"And beauty," she said.

Jake sent her an agreeable nod.

"You did just fine today, watching our line of stampeders up the Chilkoot," he told her.

She smiled, happy to finally be on her way up the Golden Stairs.

"Get yourself settled and help me get dinner going for this hungry group," Jake asked of her.

"Be right there," she assured him, then picked a spot to set up among the campers already circled near the log cabin.

"Hey, Abby," one of the college buddies greeted her. "How's it going?"

"Hi, Matt. Good," she said and plopped her gear down.

"Here, let me help you with that," he offered and jumped up quickly.

"I can—"

Matt had already taken her tent from her and started to set it up before she could say another word. She didn't need anybody helping her.

"So, you go to the School of Mines?" he said, making easy conversation while he worked.

"Yes."

"A freshman?"

"Yes . . . well, no. I'm a sophomore."

"Me, too. I go to CU. We're not far away from each other," he pointed out, giving her a wink at the irony of the moment. He wasn't just referring to the short distance between Golden and Boulder. "There. Done." Matt finished and stood up.

"I need to help Jake get dinner. Thanks again, Matt," she said and took off. She wasn't good at this sort of thing . . . talking to guys. She didn't want to give him a chance to say anything more. He seemed nice enough, just trying to be friendly. He made her uncomfortable anyway.

Too excited about tomorrow, Abby couldn't sleep. The summer night had turned cold. Snug in her down sleeping bag, the chilly temperature didn't keep her up. Thinking about tomorrow's climb to Sheep Camp did. Fog could move in, or rain, even snow. It was the same in Colorado at this altitude. Abby imagined herself camping in this very spot during the Klondike rush. Would she have traveled in a party the same as now or would she be alone, like so many of the old miners had been? Alone, she thought. No, she *knew* she'd be alone. Things wouldn't be different in a different life. She shrugged off her somber mood and focused on the coming day.

Tomorrow would be a good day. She could feel it in her bones.

The views opened up as Abby ascended toward Sheep Camp. The elevation gradually rose. The climb remained relatively easy, despite rough, rocky sections and boot-grabbing boggy spots. She might be the only one on the historic trail, the way it felt to her now. The allotted number of hikers covered the trail, but no more than fifty per twenty-four hours. During Klondike days, the number would have been in the thousands, stretching from Dyea to Sheep Camp. Eleven miles of humanity, crowded together in hostile conditions, no matter what time of year.

Abby strained to search out artifacts between the camps. Reportedly at higher elevations, broken teapots, wagon wheels, horse bones, shoes, and even graves could be spotted. It was possible she'd discover any of those artifacts at lower reaches, and she meant to keep a sharp eye out. *Especially for graves,* she suddenly thought and felt goose bumps rise at the notion. The Slide Cemetery was miles away at this point, and she had no reason having goose bumps. She pulled up short and rubbed her arms to chase away the eerie sensation.

"Abigail . . . Abigail . . ."

She refused to turn around and see who called out. She refused to be held captive to ghosts and had to stop thinking they were following her up the Chilkoot! Besides, she hurt inside thinking about ghosts. Unexplained things were just that: unexplained things. She couldn't assign any more meaning to her situation than that. If she wanted to find answers, she needed to keep a cool head and not give in to fantasy. The hair at the back of her neck bristled as if something had come too close for comfort.

Abby took deliberate steps up the trail and kept a wary eye out for bears. Matt and her group hiked farther up the trail. She'd best catch up and keep her guard. A fine lookout she was, worrying about ghosts and not real people in real danger. She pushed her North Face beanie cap just off her ears and tuned in to the forest, listening for any sounds that might alert her to danger. Consciously she listened for bears; subconsciously she listened for ghosts.

Abby followed two paths at this point—one rooted in science and nature, and the other in pseudoscience and apparitions. Somewhere in between she'd find her answers to the unexplained. In her heart of hearts, she knew she had to find out what the handsome westerner wanted from her. She couldn't let him go until she did.

"Abby, what's wrong?" Jake ran over to her the moment he spotted her arrival at Sheep Camp, worried she'd been an hour behind them.

"I don't know," she answered honestly before she slipped to the ground.

Matt watched what happened and came running over.

Jake knelt and removed Abby's pack while Matt supported

her head and shoulders.

Abby didn't fight them. She had no energy. Her body had given out with no warning. She fought to recall what happened. She remembered coming upon what she'd thought to be a grave along the trail. When she bent down and ran a careful hand over the mounded area, she looked up the mountain to an unseen ravine, as if the grave were *there* and not under her shaky fingers. It took everything in her to get up from that spot and continue up the trail. She'd felt pulled back to the site, which was almost like a magnet refusing to let go. The eerie sensation held her still. Her chest pulled. Her heart felt as if it had stopped, her energy was so low at this point. Numbness set in, not pain.

Jake did a CPR check on Abby, making sure of her breathing and her pulse.

Abby let him, unable to protest or move. She must be sick with the flu. Worthless flu shot! Next year she'd pass on the phony inoculation. Her body ran hot and cold, and her brain wanted sleep.

By this time the ranger stationed at Sheep Camp knelt beside Abby, along with Jake and Matt. The ranger had paramedic training.

"Abby," Kirk Brady said to her after learning her name and listening to Jake's accounting so far. "Can you tell me your last name?"

"Gray."

"Can you tell me where you are?"

"Sheep Camp."

"Can you tell me the names of the two men here with me now?"

"Jake and Matt," she answered, almost irritated. She just needed to sleep!

"Are you in any pain?"

"No."

"Do you have diabetes or any medical problems we should know about?" the ranger quietly asked, meanwhile looking for a medic-alert bracelet and assessing her situation.

"No . . . please just . . . let me . . . sleep," she managed to say.

"No worries, Abby. We'll let you sleep," Kirk assured her. "We're going to help you stand, all right?"

She nodded yes to him and let the three help her up. She felt as if her mind had left her body as she was being moved by others. In her mind's eye, she watched the ranger, Jake, and Matt help her to the warm cabin and then onto the cot provided, and felt removed from the scene. Awash in relief the instant she sensed the canvas cushioning at her back, she could stop watching, stop talking, stop listening, and pass into heavenly sleep.

Eli checked his pocket watch, noting the time Abby arrived at Sheep Camp. The important hour had passed. He'd no way of knowing what happened. Unable to stand still, he took off for Dyea's tidal flats. He needed to walk off his worries.

CHAPTER TWENTY-TWO

Abigail dragged herself and her heavy pack to the Scales. It had taken all day. Others did the same, in front of and behind her. There had to be people still on the trail below her, forced to camp in place for the night. In her mind's eye, Abigail saw the line of stampeders from Dyea to the Scales, unbroken, stretching from camp to camp with people all along the way stopping when they couldn't go another step.

By afternoon they'd all lost the sun, and it was snowing again, making visibility poor. Abigail had trudged through knee-deep white powder, with no idea how much snow had actually accumulated on the trail that day. Footprints in the snow ahead quickly disappeared. Stampeders climbing in front of her made a path, but it got covered over quickly. Abigail couldn't feel her feet anymore, but managed to keep to the trail and reach the Scales. Desperate to set up some kind of camp and get warm in the blinding howl, she fumbled her way around the flat terrain.

Shouts carried through the snow. Abigail couldn't understand the shouts and didn't try to. All she wanted was to get warm and find shelter from the weather. The winds picked up, making it harder to see. Her face numbed at the icy assault of the newest storm. She dropped her gear and pulled her canvas tent and wood posts from the pack. She'd brought little else on this first trip, save what she had on her person and what she thought she'd need the first night. Every pound counted.

Mentally she'd added the weight and brought what she

thought she could manage: a tin of beans, a small sack of dried fruit, the metal cooking sheet of her small, collapsible stove, matches, two candles, her lantern tied to the pack, her shovel poking out, her knife, and her pistol. She'd bring her stovepipe next time. Tired and sick, she didn't even try to carry more. Glad to make it to the Scales, she could hardly believe she'd done so on her own. God knew who helped her. Abigail paused, knowing He must have.

Others set up close by at the Scales; she could see that much at least. Despite their company, she felt alone on this cold mountain. Along the way today, a man's voice called out to her, but no one was there when she turned around. Disappointed not to see Elias, she thought she had to be making the voice up in her head. *I am no beauty,* she'd reflexively lamented, and then turned away from his distant memory and kept to her climb.

Knowing she risked frostbite, Abigail removed her mittens anyway to better set up the wood braces, and stretched her canvas tent from post to post. If she didn't have shelter, she wouldn't survive the night. A few strikes of her shovel pounded each of the posts deep enough to hold in the uncertain glacial bank. The movement caused her head to pound and her gut to wrench worse than before. Her vision blurred and forced her to rip off her snow glasses. This action didn't help much. Her eyes stung from the day's glare.

She strained to see through the wind and flurry, at last able to distinguish the outline of large tents grouped together, and one off to the side. Probably restaurants, hotels, and saloons. Tent towns all looked alike to Abigail; the numbers of their occupants the only difference. The tent off to the side could be the aerial tramway office she'd heard about. The cables and ropes ran from the Scales to the summit. She couldn't make out the lines in this weather. Anyhow, she didn't have money to pay for the aerial tramway service and have her goods carried up the Golden Stairs to the summit.

I have to get 2,000 pounds up from Sheep Camp here to the Scales! The thought overwhelmed her. Her goods would be weighed here, and she needed to have the right amount to continue. Could she do it? Her heart said yes, but her body said no. She needed to get through this first night at the Scales, and then she'd worry about the next, then the next, then the next.

Disheartened and shivering, from the reality of her situation as much as from the cold, Abigail crawled inside her tent. Her teeth chattered and she struggled for calm, at the same time moving her fingers and toes in an attempt to get her blood flowing. How was she to get the rest of her cache to the Scales? In the best of weather and the best of health, her labors seemed endless. In this snowstorm and feeling so poorly, she doubted herself. She couldn't give up when she'd come so far, but in that moment, she realized she might not make it up the Golden Stairs to the gold fields beyond.

Shaking, Abigail curled up on her camp blanket and tried to steady herself. She had her mittens on, her wool cap, and everything else she'd worn up the mountain. Some feeling had returned to her feet, and she worked them harder inside her German socks and boots. She had no wood for a fire. When she felt able enough, she'd pry open a tin of beans and force them down. Keeping even a handful of snow on her stomach would be hard. Maybe she'd have to wait a day and get better before she descended to Sheep Camp for her next load. She choked back tears. If she did that, she'd lose her place in line, and she couldn't afford to miss this one chance to have her own jars of gold dust, and buy the security she'd dreamed of having—her own home and safe shelter.

The storm howled outside. Abigail curled up in a tighter ball to defend against the roar and rumble. It wasn't just the wind; was something else rumbling? It wouldn't be a thunderstorm, but something rumbled like thunder. The ground beneath her shifted. It had to be her imagination. Still shaky, she reached for her lantern, needing the companionable glimmer to keep her company.

Despite unsteady, numb fingers she managed to light a match and then the candle inside her lantern. Its tiny glow brightened her spirits. It was a little thing but it meant everything to her just then. When the glimmer burned out, she'd be left alone on this mountain. She had one more candle and would use them both. She'd bring more next trip. Before she put her mitten back on she unwittingly put her hand inside the deep pocket where she kept her gold nugget and Elias's note, and encircled them in her damaged palm. This motion soothed her, and her shivers diminished.

When Abigail realized what she was doing, she drew her hand out of her pocket. She was glad she hadn't tossed Elias's note away, as she'd thought she would have by now. The candlelight flickered. She watched it. If she wanted, she had enough light to read Elias's note. Instead she reached for the pencil and paper she kept in another pocket, forcing her fingers to work. She needed to talk to someone, to set down her feelings about this night. She could take her letter down to Sheep Camp and put it in the mail for Dyea. This thought brightened her spirits just as the glimmer from her lantern had, and she didn't feel so alone.

Abigail woke up to chaos—to nightmarish screams, frightened curses and shouts, unsettled darkness, pounding snow and freezing temperatures—to hell on earth. Her tent had collapsed on top of her, and its weight nearly suffocated her. She fought for breath and listened to the faint cries around her.

"Grab your shovels!"

"We've gotta dig 'em out!"

"Get up!"

"They're buried!"

"There's not much time! Get up and help!"

"Avalanche! Avalanche!"

People thudded by overhead, Abigail could tell. She felt their vibrations and heard their muffled cries. She struggled to lift herself but couldn't move. She lay facedown and couldn't turn her head to catch her breath. *Dead space!* She didn't have much room to breathe. Her lantern pressed against her cheek and created a tiny air pocket between her face and crushing snow. She sensed the latter, since she couldn't open her eyes. Then she understood . . . *she'd been buried in an avalanche!*

She tried to spit but couldn't. Even if she could move her limbs, if she couldn't spit, she wouldn't know whether to dig up or down. Unable to cry for help, she tried not to panic. She'd wait to die. That's all she could do. She struggled for calm and peace in this deadly moment and regretted not being able to clasp her gold nugget and Elias's note and hold them close. She imagined Elias's arms embracing her, and she let him hold her this last time.

Then she prayed.

The Lord is my shepherd, I shall not want. He maketh me to lie down in green pastures. He leadeth me beside the still waters. He restoreth my soul. He leadeth me in the paths of righteousness for his name's sake. Yea, though I walk through the valley of the shadow of death, I will fear no evil, for thou art with me. Thy rod and thy staff they comfort me. Thou preparest—

"Help me dig here, will ya?"

Abigail heard the faint, disorienting voice well enough to silence her prayer and make her listen through the fog of death.

"Here! Dig here!"

Shovels hit the snow above her, the sound unmistakable. Rescuers! The voices of men who were digging her out of her icy grave. *One of them might be Elias!* But he wouldn't be here;

he couldn't be, she knew.

"Get this tent off, fellas!"

With the weight above lifted, Abigail could breathe.

"He alive?" one of the men asked, having to yell over the storm.

"He's a she, and yes," another rescuer said when he pulled Abigail up from the ground. "What's your name?" he asked, helping clear the snow and debris from her. It still snowed heavily so this did little good.

"Abigail Grayce," she said, more as her own testament of life than to answer the men who'd just saved her. She managed to stand on wobbly, half-frozen feet.

"I'm Archie Burns. Are you all right?"

"Yes." She'd remember his name.

"We could use your help then, Abigail. Can you grab your shovel and help us dig?" he asked, then disappeared into the storm.

Abigail didn't have time to think about having almost died, but tried to get her bearings in the aftermath of the avalanche. It still snowed heavily. She bent to her scattered pack and found her shovel, then automatically checked that her treasured bundle was safe in her deepest of pockets. Strangely, she didn't feel ill as she had last night. The idea she'd survived the avalanche revived her. So did the fact that others cared enough to dig her out. They showed kindness to her when she'd believed no one on the Chilkoot would.

"Over here!" a man shouted.

Abigail saw him and trudged over to the snowbank where he stood, and she began to dig alongside him. The winds howled and made conversation impossible. If anyone buried below her called out, she prayed she'd hear them. Who knew how long they'd been trapped? If the avalanche had just hit, the people buried here could be rescued, she believed, if they had enough air to live. If much more time passed, they would die. She'd almost died. The truth made her dig harder. More rescuers came to help. The frenzy of digging out victims in the swirling storm added to Abigail's panic over their situation.

She'd lost all sense of the time of day or night, or how much air those folks buried had left. More avalanches were likely to be triggered. The rumbles she'd heard before she fell asleep had been snowslides, she realized. Everyone at the Scales faced a grim reality. No place here was safe. Abigail kept digging; digging was the only place she dared put her attention.

The Tlingit knew this. He'd tried to warn me, and I didn't listen. "*Tleik. Dleit kaadi,*" he'd said. *No! Avalanche!* Now she understood his warning. He knew the trail and knew better than to go on under present conditions. She should have known better, but she'd risked leaving anyway. A poor choice; she wondered if she'd live to regret it.

Sometime later all twenty of the buried stampeders had been rescued. No one tried to go back to sleep, for fear another avalanche might catch them unawares. Abigail counted over a hundred people she'd spotted digging and knew there must be more; maybe two hundred who'd already camped or were living at the Scales. In the continuing storm, it was hard to count everyone. Five feet, at least, of new snow had fallen in the past days, she guessed. All that snow and two days of warm winds had created the springtime avalanche danger. The poor choice she'd made in deciding to leave Sheep Camp haunted her.

Screams echoed from across the Scales. Another slide! Abigail rushed toward the mayhem to help dig people out and try to save as many of them as she could. She forced herself to keep moving through her own aches, pains, and exhaustion. The slice across her cheek stung, but the mark was a symbol of the lamp that had saved her life. *Her lamplight had saved her life.* She prayed those buried in the latest avalanche had something of a similar nature to save their lives and provide them with enough air until they could be rescued.

Abigail clutched her shovel. Three people had been buried in the second avalanche, and all had been rescued in time. Twenty-three stampeders had been buried by the two slides, or so the talk circulating across the Scales said. They'd all been lucky. How long would their luck hold? Abigail asked herself. She kept her shovel close and knew everyone at the Scales should do the same.

If more slides hit, she'd have to begin digging instantly. Moving with the slide would be her only hope: to keep hold of her shovel and keep moving, working her body to create an air pocket once the slide ended. After that, there'd be no chance for movement; there would be no air after the slide turned snow into cement. There was no telling how much snow and ice would settle on top of her . . . five feet . . . fifty feet. If she knew the right way to dig, she might survive a five-foot slide but not a fifty-foot one. Rescuers wouldn't be able to get to a person in time if he or she were buried under fifty feet of snow. She forgot about danger from frostbite. If another avalanche hit, her only hope would be to see which way her spittle fell, and then she'd know which way to dig.

The morning light did little to improve visibility. Abigail didn't have a timepiece, but she knew today was Palm Sunday. She should be in church this morning instead of on the Chilkoot facing her Maker. Unbeknownst to her family, she'd sneak off and go to church in whichever mining town they lived. She had a friend in the Lord, and worship always improved her spirits. Her family had bullied and tormented her, but the Lord had always saved her. Would He now?

"Go! Go!" Shouts tumbled down from the Golden Stairs.

"Evacuate!"

"Go down now!"

Slides rumbled down near the Scales, but didn't strike here. Abigail's weak pulse thudded. She stayed put and watched the group of men file down from above the Scales, and listened for more words of warning. It was snowing, but she could make out their figures and felt their panic. She held onto her shovel and waited.

Time has run out for us.

CHAPTER TWENTY-THREE

Goods lay scattered over the Scales as far as Abigail could see through the heavy snowfall. Uncovered tents and snatches of gear from the two-hundred people camped here lay as if remains of the dead. She had half a notion to sit down in the whipping wind and wait for the next avalanche to bury her here, and not heed the calls to leave. Whether she had a grave at the Scales or at Sheep Camp made little difference to her now. But a part of her did want to live.

"Here, grab onto this!" a man suddenly yelled and shoved a length of rope at her.

Abigail took one hand off her shovel and accepted the rope. She couldn't tell if he'd come from the group who'd just descended or had already been in camp. Chaos erupted around her, but she kept her focus on the rope in hand. A man in front of her held onto the same thick rope, as did a man in back of her. People shouted orders.

"Alternate sides of the rope, and don't let go!"

"Take your shovel with you and that's all!"

"We have to get down to Sheep Camp!"

"Get moving!"

The rope jerked, and Abigail fought to get a tighter hold on it. The sudden tug caused her to stumble, but she picked herself up, then somehow scrambled to the other side of the rope, opposite the men in front and in back of her. She lost all sense of anything except for the rope in her wounded hands. How many people held onto this same lifeline, she'd no way of knowing. They all feared for their lives, their terror palpable to Abigail, despite her icy, battered hands and heavy mittens. Fear ran through her as an electric current might.

She stumbled again when the rope dropped down hard, and she struggled to hold on and keep her footing. Yanked along, she took her first step off the level terrain of the Scales and began her descent to Sheep Camp. Snow blinded her. Her sense of confusion deepened. Nothing seemed to have a beginning or an end. The cold penetrated to her bones, numbing her limbs and freezing her hope. Utterly dispirited, she kept going . . . one unsure step after another.

Abigail and some two-hundred other people sharing the rope line had no way of knowing the fate of the twenty crewmen from the Chilkoot Railroad and Transport Company, who, due to poor visibility, had taken a turn off-course into a dangerous ravine. Those same men had made their descent from the summit earlier that morning, shouting warnings to the folks at the Scales and providing them with two-hundred feet of rope to help guide them to safety. Then the crew started their own descent before the roped evacuation commenced at the Scales.

In single file, alternating sides along the rope—the general intent being to have the strongest at the front of the line and the weakest at the rear—frantic stampeders descended the Chilkoot and followed the footprints of the crew that had gone before them. They had no idea the crew had taken a deadly turn.

Instinct forced Abigail's hand off the rope. Willpower forced her forward the instant she heard a terrifying roar crashing behind her. *Stay conscious* was her only thought before impact.

Everything hurt. Everything blurred. Then everything shut down.

Abigail didn't hear the voices buried with her under the snow; those of the people caught up in the same ten-acre avalanche as she. Some victims swore. Some prayed. Some said their good-byes, while some carried on calm conversations. Some stampeders buried by the avalanche had more time than others for hope of rescue.

Elias had spent a restless night. He'd slept little. Worries about Abigail haunted him from the moment his head hit the pillow. He needed to make a decision about whether to go after her or not. The right or wrong in any of this didn't matter; he didn't care if she gave him the mitten again. He dragged himself out of bed and pulled on his clothes. Nate would have the coffee on. Coffee and work might help him figure out what to do.

Today's *Dyea Press* had been tossed on the bar, and Elias picked it up as he sipped his coffee. He set his cup down hard when he read the headline. The news burned more than any spilt coffee might:

Monday, April 4, 1898, Dyea Press
Special Bulletin!

A DISASTROUS AVALANCHE!

First authentic list of fatalities updated.
Complete details as far as can be procured.

MANY ENCOUNTER SUDDEN DEATH
ON THE TRAIL

A snowslide near the Scales engulfs hundreds.

Fearful loss of lives.

Total number of dead reported to be over forty.

Tramway employees declared missing.

List of dead.

Elias seldom got scared, but he was good and scared now. Dread shot through him like a bullet. He fought the urge to throw the paper away and didn't want to read the "List of Dead." But he had to. He strained to bring his blurred vision into focus and read down the list. Abigail's name wasn't on it. He didn't feel relieved. "As far as can be procured," the front page had said. That could mean anything. Abigail could be dead or alive or gone on to the Yukon, for all he knew. He had no idea of her whereabouts. He sure as hell needed to find out it wasn't below the Scales yesterday morning!

"Boss." Nate came up to Elias in a hurry. "You've seen the news? This is bad, real bad."

"Yeah," Elias grumbled. "I'm going up to help, Nate. Will you and the boys watch this place for me? I don't know how long I'll be."

"Sure thing, boss, but I bet there are plenty folks at Sheep Camp to help dig out. Everyone of 'em is bound to have a shovel. No need for you to go unless you're worried about somebody special."

"Like I said, I'm going up to help," Elias made clear.

Nate understood.

"I should make it by nightfall," Elias said. "Tell the others, will you?"

"You bet. Don't worry about things here. Me and the boys will keep old Soapy out." He tried to make a joke of it.

"Don't anybody get hurt over this place, Nate. I don't want anybody else dead," Elias warned. "Got it?"

"Yeah, boss. Got it."

"Appreciate it, Nate. I really do," Elias said and meant it. Nate had his back. Elias had Nate's back and those of his employees. They watched out for one another. It was painfully obvious to Elias that he'd never had Abigail's back. If he didn't find her alive, he'd bury her all proper. If he didn't find her at all—he couldn't think about the likelihood of never seeing her again. He wanted her, dead or alive, and would go to his grave trying to find her.

"Watch yourself, boss," Elias heard Nate call behind him. Elias raised a hand in recognition and never looked back. His gut wrenched. He felt helpless. His Colt Six-Shooter couldn't help him out of this one. He needed to protect Abigail. Elias studied his hands. Empty of his gun, they were all he had to give Abigail. She already had his heart.

Elias was hours up the trail before he realized he was moving forward when no one else was. The line up the Chilkoot had stopped. He'd picked his way past stampeders camped all over the place, scattered from Dyea to Canyon City. He hadn't stopped to talk to anybody along the seven-mile stretch between the two. The day had turned cloudy but didn't snow, and Elias kept on through the muck, mud, and slush. Whether the trail narrowed or widened didn't matter. He didn't have to fight the sun, just the cloying damp and his own fears for Abigail. In four miles' time he'd find her. This single purpose kept his feet sure on the unsure Chilkoot Trail.

His six-shooter came with him. It was a part of him he'd refused to leave behind. A body had to be well-heeled. It was the only way life worked for him. He might need his gun to protect Abigail, after all, he thought somewhere in the recesses of his mind. Although not a praying man, Elias found himself praying.

Dear God, she has to be alive. She can't die on me. Don't let her, all right? Elias bargained with God. His throat seized on him, as he tried to pray for Abigail. He didn't deserve the Almighty listening to him, but Abigail deserved His help. Elias might have one foot in Boot Hill, but Abigail never would.

The trail started to rise and Elias climbed with it. When the going got rough, he toughened himself to changes in the terrain and conditions. He didn't know what to expect next on the Chilkoot. He hadn't thought much about the terrain when he'd set out from Dyea in the early morning. The avalanche had happened yesterday, and there was no telling what was going on at Sheep Camp. No telling how many were dead, how many were alive, or how many had given up a search. Elias set his jaw. He'd never give up searching for Abigail. He was committed to the trail and to her. There was no going back.

Elias made it to Sheep Camp late in the night. The size of the camp surprised him, even though he'd heard about it for months. All he could think about was how much harder it would be to find Abigail in this jam-packed camp than if it were more sparsely populated. People milled about him in every direction, just as in a typical boomtown. But it didn't sound like any boomtown Elias had ever been in before. The silence caught him and made him stop at last, after his eleven-mile journey to get here.

Sheep Camp felt like a graveyard.

All shut down.

It hit him again that Abigail might be dead, lying here somewhere all by herself.

Fear for her made Elias move his feet, one uncertain step in front of the other, as he tried to find the rescue center for the victims of the avalanche. He bumped past a lot of men before he stopped to ask one of them where he could find whatever was being used as a morgue. The undertaker was the last stop in this life. Right now every man who passed him looked to Elias like an undertaker.

"There's a tent set up for the bodies, yonder at the edge of camp. Keep goin' straight past these restaurants and saloons, and you'll run into it," the stranger told Elias.

"Thanks, mister," Elias said and picked up his pace down the crowded tent-and-wood-frame street. Dim lantern light drifted outside from the structures, enough to guide Elias to the make-do morgue. The cloudy twilight sky had turned dark. Elias faced down the street into the grim reality that awaited him at the edge of Sheep Camp.

Once he arrived at the newly created morgue, Elias hesitated to go inside the large tent. Fear held him to the spot. Thoughts of Abigail held him back—thoughts of her tender expression, her hand at his cheek, her bluest of eyes, and her soft curves against him. He didn't want to let go of her image in life, and he was afraid to go inside the morgue and risk seeing her image in death.

"Sorry," a man said when he bumped past Elias to go inside the morgue.

Elias reflexively followed him. He took a deep breath, exhaled, then threw open the flap for himself and entered. Ill-prepared for the grim scene of so much death and misery in one place, and so many people hunched over bodies and their effects, Elias's first instinct was to take out his Colt Six-Shooter and chase all the interlopers away. If any one of 'em picked over Abigail, or probed at her effects, he'd shoot the bastard!

"Help you, son?" A graying stranger came up on him.

"Yeah," Elias heard himself answer and eased his gun hand. "All the bodies in here identified?"

"No. People are going around trying to assign names to bodies. We have a list so far. Who are you looking for?"

Elias cleared his throat.

"Abigail Grayce."

"C'mon over here, son, and I'll check the names we have."

Elias mutely followed him over to a sawbuck desk and fixed his attention on the papers spread there. Lantern light filled the space. It looked like there was more than one list.

"How many lists you got there?" Elias asked, already scared.

"Three now," the man answered and scooped up the slips of paper. "Let's see. On this one there's only one woman, a Mrs. Ryan of Baltimore, Maryland."

Elias didn't move a muscle.

"On this second one there's a woman by the name of Mrs. Anna Moxon of Jefferson County, Pennsylvania," the man read, then looked at the third list.

Elias watched the paper in the man's hand crinkle and he prayed.

"Let's see, son. There's a woman on this list but she hasn't been identified. Sorry, but you might want to go have a look at the bodies here and see if you can find Abigail Grayce. There are more bodies that just came in. They're being brought in all the time. Likely, we'll keep up the search another two days or so, the area of the avalanche being so big. No telling how many are dead," the newly appointed coroner said and shook his head woefully.

"Is there another tent besides this one—with bodies? I mean, if she's not here, can I look somewhere else?"

"Yes, up the mountain on Long Hill, at the Stone house. The Alaska Railroad and Transport Company has turned their engine house for the tramway into a temporary morgue. A lot of men, maybe ten at least, have been dug out near there so far and taken to that morgue."

"Any women, you think?"

The coroner shrugged uncomfortably.

"I don't know. Could be."

Elias tipped his hat brim in thanks to the keeper of the lists and turned to the sea of tarp-covered bodies lining the tent floor. He hated to join in the mix of people hunched over the bodies, but he didn't have a choice.

CHAPTER TWENTY-FOUR

Elias pulled each tarp up off each face of the dead, one after the other, of those for whom no identification had been made. The bodies identified had tags with their name recorded. He bent to the unnamed dead and lifted the cover over them with shaky fingers. The instant he could see the face wasn't Abigail's, he re-covered the face gently as he could, in a rush to go to the next body and find her. But then, he didn't want to find her stone-cold dead. That's what all the faces here were: dead faces. He'd seen dead faces before, but never like this; never lined up in canvas coffins ready for burial on cemetery hill.

There was one face left, one last body to kneel beside, and he hoped it didn't belong to Abigail. The hubbub in the hasty morgue grated on Elias to the point where he couldn't lift the last tarp off this last body. None of this was right. *None of us should be in here going over these bodies like animals going over kills.* He didn't want to pick over any more remains and needed to get out of there. He didn't want to find Abigail under the tarp. So shaken up he couldn't move, he knelt there for long minutes.

"Son." The coroner came up on him. "I'll do this for you," he said and gently lifted the last cover over the last face, for Elias to see.

The face was a woman's face, but it wasn't Abigail's.

Elias spent the rest of the night in a room he'd found, and caught a few hours of sleep. He had his own shovel now to help dig out bodies buried in the avalanche. Who could still be alive after so long a time? No one, he knew. He'd convinced himself Abigail had made it to safer ground on the other side of Chilkoot Pass, and gone on to the Yukon. First thing in the morning, he'd check the morgue on Long Hill just to make sure she wasn't one of the faces of the dead, before he'd pitch in to help dig out more bodies. The coroner had said they'd search for two more days. Elias would stay and do what he could to help. Somewhere inside him, he knew he might put his shovel to the snow and find Abigail's body, but he wouldn't let himself think about it.

Elias dragged himself back to his room at Sheep Camp. He'd been up the past forty-eight hours, helping dig out the dead. None of the faces had belonged to Abigail. Somewhere in the hours and minutes, his mind went numb, and he couldn't think of much but the shovel in his hands. He'd lost Abigail to the Yukon, but she hadn't died a horrible death in the avalanche, buried under fifty feet of crushing snow. He couldn't imagine those moments—the moments before death—for any of those found so far. Bullets showed more mercy than the avalanche.

Sorrow weighed Elias down, and he fell into exhausted sleep.

"What'll it be?" the barkeep asked.

Elias wanted a drink more than he wanted coffee this morning.

"A shot of whiskey," he ordered, then saw another man approaching the bar in the saloon at Sheep Camp. "Make that two."

"That's right friendly," the stranger said and waited for the pour. "Name's Archie."

"Elias." He knew better than to ask a last name. Last names gave away too much about a person's past.

"Say, Archie," said the barkeep. "What's left up at the Scales?"

Elias realized that the two men were acquainted, and that Archie had been up as far as the Scales.

"The slide hit in the ravine below. Up top, we survived the worst of it. A slide hit us earlier in the morning and buried twenty or so. We got everybody dug out of that one and, next thing we know, the tramway crew came barreling down from the summit, telling everybody to get out. Most everybody did," Archie told the barkeep. "We all know what happened after that."

Elias's heart thudded. *Buried twenty or so,* Archie had said.

"Any women in that twenty or so?" Elias asked.

Archie finished off his shot and turned to Elias.

"One at least. It was snowing and blowing so hard, you couldn't see much but the shovel in front of you."

"Did that one woman have a name?" Elias managed to ask past his tight throat.

"Matter of fact, yes. I dug her out myself. I remember her name. Abigail Grayce, she'd said. A little bit of a thing as I recall. Too bad she evacuated down the mountain with the rest. If she's not alive, she's gone. A hell of a way to die," Archie said and shook his head.

Elias slammed his whiskey on the bar, spilling it. Abigail wasn't here at Sheep Camp, alive. She died in the snowslide— *four days dead!* The urge to find her struck him hard and deep. He had to find her and bury her proper. He'd bury her in wildflowers and silk and tend her grave until his last day. He couldn't leave her alone on this cold mountain. He wouldn't.

Archie Burns watched Elias exit the saloon in a hurry and guessed he must have known Abigail Grayce.

Elias bumped into the line of stampeders already starting back up the Chilkoot when he stepped outside the saloon. The whole camp seemed to be moving out. Time was running out for them to find gold and for him to find Abigail's body. He threaded his way through the throng and headed to his room for his shovel. Where he should start to dig in the vast debris field, he had no idea. Abigail was buried somewhere in between Sheep Camp and the Scales, he knew, since Archie had told of her whereabouts before the second avalanche.

It wouldn't do any good to check the morgues for her. Both had already closed their books on the dead. Newspapers had already reported what names they had. None of the lists had the same names. Elias understood others could be lost too, the same as Abigail, and their names would never make any list.

He needed to keep a level head and be sure his every move was deliberate if he expected to find Abigail. So far, her body hadn't been found. The depth of snow could be the reason. Burying his emotions, he thought hard about where to start his search. In the deepest snow, he decided. As soon as he had his shovel, he'd strike out for the deepest part of the debris field.

"Abigail! Abigail!" Elias called over the vast snowfield. He lost his confidence about finding her in such a huge area, having dug for hours and come up short. *I'm sorry, darlin'. I'm so sorry.* In a last-ditch effort to determine where he might find her, he pivoted slowly and called woefully in every direction. It was all he had left to help guide him.

"Abigail . . . Abigail . . ."

He closed his eyes and listened with his heart, able to block out everything else. Stampeders passed by, but he didn't listen to them.

"Abigail! Abigail!" He called out in desperation.

He imagined her answering him, calling his name. He listened for her, for any sign of where she might be. She couldn't call back from the dead, but somewhere inside him, he wished her alive.

"Abigail! Abigail!"

"Elias."

His shovel dropped to the ground when he heard the raspy whisper. He ran shaky fingers over his face and through his damp hair, wanting to believe the voice was Abigail's and not a voice in his head, but he knew the truth. It couldn't be her calling out after four days. He shouldn't be chasing a ghost. He'd lost her. Digging anymore wouldn't bring her back.

"Elias."

Elias picked up his shovel to get out of there and away from the voice in his head.

"Elias."

He stood his ground. The voice wasn't in his head, but right under his feet!

Abby woke up alone in the ranger station at Sheep Camp. Disoriented at first, her head quickly cleared. She remembered how tired she'd been the night before and how the two rangers had helped her inside the cabin. She sat up and suffered no ill effects . . . except for a stinging slice along her cheek. When she ran her fingers over the spot, she didn't feel any mark, but it hurt all the same. Maybe it was because of how she'd slept.

Yesterday had left her with nothing but questions. She'd fallen ill and fallen down, but why? The hike from Canyon City had gone just fine. In fact, she'd been enjoying the day so much, she'd forgotten all about any ghosts following her. Matt and his friends hiked ahead of her, and nothing had gone wrong there. She remembered looking for artifacts along the Chilkoot, even graves.

That was it!

She'd knelt and placed her hands flat on a mound of dirt,

thinking it a gravesite. Careful not to disturb anything, she'd dug her fingers in the soggy ground just enough to better investigate the area. She'd looked up toward the Scales. Her mind was a blank about what occurred after that. Abby strained to recall details, determined to figure out what had happened to her when she'd touched what she thought to be a grave. She determined to stay in that moment in time until she had answers, and would sit on this cot in this cabin until she found them.

Had she eaten wild mushrooms? What else could explain her loss of memory? There was no reason for her to have shut down. A sudden rush of air filled her lungs. Abby sat up straight and braced for the rush of phantom sensations to assault her. Everything jarred her. Everything hurt. Everything blurred . . . then everything shut down. Vivid sensations stung her, just like that phantom mark on her cheek.

I must have hiked up to Sheep Camp when I recovered from my swoon.

Abby looked at her hands and studied them as if they held more answers. Her nails were caked with dirt, which made sense. She'd been digging in the dirt, after all. Dismissing this, she mindlessly began clearing the dirt under each nail using her fingernails, with most of her attention fixed on the day to come. It was only when she looked at her hands again that she noticed white deposits in the caked grime under her nails. At first she blew the bits away as dust, but one nail had a tiny sliver of paper embedded there.

The cabin door opened and Jake walked in.

"Glad to see you awake, Abby. How are you feeling?"

The other ranger, Kirk Brady, came inside behind Jake.

Both men approached her bedside.

Abby buried her hands under the quilt and tossed an innocent smile to the rangers, still not sure what to make of the sliver of paper she'd discovered.

"We're getting you out of here this morning and back down to Skagway." Kirk wasted no time delivering his decision.

"No . . . I mean . . ." Abby sat there, confused, unsure what to say. "I mean, I'm fine and I don't need to leave the Chilkoot."

"It's the safest thing to do, Abby," Jake said. "You might feel fine now, but we have to make sure. The docs in Skagway need to take a look at you. Air Rescue is on the way."

"But the hike, Jake. I need to keep my commitment and finish the hike up the Golden Stairs with our group. Please, I'm fine," she insisted, and tried to get up.

"Hold on." Jake gently put a hand on her shoulder. "You're coming with us to Air Rescue now. Your safety comes first. Our group has already started out. Matt's got the lead. Don't worry about anything this trip," Jake insisted. "There'll be other hikes, Abby Gray."

"But—"

"Easy does it, Abby," Kirk said. He helped guide her to stand and walk out the cabin door.

Jake collected her gear and fell in behind them.

Abby tried to come up with an argument to keep her on the Chilkoot, but she didn't have enough time. She heard the helicopter overhead. She *did* feel fine, and she *was* all right. She hadn't found answers as to what had brought her here in the first place—she still didn't know what the handsome westerner wanted from her.

Now she might not see him again.

Abby almost stumbled at the turn of her thoughts—that she had deep feelings for a ghost. This whole trip had spiraled out of her control. The rangers didn't have to hurry her along at this point. She couldn't get away from Sheep Camp fast enough.

Eli didn't wait for her in Skagway. Time had run out.

CHAPTER TWENTY-FIVE

Abigail realized she had enough room to breathe and to spit the instant the avalanche hit. She'd managed to stay conscious and still had her wits about her. Her right arm jutted up. Her left forearm and hand were inches in front of her face, maybe more. She couldn't see in the blackness, but she had a sense of her buried position and her luck of having created breathing room by swimming through the avalanche.

She spat the snow from her mouth, then tried to form spittle. This took effort. She remained eerily calm and tried again and again until she felt the line of spittle trickle down her chin. That meant she had to dig up. But that was impossible; she couldn't move, except to spit and breathe. She had to wait for rescue. That was the only thing she could do. She listened for any voices coming from any direction, and had no idea how many feet of snow buried her. She didn't hear anything. At best, she might have an hour of air, she calculated.

Wait for rescue.

That was the only thing she could do.

She'd say her goodbyes now . . . to the unknown miner in Cripple Creek who'd given her her precious gold nugget . . . to Mary at the Women's Exchange . . . to Amos at the *Rocky Mountain News* . . . to Maud and Francesca and Lilly and Simone . . . to Martha in Dyea . . . to Archie at the Scales . . . and most important of all, "to Elias," she whispered.

"Elias," she repeated, imagining him calling her name.

"Elias," she said one last time in loving goodbye. "I will alwa—"

Just then something struck the ground above her. Vibrations echoed down, and the snow around her began to shift. She didn't want to let herself hope for rescue, but she could swear the bangs and pounding came from shovels.

"Abigail . . . Abigail . . ."

Elias? It couldn't be! She shut her ears and her heart to her dreams of Elias in these last moments before death. She had to let him go and ignore the disturbance closing in on her.

"Abigail . . . Abigail," Elias whispered and threw his gloves onto the snow. He took the small hand he'd uncovered in his and held on. He didn't let himself think she'd be alive after four days. He'd found her and wouldn't let go this time. Others had come to help him dig, and he would let them uncover her body. He dropped to his knees and held onto her hand, dreading the next moments. "Be careful with her," he pleaded of the others.

The three men helping Elias kept to their task, methodically digging, just as they'd done for the past four days. They'd found one more body here. They'd return to their place in line up the Golden Stairs the moment they finished digging. The spring thaw opened up the Yukon River. They had five-hundred miles to navigate before they'd reach the gold fields. Once they passed muster with the Canadian Mounties and made it to Lake Bennett, they had boats to build, and there was no telling how long it would take 'em to get to the river. None of the three diggers had any tears left, even for Abigail.

Elias did. He didn't wipe them away this time but kept hold of Abigail's cold, stiff fingers. There was no easy way to get through this. He reflexively clasped her hand for solace and waited for her body to be recovered.

Her fingers moved!

Elias let go and stood up, wanting to run from the scene. He was conjuring ghosts! That Bible talk with the preacher in Dyea haunted him now—when he'd said Lazarus had raised from the dead four days after dying and being buried. *My God, here I am thinking the same about Abigail.*

"Look it! She's moving!"

"She ain't dead!"

"Somethin' wrong here, fellas. She must a jus' got buried," the third rescuer said.

The three men stood over Abigail in disbelief at what they saw. She appeared to be alive, moving just enough to indicate life. To a man, they shot accusing looks at Elias, as if he could explain what happened here.

He couldn't. He lowered himself to the ground: to her. She was *real* and not a ghost.

"Abigail," he said in a gentle rasp. "Abigail."

The rush of air to her lungs shocked her. The suffocating pressure that had held her trapped lifted away. Dazed and disoriented, Abigail responded to the voice calling her name, and began to feel needle pricks in her limbs as her circulation returned. She dared not open her eyes, afraid to believe she'd survived the last avalanche. Straining for calm, she tried to make sense of the moment, when all she could see in her mind's eye was the girl in the funny cap looking up at the second-story window of the Red Onion Saloon—*the girl who never looked at me, but looks just like me.*

"Abigail . . . Abigail . . ."

Elias! Praise God, it *was* Elias! She instantly opened her eyes to the reality that Elias had found her and that she'd survived.

"C'mon, darlin'," he coaxed her gently.

Abigail couldn't speak yet but let Elias help her turn over and sit up. She squinted in the sunlight, and had to shut her eyes against the painful sensation. When she tried to stand, she couldn't support her weight and collapsed against Elias.

"Easy does it," he said and lowered her to sit on the ground.

The three men around Abigail and Elias left; no doubt confused by what they'd just witnessed. None could explain how the woman in arctic clothes was still alive after four days buried. They wouldn't talk about this to other folks. No one would believe them. Hell, they couldn't believe it themselves. They quickly buried the unexplained incident under the snowy Chilkoot Trail and would let it lie there. Their minds were already back on the Golden Stairs ahead.

Abigail fought for clarity.

"Elias," she whispered and put her hand to his cheek. "Elias . . . this is real, isn't it?"

"Yes, darlin'."

She ran her fingers over his face and stopped at his mouth, as if to make sure he was really there with her.

Elias kissed her fingers, for the same reason.

"You . . . you came for me, didn't you?"

"Yes, darlin'."

"I dreamed you here," she admitted.

"Maybe," he said and smiled.

Abigail suddenly became aware of her cumbersome clothing and sodden boots; their heaviness weighed her down. She was surprised everything hadn't been ripped away in the powerful avalanche. She hadn't been killed. That surprised her, too.

"Elias, how did you get here so fast? The avalanche couldn't have happened more than an hour ago, and yet you're here?"

"No, darlin'. It happened four days ago."

"That's impossible. Look around you . . . it's . . . it's—"

"It's all cleaned up, darlin'."

Abigail squinted at the landscape and didn't understand. Where were all the rest of the victims who'd been buried along with her? Where were all the rescuers digging them out, as she'd just been? In the distance she spotted movement and soon recognized the black line of men and women still climbing the Chilkoot, as if the avalanche had never happened.

"Elias," she said and looked at him. "I don't understand."

"Neither do I," he confessed, worried that she might be injured. "Do you think you can stand?" He wanted to get her mind off what had happened and get her moving.

"I'll try. Help me?"

He didn't answer but slipped his arms under hers and helped her up. She was too wobbly to stand on her own. He scooped her up. He'd carry her back to Sheep Camp.

Abigail didn't object and snuggled against him. She'd never felt as beautiful as she did in his arms.

"Thanks," Abby said to the discharge nurse, then quickly exited out the front door of the Skagway Clinic. She'd been kept overnight as a precautionary measure. The doctor gave her a clean bill of health this morning and signed her release. Abby didn't wait for anybody from the Skagway Ranger Station to escort her from the clinic but struck out on her own. She slung her backpack over a shoulder and started down Broadway Street. She needed to think about things and wanted to be alone.

The Red Onion was there, up ahead. She kept walking toward the saloon, then veered across the street to the bench and plopped her backpack, then herself, onto it. Few tourists roamed in and out of the stores dotting Broadway Street this early July morning. Abby spotted an eagle perched atop the Red Onion, then watched the majestic bird soar away. How it must feel to fly like an eagle. Magic, she thought. Immediately she put her hands in front of her and studied her fingers. Is that what all this is: *magic*?

She remained bewildered by the fact that her fingernails were sparkling clean when she looked at them after she'd boarded the helicopter, when only minutes before they'd been caked in dirt and bits of paper. Abby tried to process how this could have happened. It had nothing to do with magic she tried to convince herself; yet . . . who knew? Abby leaned back against the wood bench, frustrated at the realization her mind had returned to the subject of ghosts. She exhaled sharply and rested her arm on her backpack.

Her fingers draped over the zippered compartment where she kept her valuables tucked away: her tickets, her money, her certifications and trail maps. As was her habit, she unzipped the secret pocket and ran her fingers inside to make sure of her things: that nothing had gone missing. She knew by hand everything contained in the pocket. Most of her attention was still on the Red Onion and the closed second-story window. No lace curtains blew outside today. No female hand reached out to draw them in. Everything looked as it probably had looked a hundred years ago. A hundred years since the window had last been opened . . . as if no ghosts ever dwelled inside.

Abby's fingers stopped on an object deep inside her backpack pocket. It wasn't a coin but something her fingers couldn't read. She took her attention from the Red Onion and looked inside the pocket, carefully moving her money and papers to the side.

The instant her fingers touched the heart-shaped object, she saw the gold nugget. In that instant, a noise from across the street jarred and made Abby look up. The second-story window of the Red Onion opened, and lace curtains gently blew in the morning breeze.

Lydia.

A filmy white arm extended through the open window to draw the curtains inside.

Abby watched, transfixed.

The figure didn't leave the window, but stayed there, its attention fixed on Abby. The apparition smiled in greeting, gave a soft nod, and then faded from view.

The nugget slipped from Abby's hand and landed with a ping on the bench. She instinctively scooped it up and closed her fist around the gold as if it might vanish, the same way Lydia had just disappeared. Abby knew Lydia wasn't real, but the nugget felt real. She slowly opened her hand and studied the heart-shaped nugget. The precious metal sparkled in the sunlight. It warmed her hand on this chilly morning and made Abby think it held more value than that of the gold itself. *Magic,* she immediately thought. Ridiculous! Faulty theory! Yet she thought magic all the same.

Abby chanced another look at the second-story window. The ghost inside the Red Onion knew where this came from. Then Abby caught herself and shoved the nugget into the deepest recesses of her backpack pocket and zipped it shut. A more likely scenario was that she somehow found the nugget along the Chilkoot and unknowingly scooped it up. These mountains and rivers still drew miners today. There was still gold to be found. She must have found the nugget somewhere along the way.

Abby got up, slung her backpack over one shoulder, and struck out for the Skagway Ranger Station. Guilt about having the gold nugget in her pocket dogged her steps. The Chilkoot was the largest outdoor museum in the world. She couldn't help but think she'd somehow stolen an artifact and was on a nanny cam in one of the park ranger stations. *I'd return this if I could,* she told herself; all the while knowing she never would . . . because, if she returned it, she'd lose her connection with Lydia and the handsome westerner.

★ ★ ★ ★ ★

"Are you sure you're up for staying the rest of the summer?" the ranger asked Abby when she arrived at the Skagway Station. "Jake told me what happened. The doc at the clinic filled me in on the rest."

"Yes, I'm fine," Abby said. "A touch of the flu, that was all," she said and tried to bite back the lie. Convinced she needed more time in Dyea to ghost mine, she didn't want to leave until the end of her internship. She thought longingly of the Golden Stairs and hoped for another chance to climb them. She'd come so close.

"Young lady, if you want to stay, you need to give me your word you won't step outside our guidelines and go off on your own again. We came to pick you up at the clinic only to find out you'd left. Alaska is no place to go off on your own in town or out of town. Got me?"

"I understand." She knew the park rangers felt responsible for her safety.

"You sure?" he asked again and raised an eyebrow.

"Hundred percent," she replied.

"All right then, Abby Gray, let's get you to the ranch in Dyea and onto the horse trail back in time," the ranger said, sounding more lighthearted than before.

Back in time. His words, not hers. That's precisely where she wanted to go.

CHAPTER TWENTY-SIX

"Well, I'll be," Archie Burns muttered when he recognized Elias coming into Sheep Camp with someone in his arms—someone alive, not a dead body. Abigail Grayce, Archie thought right away. No one should be alive after having been buried four days, yet the slight woman had survived not just one avalanche, but two! Folks around the store owner didn't appear to notice anything in particular about a man carrying a woman back into camp; no doubt she was hurt or exhausted and needed rest before finishing this next section of the climb. Archie knew different.

He remembered Abigail Grayce's name from the Scales.

He remembered Elias had gone searching for her.

Damned if he hadn't found her, Archie thought, amazed. It had to be the work of the Lord, Archie thought. Archie finished resupplying his goods in Sheep Camp and set out for his general store at the Scales. He thought about the miracle he'd witnessed and knew he wouldn't see the likes of it again.

Elias didn't put Abigail down until he could lay her on his bed at the makeshift hotel in Sheep Camp. Neither of them had said a word on the way down the mountain. They didn't need words; only each other. She didn't protest when he began to unfasten her clothing and get her out of her burial shroud. Her limbs ached, but she helped him when she could. He didn't have anything with him except the clothes on his back, so he immediately stripped off his shirt and wrapped it around Abigail. That was the moment they both realized they'd been given more time together, when just a short time ago neither believed they would see each other again.

Elias crawled under the quilt with her and pulled her close. She needed food and water, but he needed to feel her heart beating against his . . . for only a few minutes more.

"I love you, darlin'. I'll never let you go again," he promised.

"I know," she whispered. "I know."

Abby cradled the heart-shaped nugget in her hand. It had been three weeks since she'd found the gold piece in her pack, and three weeks had passed without a single sign of ghosts. More important, no one had called out her name in her dreams or in the light of day. Instead of being comforted by this, she was upset. Where could *he* have gone? A shudder ran down her spine and brought goose bumps to her flesh. *Of course!* Abby finally put the two together—her name whispered in the Slide Cemetery and the handsome westerner who had followed her. Why hadn't she thought of the two phenomena together before?

Now it might be too late to find him or any clue that might lead her to him. He was gone, she knew. Somewhere deep down, she knew he'd left and would never call her name again. He must not have wanted anything from her after all, or else he would have appeared again. Three weeks had passed and . . . nothing. On horseback tours she'd conducted, winding in and around the Dyea tidal flats and forested terrain . . . nothing. What had she thought, anyway? That she'd follow him into his ghostly world and they'd live happily ever after? Of course not! But she'd wished it.

In a week's time, her internship would be over, and she'd fly back to Colorado and to the School of Mines. She hated to face the truth—she'd leave without realizing her golden dreams of

271

love and happily ever after. She certainly couldn't print *that* in the *Oredigger*! If she admitted she'd been chasing ghosts in Alaska instead of Klondike gold-rush history, she'd lose her multiple scholarships and any credibility she might have garnered as a mining engineer. Abby vowed never to speak of this slip in time to anybody, even Ebony.

A slip in time, Abby mused, still cradling the gold nugget in her palm. *Is that what all of this has been?* Einstein believed times could coexist: the past, the present, the future. The lines between them could blur. Abby believed it, too, at this point. Intellect didn't help her feel better. Einstein didn't have all the answers. *What are you supposed to do if you want somebody who exists in another time, Albert?* That inconvenient problem should have been addressed in your papers and texts.

Einstein had possessed intellect but no heart.

The gold nugget in her palm annoyed her, and she shoved it inside her backpack pocket. Maybe it was a bad idea to hold onto the souvenir. Maybe it belonged in the Klondike Gold Rush National Historical Park and not with her. She'd consider returning it. She might be better off if she let this memory go.

Abby fumbled around her cabin for her North Face cap. She wouldn't work this last day without it. She looked under the bed and spotted the covering—which was exactly what she'd used her cap to do—to cover as much of her as possible. Her hair was a mess and her complexion dull. She snatched up her cap and shoved it down over her ears. As usual, she'd not glance in the mirror before she left. She'd already brushed her teeth, at least she thought so.

Last night she'd caught an hour or two of uneasy sleep and hoped it was enough to get her through the day. She had a horseback tour to guide and couldn't make any mistakes. Many tourists had little experience with horses, and she had to give them careful instruction and watch them closely. The ranger with her would do all the talking today, so at least she didn't have to worry about that. Dispirited for weeks now, the idea of having to talk about Dyea and its history didn't appeal to her at all. There was no particular reason for her mood, she told herself. After all, the tour didn't include a ride through the Slide Cemetery, which was the one place she'd taken care to avoid since leaving the Chilkoot.

And the one place I haven't been to see if he would be there, calling my name! Already late, she fought the overwhelming urge to go back to her cabin and check the mirror. She knew she looked a mess and hoped the handsome westerner wouldn't notice.

He *would* be there.

Scared and excited at the same time, she couldn't wait to get to the stables and start working.

Abby hadn't gone back to her cabin to clean up after her last day at work, as she'd promised herself she would. She was in too much of a hurry to return to the Slide Cemetery. She wasn't accustomed to worrying about her looks and totally forgot. The only face she wanted to see was the handsome westerner's, smiling at her. The only voice she wanted to hear was his, calling her name. She left all her years of research and hard-learned scientific principle behind, wanting to be with him, no matter what it cost her. She was so caught up in her own longings, she forgot he'd wanted something from her; he didn't want her.

She'd reached the Dyea town site and hurried through thickets and ruins, past the only wall left standing, past its window, door, and attached length of fence, past cabins forgotten and ghosts left behind, in order to get to the Slide Cemetery in time. At dusk the Alaska summer sky would still provide light, but he might not wait for her if she were too late. She doubted any tourists would still be in the area, so she and he would be alone at the cemetery. She couldn't afford to be afraid as she'd been the last time. This time his voice wouldn't chase her away. This time she would stay and find out his name.

Abby was inside the Slide Cemetery before she noticed. She stopped short when she realized where she was. Her heart pounded. Out of breath and suddenly frightened, she gulped hard and fought for calm. The quiet evening frightened her as much as the headstones that surrounded her. She slowly pivoted and did her best to face each one. He might call to her from any of the graves. She'd been in this same graveyard before when he called, "Abigail . . . Abigail . . ." She waited anxiously to hear the same rasped whisper calling her name. She was sure it would.

Minutes turned into an hour. He wasn't coming. Abby didn't have the courage to move, but she needed to. If she went to each grave and read each name, then he would see and know she was here, waiting for him. It took everything she had in her to fight the fear that she'd lost him and would never even know his name. She forced herself to take the steps needed to visit each grave.

"E. D. Atwood. Died April 3, 1898," the first headboard read.

"Thomas Culleden. Died April 3, 1898."

"Frank Sprague. Died April 3, 1898."

"George Uhlin. Died April 3, 1898."

"W. Carl. Died April 3, 1898."

"Walter Chapper. Died April 3, 1898."

"Con Gephard. Died April 3, 1898."

"Allen Gray. Died April 3, 1898." Abby took more time at this grave. The name matched hers. She wondered if he'd been a relation.

Abby stopped at all the graves, those with names she could read, as well as those marked "unknown." When the graves ran out, she had to face the truth. The handsome westerner had likely died in the Palm Sunday Avalanche, April 3, 1898, or in Dyea during the time of the Klondike Gold Rush. His ghost—if there ever were such a thing—had gone on and left her alone, standing here on this otherwise ordinary southeast Alaska summer's eve.

Tears trickled down her cheeks. She quickly wiped them away; she was through with ghost mining.

"May you all rest in peace," Abby whispered, and she left the Slide Cemetery and its ghosts behind, each to their own place of honor in gold-rush history.

Abby tried to put her travel time to good use on the ferry and on the plane back to Colorado. She finished the articles on her internship she needed to submit to the scholarship board and the school newspaper. Once she'd finished the articles, she'd be through with Alaska and her veer off-course into ghost mining. The past months needed to stay dead and buried. She couldn't allow herself to go off the grid again, away from gold mining and engineering. Her emotions had run amuck, obviously, and she was tired of trying to figure out why.

Emptiness filled her days and nights, and took up all her time. Tasked with finding the energy to go through the motions and get back to her old self, she needed to focus on school. She didn't think she could feel worse than she did now, but if she lost her scholarships—

Abby couldn't let herself think about that particular danger.

School, that's all she had to hold on to . . . *school.*

"C'mon girlfriend, let's go to the Red Onion," Ebony suggested. She hooked her arm in Abby's to pull her along.

"No, Ebony, I've got too much homework. Besides I have to help out at the hostel tonight," Abby protested and stopped on the sidewalk, trying to break free of Ebony's hold.

"Oh, no, you don't!" Ebony said, holding onto Abby as she started for the saloon. "You've done nothing but study since you got back from Alaska. The rest of the time you mope around as if you just lost your boyfriend or something." Ebony stopped walking and let go of Abby. "Is that what this is all about? Did you meet a guy in Alaska and he's broken up with you? That explains it," Ebony declared.

"No," Abby lied.

Ebony suddenly gave Abby a hug, not believing her.

"You need a beer. I need a beer. We're going to the Red Onion if I have to drag you there, Abby Gray!"

The mere mention of the Red Onion agitated Abby. The thought of going inside the haunted place scared her.

"I can't, Ebony. I have to go."

"Yes, *we* have to go to the Red Onion and get that beer," Ebony insisted and hooked her arm in Abby's, holding tight this time.

Abby let herself be led without protest. She knew Ebony wouldn't give up.

"At least let me pay," Abby grumbled, realizing the Red Onion Saloon was just around the corner. She'd faced her ghosts before, and she could do it one last time. After braving the place this time, she wouldn't walk this path again.

"Deal," Ebony said.

"Wait, wait. Hold up," Abby said when they stood out front of the Red Onion. "I want to get my money out of my pack first." She propped her backpack on the bench in front of the saloon and rifled through her carefully guarded, zippered compartment.

"No worries, Abby, I can pay," Ebony offered, seeing her friend struggle with the heavy pack. "Why do you carry all that weight around every day? Really, you look like you're going on a dig every time you go to class," she teased.

Abby knew she had a ten-dollar bill somewhere in the hidden pocket and groped for change, too. Just then her fingers touched an object she'd forgotten about: the heart-shaped gold nugget. She closed her fingers around the memories held inside the gold, and let herself remember forgotten dreams one last time.

"Are you gals coming in?"

Abby froze. She thought she recognized the voice. The gold in her hand singed her fingers, and she let it fall back in place. This was a bad idea, coming to the Red Onion. She realized she couldn't face her ghosts after all, and never looked up to see who the voice belonged to.

"You go on in, Ebony," she said past her tight throat. She kept her head down and couldn't face the voice she'd just heard. "I'll see you later," she called over her shoulder to Ebony and took off down the street, leaving her backpack behind.

"Abigail! Abigail!"

She kept going.

"Abigail! Abigail! My name's Eli Cole!"

Eli Cole! She stopped in her tracks, so jarred by learning *his* name and the fact he appeared to be real and was calling her name.

By this time, Eli had reached her.

"You," she turned to him and whispered. "It's you."

"Yes, darlin'. I love you. I'll never let you go again," he promised.

She'd never felt as beautiful as she did in this moment.

"I know," she whispered. "I know."

POSTSCRIPT

Abigail Grayce and Elias Colt spent the rest of their lives together, traveling first to Nome—the next gold-rush boom-town—and then back to their roots in Montana and Colorado—back to the Old West.

Abby Gray and Eli Cole made a life together in Colorado, building a cabin in the foothills outside Golden; with Abby in mining and Eli managing the Red Onion Saloon; neither choosing to leave the Old West.

What brought them together made little difference.

What kept them together made all the difference.

One could argue Abigail Grayce and Abby Gray embody the same person existing in different times, or personify two different people existing in the same time. A similar argument can be made for Elias Colt and Eli Cole. Whether talking about ghosts or about God, it can be argued that it's possible to hold a belief in both, close, at the same moment in time. While this argument remains open-ended, I believe love is not a subject for argument. Love is a powerful connection, able to withstand the test of time—past, present, and future.

ABOUT THE AUTHOR

My nine, published novels to date are with Five Star, Gale/ Cengage. What started as a pastime in my mountain "writing spot" turned into the realization of my dream to bring my own voice to my own fiction page in frontier history. My early novels reveal my love of historical romance, while later works uncover my bent for *western spirits*, in fact and fiction. Old West history is ever the star. I'm just here to record moments in time.

Past works include: *Matchmaker, Matchmaker; A . . . My Name's Amelia; The Parlor House Daughter; Meggie's Remains; Hearts Divided* and *Hearts Persuaded* (The Quaker and the Confederate); *Arctic Storm, Arctic Shadow,* and *Arctic Will* (Watch Eyes Trilogy). I now make my home in California.

The employees of Five Star Publishing hope you have enjoyed this book.

Our Five Star novels explore little-known chapters from America's history, stories told from unique perspectives that will entertain a broad range of readers.

Other Five Star books are available at your local library, bookstore, all major book distributors, and directly from Five Star/Gale.

Connect with Five Star Publishing

Visit us on Facebook:
https://www.facebook.com/FiveStarCengage

Email:
FiveStar@cengage.com

For information about titles and placing orders:
(800) 223-1244
gale.orders@cengage.com

To share your comments, write to us:
Five Star Publishing
Attn: Publisher
10 Water St., Suite 310
Waterville, ME 04901